I0536944

Books by Anina Collins

The Eleventh Hour (Poppy McGuire Mysteries #1)
After Hours (Poppy McGuire Mysteries #2)
Top of the Hour (Poppy McGuire Mysteries #3)

TOP OF THE HOUR

ANINA COLLINS

The Top of the Hour is a work of fiction. Names, characters, places, and events are the products of the author's imagination. Any resemblance to events, locations, or persons, living or dead, is coincidental.

2016 Eight Feathers Press, LLC

Copyright © 2016 Eight Feathers Press, LLC
Print Edition

All rights reserved. Without limiting the rights under copyright reserved above, no part of this publication may be reproduced, stored in or introduced into a retrieval system, or transmitted, in any form, or by any means (electronic, mechanical, photocopying, recording, or otherwise) without the prior written permission of the copyright owner.

Published in the United States
ISBN: 978-0-9972153-4-2

Book Cover design by Natasha Snow Designs
www.natashasnowdesigns.com

Top of the Hour

Controversy sells as much as sex, and nobody knows that better than the local radio morning DJ who loves to talk politics. His shows enrage people, but who hated Lee Reynolds enough to shoot him point blank and leave him for dead in the woods outside of town?

Poppy and Alex have no shortage of suspects and for once aren't at odds on who they like for the crime. But all is not well between the partners. This time, murder has brought with it a new love interest for Poppy, but Alex isn't happy with this turn of events.

Will he lose Poppy, the one person he trusts in Sunset Ridge?

Chapter One

ALEX'S CALL CAME in just after seven PM, rousing me from a painfully dry article on winemaking I'd been trying to get through for the past two hours. I knew by the sound of his voice when he said my name that our newest case was no ordinary stolen decorative scarecrow taken from someone's front porch. Jumping in my car, I raced up the road past the Hotel Piermont to a wooded area teenagers had long used as a not-so-secret place for their parties after football games and parked next to two police cruisers and the coroner's van.

The air smelled earthy from the decaying red and yellow leaves that carpeted the ground beneath my feet. I loved this time of year for just that smell alone, but it was more than that. Autumn in Sunset Ridge wasn't like it was in New England, where I was sure every picture ever taken of fall had been snapped. There as you crunched your way over fallen leaves, your cheeks were treated to the brisk wind and chilly weather and the nights got downright cold. The fall season in the mid-Atlantic region, on the other hand, was best described as the best of both summer and autumn. Our days still warmed to the high sixties and sometimes even the seventies, and nighttime temperatures made a sweater necessary but not much more.

It was with all these thoughts rambling through my brain that I trudged up the hill toward where Alex, Craig, and Donny stood surrounded by lights all focused on a spot just beyond them. As I reached the three men, I took a deep breath of that heady dead leaf smell and exhaled, surprised at how winded that short walk had left me.

"Whew. I need to get into shape, it seems. No more danishes from The Grounds from this point on," I joked as Alex and Craig chuckled in response.

"At least you're in better shape than this poor guy," Alex said in a somber voice. "No more anything for him."

I looked down at the ground and saw a man lying face down on his stomach about five feet away. Dressed in jeans, he also wore a dark sport coat with an unmistakable bullet hole and bloodstain through the center right between his shoulder blades. A white bullseye drawn around the hole directed my gaze to it immediately.

Turning to look at Alex, I asked, "Someone think we needed help figuring out what killed him? I'm feeling like we should be insulted."

He gave me a tiny smile as he tried to remain more professional. "I think the killer had something else in mind. This is Lee Reynolds."

My head pivoted back to look at the dead man in front of us and I stared down to see something familiar in the body. Lee Reynolds had been the local version of a morning shock jock on AM 790 WXSN for the past five or so years. Offending people on a daily basis had become his trademark. Now the bullseye made sense.

"Wow, I didn't realize that before now. Did you ever listen to his show?"

Craig leaned around Alex and raised his hand. "I did every morning. It was pretty addictive, actually. I didn't even agree with most of his opinions on anything, but after the first couple shows, I couldn't stop myself from listening."

Looking over at Craig and then over at me, Alex mumbled, "Yeah, like a verbal train wreck. It looks like we're supposed to believe one of those people he angered with his opinions finally got to him."

"Do you?"

He stood silently looking down at our latest victim and shrugged. "I believe nothing right now other than Lee Reynolds is dead and someone shot him. Until I hear anything more, that's all I can believe."

Donny looked up from where he crouched next to the dead man and said, "Well, I can tell you it was a .38 that killed him and the murderer drew around the wound with what looks like regular sidewalk chalk like kids use to draw with."

"Did we find the piece of chalk he used?" Alex asked no one in particular.

Craig shook his head. "Nope, not yet. There's a lot of brush and leaves here, so it might take us a little while."

"Search this entire area within a few hundred yards. Our murderer may have thought they were smart and threw it as they ran away, assuming they threw it at all."

"Got it. I'll let you know what I find," Craig chirped as he switched on his flashlight and took off to begin his search.

"Can you tell us anything else, Donny?" I asked,

hoping some kind of forensic evidence might help us start our investigation.

Even though he didn't have to answer to me, the coroner for Sunset Ridge always did and always with a smile. "I'm guessing he's been dead for a couple hours."

"Why?" I asked as I stepped closer to the body, curious why Donny was able to be so precise. It was completely uncharacteristic for him.

He pointed at Lee Reynolds' shoulders with his pen. "Rigor mortis has begun to set in. See how stiff he is up here especially? That tells me the murder likely took place around dinnertime, say four or five."

I heard a voice come over Alex's radio announcing a car accident had occurred at the corner of Simpson and Ford Streets. Distracted for a moment as he answered the call, I returned my attention to Donny and asked a question I realized Alex may have asked already.

"Did the murderer take anything from him, Donny? Did you find anything on him?"

He shook his head. "There's nothing on the body but his wallet with some money, pictures, and credit cards. It doesn't look like they took anything."

"Alex, I'll come back with Jason and search for that chalk after I handle the fender bender over on Ford," Craig yelled as he ran toward his squad car.

Nodding, Alex answered, "Okay, but get back here as soon as possible. I don't want it raining before we have a chance to find that chalk."

As Craig sped away, I nudged Alex's arm. He looked down at me and with a smile I told him what the weatherman had happily announced that morning as I watched the seven AM local news.

"They're not expecting rain for at least the next four

days. I saw it on the weather this morning."

"Good. We need to go speak to Lee Reynolds' wife, so we don't have time to go searching the forest floor for a piece of kids' chalk."

"Are we doing that now?"

He looked at Lee on the ground at our feet and took a deep breath. "Yeah. No point in putting off the inevitable. I'm hoping she'll be able to tell us something about who might have wanted to do this to her husband."

We turned to walk back down the hill and I asked, "Are you thinking she's the prime suspect at this point?"

"That's usually the case, but I'm not thinking that this time." He turned to look at me and smiled. "I'm keeping an open mind until you tell me what you know of Mr. and Mrs. Lee Reynolds."

I watched where I stepped to avoid tumbling down the hill and landing flat on my back. Once we reached level ground, I headed toward my car as I broke the news to him that I couldn't help him with any juicy tidbits this time.

"Not a thing. I've never spoken to either of them, and that morning rabble rouser thing isn't my shtick, so I know nothing of him at all, other than what he did for a living."

Alex opened his car door as I reached mine. Shaking his head, he put on a look of disappointment I knew was fake. "You're letting me down, Poppy. I can't be on the top of my game without you clueing me in behind the scenes about the sordid details of people's lives."

I chuckled at his teasing. "Officer Montero, if I'm not mistaken your former job title was detective. Looks like you're going to have to detect the clues this time."

"It's not the same," he said with a smile. "I'll meet you at your house and we'll go from there, okay? See you in five."

I gave him a salute and hopped into my car to head back to my place. As I drove there, I tried to remember if I'd ever seen Lee Reynolds or his wife in McGuire's, but I couldn't think of a time they'd ever been in. He was something of a local celebrity, so maybe he'd spent his time at Diamanti's instead, but I'd never seen them there either. Perhaps his fame made going out in public difficult. Local radio DJ wasn't much, but in a small town like Sunset Ridge, it was more than most people could lay claim to.

WE PULLED UP to the Reynolds' brick townhouse on Colonial Drive, a newer section of town developed for younger residents who preferred the freedom from mowing the lawn and raking leaves in a yard. The area had three sections of twelve townhomes each arranged in a horseshoe design along Colonial, Regimental, and Union Drives.

"I'm always impressed at how different this part of Sunset Ridge looks from the Victorians downtown," I said as I opened my car door to get out.

"I've only been here once or twice. Both times were trespassing complaints, I think," Alex said as he rounded his side of the car to join me.

That didn't surprise me. While the people who lived in the townhouses were basically as friendly as anyone else in town, they seemed far more concerned with belongings and property, in my experience.

"Well, it seems that murder has come to this part of

town too."

He pointed toward the red door at 114 Colonial Drive. "That's the house there. Her name is Jessica Reynolds."

As he knocked on the door, I braced myself for what was to come. I wasn't sure when this part would get easier, if it ever would. Each time I watched Alex break the news to the family member left behind, my heart ached for them. I knew he usually suspected them in the demise of their loved one, but I also had a sense he felt bad for them too.

A petite woman with long brown hair and striking green eyes opened the door and focused on Alex's police badge. "Is something wrong, officer?"

"I'm Officer Alex Montero and this is my partner Poppy McGuire, Mrs. Reynolds. There's been an accident. Can we come in?"

She buried her face in her hands and sobbed, "Oh my God! What happened?"

Alex reached out to gently touch her shoulder. "Can we please come in and talk for a few minutes? I think it might be better if you were sitting."

Jessica Reynolds nodded and let him help her inside to a black leather couch in the living room. They sat down next to one another, so I found a seat in a matching recliner across from them and watched as he told her what had happened to her husband. She broke down and sobbed even harder at the news that someone had shot him in cold blood.

"Why would anyone do that to Lee?" she asked as she wiped the mascara that had run under her eyes.

"We were hoping you might be able to help us with that very question. I know it's difficult now, but we want to find the person who killed your husband, Mrs. Reynolds," Alex said in his kindest voice I knew was genuine.

She sniffled and nodded. "Please call me Jessica. I know you probably think the person my husband was on the radio deserved someone doing this to him, but he wasn't like that. That persona was just for the show, nothing else. In real life, he was a pussycat. I used to tease him that if people ever found out what kind of man he really was, he'd lose his show in a second."

"Other than disgruntled listeners, did he have any real enemies?" Alex asked as he took out his notepad and pen from his blue windbreaker.

"No, I can't believe he did. Anyone who met Lee in person could see how good he was."

While his wife protested the idea that someone would confuse the online personality with the real man, I imagined Lee Reynolds had offended a lot of people with his ultra-conservative rants every Monday through Friday. He wasn't exactly that pussycat she described every morning when he was bashing every liberal politician and social program for all it was worth.

"Did he ever get any threats against him?" I asked, imagining every angry listener had thought about giving Lee a taste of his own vitriolic medicine at one time or another.

Jessica turned to look at me and without missing a beat, she answered, "Not here, but maybe at the station. You have to understand Lee never brought his work home with him. Who he was at work was just that—his work persona. When he left the station, he wasn't that man anymore."

"We'll make sure to check at his work for any leads,

Jessica. Now I have to ask this, even if it seems wrong," Alex explained with a sympathetic smile. "Were there any problems between the two of you?"

Her eyes grew wide at his question and she shook her head violently. "Oh, my God! No! How could you ask that? We were just two normal people living our lives."

I reached over and lightly touched her arm, giving it a gentle squeeze. "It's okay. We have to ask because the police always look at the wife first. It doesn't mean we think anything like that is the case here, though."

She gave a heavy sigh and nodded her understanding. "We were blissfully happy. Really. I bet everyone says that, but we were. Things were so wonderful recently. We were planning to have children soon since he was making good money at the radio station."

"I'm so sorry," I said, truly hoping the woman in front of me was innocent. I knew Alex hated when I got attached to suspects, but just the way she talked about them wanting to have children made me want her to not be involved in his death.

Alex directed her attention back to our case. "Did Lee have a cell phone? We didn't find one on him."

Jessica nodded. "He always had his cell phone on him. Always."

"What time did you expect him home?"

She frowned as she recounted the last time she spoke to him. "He said he had to work late tonight, but that was nothing new. He worked late every Thursday. I expected he'd be home at the same time he always got home on Thursdays. Around six."

Alex jotted down the details in his notes while I

again expressed my sympathy for the loss of her husband. When I looked into Jessica's eyes, I saw what I believed was real sadness. Whatever Lee Reynolds was to the rest of the world, he was the man she loved and now he was gone.

By the time we got back to Alex's squad car, I was dying to know what he thought about the case so far. Once we closed our doors, I turned to him and asked, "Did you catch how she said he always worked late on Thursdays? What do you think of that?"

The corners of his mouth hitched up slightly before he turned to face me. "I was interested in how she said things were so wonderful recently too. I wonder how things were before."

Deflated that he already suspected Jessica of being involved, I slumped back in my seat. "Do you ever not think it's the person who loved the victim right off?"

"You make me sound like some ogre, Poppy. I go where the evidence takes me."

"Well, how about we go to WXSN and look for evidence there? Like maybe we can find out what he did each Thursday?"

Alex chuckled at my suggestion. "And clear the grieving Mrs. Reynolds while we're at it?"

"I wouldn't be opposed to that, so start the car and let's go. You're ruining all the good feelings I got from Jessica."

He put the car in drive and headed down Colonial Drive back toward town. "I knew you'd think she was innocent. I swear you're too soft sometimes, Poppy."

I poked his shoulder. "I take exception to that. I'm not soft. I just believe in people actually being in love. Is that so bad?"

As he turned the corner off Colonial, he rolled his eyes. "It's not bad. It's just not how real life works. I've seen too many cases where the loving husband or wife is anything but."

"Well, let me keep my illusions, okay, at least until we hear what the people at the radio station have to say?"

Alex laughed and pointed toward the WXSN tower with the bright red light atop it that loomed in the distance. "Far be it from me to be the cause of you becoming jaded. Let's see what the people at the radio station have to say about our victim, and then we'll see if Jessica is still a person of interest."

THE BARELY LIT lobby of the WXSN building stood empty, except for a single security guard sitting at his post just inside the double glass entrance doors. We approached him and Alex flashed his badge and told him we needed to speak to someone in charge, so the guard quickly ushered us back into where the offices were located. A woman with burgundy colored hair and matching long fake nails sat at her desk typing on her computer and didn't seem to even notice when we walked up to her desk.

Clearing his throat, Alex looked down at her and waited for her to acknowledge our presence, but still she didn't look up. I saw white wires coming from her ears and knew why. Miming the idea of her wearing headphones, I pointed at my own ears and said, "She can't hear us because she's listening to music."

He smirked and banged his hand down on the desk next to her keyboard so loudly it echoed throughout the office area. The secretary nearly jumped out of her skin and stood up, yanking the earbuds out of her ears.

"What the hell?" she screamed before she recognized a policeman stood in front of her.

"My name is Officer Montero and this is my partner. We need to speak to someone in charge here."

Still flustered, the woman sat back down on her office chair and picked up her earphones. "There's nobody but me in the office at night."

Alex leaned down so his face was right in front of hers and in a low voice said, "Then you'll have to do. What's your name?"

"Mercedes. Mercedes Sinclair. What's up?"

Standing to his full height, Alex pulled out his notepad and pen and asked, "What can you tell me about Lee Reynolds, Ms. Sinclair?"

She flailed her hands around making me worried she might slice her face with those purple-colored talons of hers. "Nothing. He did the morning show, and I work nights. We never saw each other."

"What time does your shift start each day?" he asked as he made notes about her name and her job at the station.

"Six. I usually get here around quarter to, though."

Alex looked up from his notes and arched a single eyebrow. "And you've never had occasion to see Lee Reynolds not even once? How long have you worked here?"

Mercedes seemed confused by his questions, likely because he was treating her like someone he had real evidence against. I had no idea why he was acting like that, but I assumed he had a sense that this woman who obviously loved adding color to her body wasn't being as forthright as she should be with him.

"I swear I never saw him in the three years I've worked here. He works early morning hours, so why would I? But Jake Warren is here and he definitely knew him. They're both DJs, so I'm sure they see each other in meetings and things like that."

Alex turned on that smile he wore whenever he was happy that a witness told him something he wanted to hear. "Where would we find Mr. Warren, Mercedes?"

She spun around in her seat so her burgundy hair twirled around her head and pointed a purple-tipped finger toward the back of the office area. "Right in there. He's the only DJ in the building right now."

We left the rattled night secretary for WXSN and headed back to speak to the early night shift DJ. Popular because his show featured eighties and nineties rock hits, Jake Warren was a favorite of many listeners in Sunset Ridge, even those too old to know much about the music he played. I'd seen him once or twice at events *The Eagle* organized with the radio station and remembered him to look like an aging rocker from the time period he seemed to love.

He sat alone behind a wall of glass and in front of a microphone speaking to his audience about how great those days used to be when men wore their hair long and the music rocked. Alex signaled to him to come out into the room where his producer sat, and while he arranged for some Led Zeppelin song that would eat up the next ten minutes of airtime, Alex questioned the man in front of the controls about Lee Reynolds.

"I knew nothing of him, to be honest. I only work with Jake here. Someone else does the early shows."

"So you've never even spoken to him? What time

does your shift start?"

"Four. I usually get here by three-thirty, but I've never talked to Reynolds."

Jake Warren came into the room where the three of us stood and told his producer to watch the time. Turning to face us, he asked, "What's up? That old drug charge catch up with me?"

I looked at the man standing in front of us and couldn't help but imagine him in a full-blown mullet back in the day. His brown hair still hung past his shoulders, but now it was pulled back into a ponytail. He looked like he hadn't shaved in a few days so his scraggly beard with patches of grey stood off his face at attention. His clothes consisted of a faded black and grey Alice Cooper concert t-shirt that had to be decades old and ripped jeans, and a dim look in his eyes told me that old drug charge would still be valid at that very moment.

"We want to talk to you about Lee Reynolds. When was the last time you saw him?"

I worked to stifle my smile at Alex's decision not to introduce himself or me, which I was sure was an indication of what he thought of Jake Warren. For his part, Warren didn't seem fazed by the fact that a policeman was questioning him about anything.

"I think I saw him a few weeks ago. I didn't really know Lee because we worked opposite schedules, and by the time I was coming in at three to begin the six PM shift, Lee was usually gone, even though he should be there until three for station meetings. Never saw him at even one in all my time here."

Alex wrote down the word *disgruntled* in his notes and asked, "How long have you worked here, Mr. Warren?"

"Mr. Warren? Dude, call me Jake. And I've worked

here for eight months."

I watched him for any indication he was lying, but his dull eyes weren't giving away any details. Alex thanked him for his help and told him in a serious voice we'd return if we had any other questions, but none of it seemed to faze the DJ. He simply mumbled something about rocking on with our bad selves and went back to work.

Chuckling at how stuck in the past Jake Warren truly was, I saw Alex roll his eyes in disgust before he turned to leave. "You wrote disgruntled next to Jake's name. Seems odd that he sounded so out of sorts about a guy he didn't know and never saw, don't you think?"

As we headed out of the office area, he nodded. "Exactly, but then again, his emotions might have been confused by what he smoked before we got here."

"You noticed that too? He's as high as a kite," I said with a laugh. "He didn't seem very nervous about talking to a cop, though."

Now it was Alex's turn to laugh. "What was I going to do? Arrest him for being a stoner? I'd actually have to see him with the drugs."

"Well, if Lee was working late like his wife said he did often on Thursdays, then Jake just wasn't seeing him. Do you think it was because he was off getting high?"

"Either that or Lee wasn't working late."

On our way out, we ran into a janitor and asked him if he'd ever seen Lee Reynolds when he worked late. The man explained he started his shift at three each afternoon, Monday through Friday, and he hadn't seen Lee in the year he'd worked there.

"Do you clean the offices or does someone else do that?"

The janitor smiled and told Alex he was in charge of cleaning the offices. I wondered why Alex didn't just demand to be let into Lee's office, but he must have had his reasons. Instead, he asked the man if he ever found anything interesting in Lee's office, and instantly the man became excited.

"I did. Wait here and I'll go get it."

As we stood there while he ran to the janitor's closet, I whispered to Alex, "Why didn't you just tell him to let us into the office?"

"Because he's a janitor and likely doesn't have the right to let us in anywhere here. I don't need any evidence we find being thrown out by some clever defense attorney because I didn't get the station manager's approval to search the office."

The man came running back down the hall toward us and handed Alex a folded piece of paper. "I found this last week when I was cleaning. It was just lying there on the floor next to his desk. I know I shouldn't have taken it, but…"

The man's voice trailed off and he hung his head. Alex opened the note and read it with a big smile on his face. Patting the man on the back, he said, "You did the right thing. Thank you. We'll come back tomorrow when the station manager is in, but you've been a great help."

The older man walked away clearly pleased from Alex's praise, and I waited for him to tell me what the note said. I knew it had to be something good by the look on his face, and then he spoke, and I had a feeling my faith in Jessica Reynolds or her marriage was about to be tested.

"I hate to ruin your belief in true love once again,

but I don't think Lee's wife was telling us the entire truth when she said they were blissfully happy. Not if this lovely note by Cherise is any indication."

I really hated the fact that people's behavior made his glee so justified.

Chapter Two

My SECOND CUP of coffee for the day hit exactly the spot I needed it to as I waited for Alex to show up at The Grounds. Wide awake and ready to continue our investigation of Lee Reynolds' murder, I didn't look forward to hearing him practically gloat about being right about our victim's wife and their not-so-perfect life together.

At least that note he found made it seem like it wasn't as perfect as she'd made it out to be.

Alex arrived at exactly nine AM right on time. Wearing his street clothes, he quickly reached for the coffee I'd gotten for him. "Thank God for this or you might have to prop me up in this chair. I was stuck at the station until after two this morning dealing with this murder case. Derek seems particularly keen on us getting this wrapped up as soon as possible."

"Why? What makes this any different than any other crime?"

He shrugged and took a gulp of his coffee. "I don't know. He mentioned something about the press being interested since our victim was a celebrity."

"A celebrity? He was a talk radio guy at a small town

radio station. I wouldn't exactly call that a celebrity, Alex."

His look of disgust told me he agreed even before he spoke. "I didn't say I thought he was anything big. I'm just telling you what's got Derek all worked up. He made me promise we'd make this case our first priority."

I had to laugh. We had no real cases to deal with other than Lee Reynolds' murder. "You mean we should put the riveting case of Mrs. Timmon's dug-up hardy mums on the back burner?"

"You think it's funny, but I'll be getting calls from her every day until I figure out which neighborhood kid is ripping up those ugly yellow flowers of hers. But yes, Derek wants us on the murder case exclusively. He's reassigned a bunch of the guys so we can devote all our time to this case."

I tapped the edge of my coffee cup against his and smiled. "Then we better get to work so you don't have to deal with your chief any more than you need to. I figure you're going to throw that note in my face since you seemed pretty happy about it last night."

Alex slipped the note out from between the pages of his notepad and held it up in front of me. "Not happy. Just interested in what looks to be an intriguing clue."

"Okay, Mr. All-Too-Interested. Read it to me again so I can enjoy this note too."

He looked around like he wasn't sure he should read me what it said in a public place, so I took it out of his hand and read it for myself. To say it was steamy would be an understatement.

I loved seeing you again last night. You definitely know how to make a girl's thighs quiver, but then again, you always have. It's been too long since I got to see that side of you. I hope it won't be the last time. Until then, think of how it felt when I did that thing with my tongue.

Cherise

Looking up from the note, I saw Alex grinning at me. "She sure does know how to send a message."

"She does," he said as he wiggled his eyebrows before his expression turned serious. "What we don't know is when that note was written, though. Was Lee Reynolds cheating on his wife or was this just some note from his past?"

I handed him the piece of paper and thought about Jessica's reaction to the news of her husband's death. He had a beautiful and devoted wife in her, so I had a hard time thinking he would step out.

"My vote is for it being from his past, but I have to admit I'm wondering why he would have kept that note as some kind of memento."

Alex didn't seem as convinced of our victim's love for his wife, though. "Let's say for argument's sake that he was having an affair and meeting this woman every Thursday when he told his wife he was working late. That would explain why no one seems to have seen him at the station on any Thursday afternoon or evening."

"I'm not a fan of this argument, Alex, but okay, let's say that's how it happened. We need to find out who this Cherise person is and talk to her."

Almost as if he hadn't heard me speak, he continued, "On the other hand, in a town as small as Sunset Ridge and with his being a sort-of celebrity, I would think that cheating on his wife would have been a dangerous chance to take. I wonder how long he and Jessica were married."

"You have a partner, you know. I'm not just a pretty face and someone to make you look less scary to the townsfolk."

He smiled like he finally heard me. "I was just thinking out loud. Do you have something you'd like to add?"

I took out my cell phone from my purse and dialed up my friend Keri Maloney at the county records office. "Even better. Just give me a minute and I might have an answer to that last question of yours."

She answered on the second ring and gave her professional spiel about how I'd contacted the county records office and she'd be happy to help me however she could, but I stopped her just as she began to give the office's hours.

"Keri, it's Poppy. Take a breath."

"Poppy! How are you? It's been way too long since we talked. What's new?"

"I need your help with something. Can you tell me how long someone's been married if I give you their name?"

A rustling sound of papers came through the phone before she said, "Yeah, sure. I just had to clear my desk a little to get to my computer. Who are we checking up on?"

"Lee and Jessica Reynolds. Can you tell me when they were married?"

She tapped on a few keys and then answered, "May 10, 2012, so they've been married for four years. First marriage for her and the second for him."

I felt my eyes grow wide from excitement at hearing there was a former Mrs. Lee Reynolds. "What was the first wife's name?"

Hearing that, Alex perked up from sitting there as he stared at the sexy note and mouthed, "He was married before?"

I nodded and then heard Keri say, "Cherise Adams Reynolds. They divorced in April 2012."

Now I was even more excited. In a rush to get off the phone and back to discussing the case, I said, "Thanks a million, Keri! I won't forget your help with this."

"You okay, Poppy? This isn't for some guy you're dating, is it?"

I knew what she was referring to. She'd known me for years and was around when I found out about Jared's cheating on me. I hated that she thought I hadn't recovered from that and would be checking up on some guy I was dating like some broken and pathetic girl even now, years later.

"No, no. I'm working with the police now and I just needed to know some details about Lee and Jessica Reynolds' marriage. That's all."

"Okay. I'm happy to hear that. We need to get together again soon, you know? It's been too long," she said in her normal voice as the last remnants of sympathy for me faded away.

"Definitely. I'll call you later this week so we can make plans. Talk to you then."

I tossed my phone into my purse and then turned back to see Alex grinning at me. "I had no idea you knew people in high places, Poppy. You never cease to amaze me."

Brushing off his compliment, I waved my hand and said, "I wouldn't call a clerk in the county records office people in high places, but Keri's good people. She told me something very interesting. It seems Lee Reynolds married Jessica in May 2012, just one month after his divorce was final from Cherise Adams Reynolds."

Alex leaned back in his chair and pursed his lips. "So now we know who Cherise is."

"That's a pretty fast turnaround, wouldn't you say? One month he's getting divorced from Cherise and then the next month he's marrying Jessica. Something tells me he's not above cheating on his wife."

"I think you might be right. I want to talk to people at the radio station this morning, but after I think we should go see this Cherise."

"How? We don't even know her address."

Alex tipped his coffee cup toward his mouth to finish the last of his coffee and then tossed it in the nearby garbage can. "I'll get Craig on finding out her address. It shouldn't be too hard. For now, let's get moving to the station. I'm hoping the daytime people have more to tell us about our victim than the nighttime people did."

WE WERE ESCORTED into the office of the station manager of WXSN, Kevin Nash. I hadn't really known what to expect, but to say I was surprised by our surroundings would be an understatement. Dark brown paneling covered the walls, and even though the carpeting on the floor wasn't shag, it certainly wasn't anything I'd consider new. Deep brown, thick, and nearly matching the color of the walls, it made the room feel like it was about to suck us in.

The chairs we sat in weren't much better. Molded plastic like those popular in the sixties and seventies, they were the same dark brown as the rest of the office and incredibly uncomfortable. As we waited for Nash to return to his desk, I leaned over to Alex and whispered as I slid forward on my seat, "Clearly lumbar support wasn't a big thing when these chairs were in fashion."

"They're more like slip and slide than sit and relax," he joked as I pushed myself up into an upright position once again.

Kevin Nash returned to his office and as he sat down behind his desk, he thanked us for coming to see him. A professional dressed in a three piece dark grey suit, he looked to be around fifty years old with tinges of grey at his temples to go along with the crow's feet next to his eyes. A lean man, he had a long face and thin lips, but he seemed genuine in his sadness over the death of his most popular on-air personality.

"We're lost here at WXSN without Lee. The phones have been ringing off the hook with fans asking if he's really dead since the local news broke the story last night. I still can't believe anyone would hurt Lee. He was a good guy, one of the few left in this world."

Alex jotted down some details about Nash and then asked, "Can you think of anyone who would have wanted him dead?"

The station manager narrowed his eyes like he was in pain. "You have to understand we loved him here. He had made our ratings soar. For six years, he handled the morning time slot, and once he settled into that political thing he began in 2011, he was golden. People may have said they hated what he had to say, but our advertising department would tell you differently. He brought in a lot of listeners, which in turn brought in a lot of advertisers. But he wasn't without his haters."

"Anyone here at the station?" I asked, getting the sense he was hinting at some interoffice issue he didn't want to come right out and talk about.

Nash shook his head and stood up. "No, nothing like that. We're a family here at WXSN. Outside the station, however, was an entirely different story."

He walked over to a cabinet and grunted as he lifted a beige sack from the bottom shelf. Returning to his desk, he deposited it in front of us and pulled open the drawstring at the top of the bag. Inside there were hundreds, maybe thousands, of letters addressed to Lee Reynolds. I peered in and was stunned at how many people had been driven to write to him just from listening to him talk five days a week.

Alex stretched his neck to look into the bag and then made a note of the letters. "Are these all hate letters?"

Nash nodded. "Most. Lee did have his fans, but as with most things in life, negative and angry people were more prone to express their opinions than people who enjoyed his show."

"This is a lot of angry people, Mr. Nash. Did Lee Reynolds feel like he was in danger?" I asked.

"No, Lee was a trooper. There were two times he and I felt like a listener might take things to the next level, so I increased security around the station. Neither time anything happened."

"Did you report these instances to the police?" Alex asked as he thumbed through the sack of hate mail.

"No, we never felt like we should bother the police with things like that. Nobody ever came around and threatened him in person. I really can't believe any of his listeners did this to him. I just can't."

Looking up from the letters, Alex raised his eyebrows in surprise at Nash's comment. "Really? He said some pretty controversial things on his show. Things that upset people, if these letters are any indication."

Nash sat back down in his leather chair folded his arms across his chest. "I know, and I guess it would be the easy answer to who killed him, but you have to understand how this job works. A personality like Lee says things to get people talking, but they're just cowards who get all worked up by the stuff he says on his show and then dash off some poison pen letter full of bluster but nothing else."

Standing from his chair, Alex said to him, "If you don't mind, I'd like to take a look at Lee's office. I'll have someone from the station come by and get these letters too and we'll see if we can find out if any of these people may have taken the next step."

Nodding, Nash agreed. "I'll show you both to his office at the end of the hall."

As we walked there, I asked him a question that had been on my mind the entire time we sat talking to him. "Mr. Nash, did Lee have any problems outside of work that you know of?"

I intentionally made my question vague in the hopes that he'd feel comfortable mentioning anything that jumped into his mind, but he merely shook his head and answered, "Lee had a great life. He and his wife were happy and I know they wanted to start a family soon. He had success at work and at home. I can't think of one area of his life that wasn't better than it had ever been before."

We stopped in front of Lee's office and Kevin Nash

unlocked the door. I walked in, but Alex stopped and said, "His wife said he often worked late on Thursdays. Can you tell me if you remember that being the case?"

Nash thought for a moment and frowned. "I haven't seen Lee past two or three in the afternoon in ages. It has to be at least six months since I've seen him in his office at that time of day. If there's anything else I can do to help, please let me know."

He walked away leaving Alex and me in Lee Reynolds' office. After a quick call to the police station to tell Craig he needed him to come by and get the sack of hate mail, Alex joined me at Lee's very neat and very bare desk.

"Notice anything missing?" I asked, sure what was not on the desk was an important clue.

Alex scanned the top of the desk and shrugged. "He was a DJ. Maybe he didn't have a laptop."

"Let me go ask the station manager. I'll be right back."

I caught Kevin Nash on the way back to his office and asked about Lee having a laptop or even a desktop computer. He confirmed my suspicion that he had possessed a computer—a laptop—and he also said it was only for Lee's use.

I ran back to where Alex stood in the office already searching through Lee's desk. "His laptop is missing. I knew it. It's a rare person who doesn't have a laptop or tablet these days."

Alex looked up at me and knitted his brows. "So both his laptop and cell phone are missing. Interesting."

"I'm going to call Jessica to ask if the laptop is there."

Before I could dial her number, Alex pulled out a

box with a pink bow tied around it from the back of the bottom drawer in Lee's desk. I had a feeling I knew what was in that box. He untied the bow, and with a pen held up a pair of fire engine red silk panties.

Panties that clearly wouldn't fit Lee's rather shapely young wife.

"The plot thickens," Alex said with a grin only a man would have on his face after finding silk panties like those dangling from the end of his pen.

"I'm definitely not getting a Jessica Reynolds vibe from those. They look like something a Cherise would wear."

I reached out to pick up the box, but Alex stopped me. "Watch. You're not wearing gloves."

"Fine. Turn over the box so I can see the lid then."

He did as I said and there on the top of the box where the bow had been were the words Sweet Nothings. Looking to me like I would know, he asked, "Is this the name brand of the lingerie?"

Not in a big hurry to discuss how often I'd visited the Sweet Nothings store in the past, I shook my head and merely said, "Nope. It's a boutique right here in Sunset Ridge."

Alex chuckled. "This town never ceases to amaze me, and for once, it's not in a bad way this time."

Blushing a little, I said quietly, "Sweet Nothings is about half a block away from the Hotel Piermont."

Not even trying to hide his amusement, he threw his head back and laughed. "It really is all about location, location, location, isn't it?"

"Ha ha. Just bag the panties and the box and let's finish up here."

As he did that, I slipped on gloves and looked

through the drawers on the other side of Lee's desk to find the usual items people kept at work. Paper clips, pens, staples, mints, a pack of chewing gum. Then in the last drawer I checked I found a day planner. Thumbing through it, I saw Lee Reynolds hadn't written much in it after the first week of January and a few notes about some political scandal that had been in the news earlier that year but had faded from public interest by spring.

"Find anything in that?" Alex asked.

"No. My guess is he's like many people and has his numbers and stuff on his phone."

Alex rose from Lee's chair and pushed it back under the desk. "I don't expect to find his phone if the murderer took it. I contacted the phone company this morning to get the LUDs and told them to keep the phone on just in case whoever took it makes the mistake of using it. Hopefully, our murderer is stupid, but I'm not counting on it."

I looked around Lee's office and saw nothing else for us to investigate. That meant we were off to check out those panties he'd had hidden.

"Looks like we need to visit Sweet Nothings. You up for a visit to the sexiest lingerie shop in town?"

He winked at me and smiled. "Since you're obviously the one who knows all about this store, lead the way."

THE SWEET NOTHINGS shop was a place that was simultaneously sweet and sexy, naughty and nice. Decorated in the softest shade of pink I'd ever seen, it also had dashes of black and red scattered around in the lace bows that hung from the ceiling above patrons' heads. The owner had thought she was staying subtle with the look of the store, but in reality, only a blind person wouldn't know as soon as they stepped through the front door what Sweet Nothings offered.

Racks of sexy lingerie dotted the space, along with shelves of panties, bras, and garter belts lining the walls. Behind the register sat bottles of colorful gels and lotions for lovers who liked to spice up their bedtime pleasures.

I'd been to the store a number of times in the past, even though I hadn't gone there for at least a year. As Alex and I walked up to the front door, I wondered if Stacy would remember me. The owner who worked the register nearly every hour the place was open, she must have seen hundreds of people since the last time I was there, I assumed, so I didn't worry about her recognizing me.

And then the bell on the front door rang as it closed behind us and I saw Stacy's blue eyes light up as she did exactly what I hadn't worried about just a minute before.

"Poppy McGuire! It's been too long since we saw you in here. Let me get your card."

She hurried to get her pink plastic index card box and spun around on her heels to meet us at the register as I scrambled to correct her assumption of why I was there. Out of the corner of my eye, I saw Alex smile and raise his eyebrows like her knowing me intrigued him.

"No, no, it's okay. We're here on police business, Stacy. We just need to ask you a few questions about a gift connected to one of our cases."

Stacy stopped thumbing through the box full of cards and looked up at me. An attractive woman with long brown hair that fell seductively around her face, she was in her late thirties and always had a flirty way about her. I watched as her gaze shifted from my face to Alex's and knew she hadn't changed since my last visit to her shop.

"Who are we? Please introduce me, Poppy," she purred as she extended her hand to shake Alex's.

I turned to see him giving her his best smile and introduced them. By the time I'd said their names, Stacy had all but forgotten I was even in the store. She batted her long eyelashes as Alex changed into work mode and began to ask her questions about the panties we'd found in Lee Reynolds' desk drawer.

Holding the bag that contained the store's box and the red silk panties, he asked, "Can you tell us who bought this item and when?"

"I'd have to get my hands on them, Alex, but they look like they're from my store," she said in sugary sweet voice.

He looked at me and then back at Stacy before he grabbed a pen from the counter and lifted the panties from the clear baggie. Holding them up by one of the leg holes, the panties slid down the pen until they were hanging by the crotch and he asked, "Better?"

Stacy's nostrils flared as she took a deep breath in. She leaned forward to look at the tag on the panties and then began flipping through the cards in her box. After just a few seconds, she looked up and smiled at him.

"Three pairs of those exact panties were sold in the past month."

"To whom?"

In her best coquette voice, Stacy answered, "My customers rely on my discretion, officer. I don't think I can betray that."

With a hint of frustration in his voice signaling his patience was already running low, Alex said, "There's no customer-lingerie store owner privilege, so I'm going to need you to tell us who bought those panties, Stacy."

I had a sense that Alex's no-nonsense way wasn't going to work with the flirty Stacy, who obviously saw this to and fro game as some kind of foreplay between them. Hoping to move things along, I asked, "Maybe if we attack this from another angle that would work. Stacy, did you sell these to Lee Reynolds recently?"

At the mention of our victim's name, Stacy's playfulness faded away, replaced by a far more serious attitude. "Yes. I can tell you that since that poor man was killed last night."

"Was Lee a regular customer of yours or were his purchases a recent thing?" I asked.

Stacy nodded as a frown settled into her features. "I sold him some very nice panties in the last two years. At first they were much bigger panties, but then his wife lost weight so they became smaller, sexier items in the past few months. He had great taste, though, and he was a wonderful customer. I was sorry to hear on the radio this morning that he'd been killed."

Now that Stacy was answering questions, Alex joined me in asking her some. "Did he ever came in with anyone or was he always alone?"

"Always alone. He told me he wanted the gifts to be surprises for his wife."

A customer entered the store and Stacy turned her attention to her. We thanked her for her help and turned to leave. I was happy that the questioning had gone as well as it did, giving us something to go on now.

On our way out, Alex stopped in front of a rack of

baby dolls and winked at me. I didn't say anything, but as my cheeks warmed from blushing, I had to admit he had great taste in sexy lingerie.

Chapter Three

A FRIDAY NIGHT in early October at McGuire's meant a bar full of customers and nearly half the tables filled as baseball began its divisional playoffs. My father called me in to help out his bartender when he saw the place filling up by six o'clock, and even though I wished I had something exciting to do on a Friday night, I didn't so I happily agreed to help out behind the bar. At least I was out of the house and not stuck inside my head thinking about Alex and that look he gave me as we walked past that rack of baby dolls.

My father's usual baseball buddies took up all the spaces at the bar, and no one could say any of them came to just watch the game. The bartender Kitty and I bounced from one empty glass to another for the first few innings while my father helped out with the tables in the back, even though I told him I would have gladly switched places. He wasn't a recovering alcoholic but someone who knew all too well his limits, so I assumed that was why he had me filling his friends' glasses instead of running tables.

Although I wasn't watching the game, I knew by the way the drinks were going down even faster by the fifth inning that whatever was happening at the stadium wasn't riveting baseball. A few of the men at my end of the bar began to loudly complain about the game being a rout for the Sox, unhappy that the team they loved to hate had surged ahead.

My father eased behind me to grab a couple bottles of beer and tapped me on the shoulder. "Everything okay up here? I thought I heard the natives getting restless."

His friend John, a man in his late fifties who spent too much time at the bar for his wife's happiness, overheard his comment and answered for me. "She's fine, Joe. Your Poppy runs this place like a well-oiled machine. You could go away on that vacation you're always threatening to take and come back to McGuire's just like you left it."

I had to smile. John had been friends with my father since I was a baby, and he probably knew him better than anyone else, besides me and his friend Albert.

Dropping a wooden chip in front of his spot on the bar, I smiled. "For that, you get a free drink. Flattery works on this girl."

John bowed his head to thank me, and my father rolled his eyes. "I'm curious, honey. How can you be so comfortable around these guys but you can't figure out how to make a move on that friend of yours?"

My mouth dropped open wide in shock that he'd said that in front of all those strangers. Well, they were practically strangers, and even if they weren't, they didn't need to know about my personal life.

Narrowing my eyes to angry squints, I groaned as he passed me on his way back to his tables. My father had clearly decided he wanted to play cupid. I hated to tell him, but he was going to be disappointed. Alex still technically was dating Bethany, even if they saw each other infrequently, and he seemed more disinterested lately than anything else. The other problem was I just wasn't sure endangering the good thing we had in our work partnership for anything more was a good idea.

I knew my father, though. If he'd gotten it into his head that there was something there between us, he wasn't going to let it go.

Best to avoid him to keep the romance chatter to a minimum. Hatching a plan to do just that, I grabbed the tray out of his hand when he returned to behind the bar and quickly told him, "Time to switch jobs. I'll handle the tables for a while, Dad."

I got away from him before he could protest my decision and found an empty table in the very back of the bar to rest my feet for a few minutes. From there, I could get a little break and keep my father from wanting to discuss the details of my personal life in front of the rest of his customers.

His words echoed in my head as I watched everyone around me have a good time. I wasn't backward or foolish, like I thought he saw me. I knew what he thought. He never considered Bethany a serious girlfriend for Alex, no matter how many times I told him otherwise. I'd even talked their relationship up a little more than it actually was in hopes of getting him off the topic of Alex and me dating at some point. Clearly, that tactic hadn't been successful.

He didn't even think my claim that Alex was still in love with his dead wife was a valid argument why we shouldn't be together. The more I told him he was in love with a ghost, the more he mentioned every time he was sure Alex looked at me like he cared or how great we fit together as partners.

Of all people, I would have thought my father would understand how a man might never be able to get over a woman, no matter how long she was gone from his life. Well, whatever my father thought he saw, I still didn't know if I wanted things between Alex and me to change.

I could never tell my father that, though. He'd just lecture me about all work and no play making me a boring Poppy and then tell me about someone he knew who worked all his life, squirreling money away for that day when he could finally enjoy himself, only to find that when the day to live had finally come, there was no one around to share his life with. Sort of like his own personal version of the grasshopper and the ant story.

So for all he knew, I just hadn't figured out a smooth way to show Alex how I truly felt. I wasn't sure I liked him thinking I was some sad woman who cowered every time a man I liked came around, but the alternatives were worse, so pathetic I'd remain.

I kept to the tables area to avoid my father as much as possible, but an hour's reprieve was all I could get. The baseball game limped to a disappointing ending with much of the bar furious about missed chances in the outfield, and when many customers began to filter out into the night, it became obvious my father wanted to talk.

Keeping my back to the bar, I wiped down each table as it emptied and collected the empty beer bottles to throw into the trash. My ears were on high alert, almost as if I knew he'd come back to speak to me at any time.

A tap on my shoulder about fifteen minutes after the game ended told me my time was up. I turned around to see my father standing there with his arms folded across his chest and a look that said he knew I'd been avoiding him.

"What's up, Dad? Good turnout tonight, don't you think?"

My chipper greeting didn't put him off, and he sat down at the table I'd just cleared. "Sit down, Poppy. I didn't get a chance to talk to you much tonight, so take a break and talk with your good old dad."

Reluctantly, I joined him and waited for what I assumed would be a father-daughter talk about following my heart. He surprised me by asking about the case instead.

"Has there been any progress on the Lee Reynolds case?"

"The murder case? No, it's just at the beginning stages," I answered truthfully, relieved we weren't going to have to talk about Alex.

"Well, if the beginning is strong, that usually indicates the rest will be."

I had the distinct impression we weren't talking about the case at all, in fact. Going the joke route, I stood up and gathered my tray as I said, "Well, thanks for that incredibly general statement, Dad. I'm going to get moving so I can get home early tonight."

Quickly walking away, I hoped he would take the hint and let sleeping dogs lie, but as he followed me up to behind the bar, I knew I wasn't going to be that lucky tonight. No, he fully intended on waking those dogs up.

Why I truly didn't know.

As I tossed away the empty bottles and put the dirty glasses in the sink to be washed, he took a seat at the bar in front of me. "I thought we might talk about something a little less general, actually, honey."

Everyone around us turned to look at me. Nothing like having your personal life laid out at the bar. I grabbed his arm and tugged him toward the storeroom, hoping he would keep his thoughts to himself until at least we were alone.

Closing the door behind him, I sat down hard on a case of whisky. "I guess I don't have a choice but talk to you about this, Dad, but do you think we could keep it in the family and not involve every person in the bar? This town already thinks I'm some kind of sad old maid. It doesn't need to hear how pathetic you think I am because I won't make a move on Alex."

My father frowned and sat down beside me on the case of liquor. Taking my hand in his, he said in his very serious Dad voice, "I'm sorry, Poppy. I didn't mean to upset you."

I looked away, already feeling like this conversation was hitting too close to home. "It's okay, Dad. Don't worry."

"Do you really care what people around town think of you?" he asked like he was surprised to hear what the fellow denizens of Sunset Ridge whispered about me.

I sighed heavily and shook my head. "No. Not really."

That was the truth. I didn't really care what people thought of me or my love life. I knew they saw me as what people used to refer to as being on the shelf too long. I didn't see me that way, though. I knew they also talked behind my back about Jared's cheating on me and running off with another woman right after asking me to marry him. That still stung, but not for the reason they thought. They saw that as proof that I'd made the wrong choice to stay in town to support my father after my mother died.

The truth was far less admirable. I hated that they talked about that when they thought of me still because I had long suspected that his leaving me for someone else was proof that I wasn't the kind of woman men truly loved.

"You're a wonderful person, Poppy. You're smart and beautiful, and anyone who knows you sees that terrific person you are."

I turned to see my father's eyes full of concern for his daughter. "You don't have to worry, Dad. I don't think I'm some misfit like people around here do."

"You know, Alex thinks you're something special too."

"Dad, why do you want to talk about this?"

He forced a smile and squeezed my hand. "Because I see two people who clearly enjoy being around each other and think maybe you aren't seeing it like I am."

"I like being around Alex. That's true. I love how his mind works while we're working on a case. I like that I can add something to our investigations because I think differently than he does. That's all there is between us, though."

My father frowned. Shaking his head, he said, "I think you're wrong. I know you like him, and I've noticed he hasn't been around with Bethany much anymore. Are you sure you aren't missing something?"

I tweaked him on the tip of his nose. "You're as bad as the old ladies in town, you know that?"

"Those women have it all over me, and you know it. I'm a rookie compared to them. I just don't want you to discount him because he was married before."

I stared at my father in shock. "Is that why you think I don't want to date him?"

"Well, you've mentioned him still being in love with her a few times. What do you call it? Being in love with a ghost? I don't want you to miss out on something because he has a past."

Sometimes my father made me chuckle. "I have a past too, Dad, and it's nothing as honorable as his wife dying young. Trust me."

"Don't sell yourself short, Poppy. One bad relationship doesn't mean a person is unlucky at love."

Unlucky at love. The way he said that reminded me of Lee Reynolds more than myself, so I seized the chance to ask my father what he knew of Sunset Ridge's latest murder victim. "Dad, did you ever meet Lee Reynolds?"

He nodded slowly. "Your victim? I did. One time at Diamanti's. It was right after he started getting big at the WXSN with his morning talk radio show."

"I never met him and I only listened to his show once or twice, but his wife told us he was nothing like the kind of person he was on air."

My father stood from our seat on that case of whisky and grabbed a bottle of water. Silently offering me one, he said, "I didn't share his brand of politics, but it wouldn't surprise me that he wasn't that person we heard on the radio in real life. How could he be? He spent four hours a day basically screaming at people for their opinions. Nobody could act like that in their real life."

"What was he like when you met him?" I asked, curious about this man who engendered such strong emotions every morning.

Looking off in the distance, my father thought about my question for a moment and turned to smile at me. "He was really nice, to be honest. I don't know if I expected him to be that abrasive person I'd heard on the radio, but I can say he was nicer than I thought he'd be."

"How did it happen? Was he sitting at the bar over there and you two happened to strike up a conversation?"

"He was eating dinner and I saw him sitting alone two tables over. He smiled and nodded, sort of a single man's camaraderie from one to another, and he asked me if I'd like to share a meal with him."

"Really? I would've never guessed that morning shock jock could ever be that genteel and nice."

I liked hearing Lee Reynolds wasn't just a raving radio guy or even the two-timing husband Alex was sure he was. It was nice to hear he had shown my father the side of him Jessica Reynolds had said existed in her husband.

"He remembered me from the bar one night when a fan got a little too friendly. I had to admit to him I'd totally forgotten that night. We enjoyed a dinner of some laughs and good food, and that was it. We never spoke again after he left me sitting there with thanks for a wonderful time."

"Did he do the whole celebrity thing and pick up the check or buy a round of drinks for the entire restaurant?"

My father broke out into laughter. "I believe he did pay for my dinner, but there was no big show of money to buy a round for everyone there. I don't think celebrities really do that, Poppy."

"Maybe not. I've never met a celebrity, so everything I know about them is from TV and movies."

"I don't know if I'd call Lee Reynolds a celebrity, to be honest. He just seemed like an ordinary single guy out for a dinner alone. Nobody approached him for an autograph or anything like that."

The locals had a way of making the most unsuspecting folks near-celebrities in Sunset Ridge, so I was surprised Lee hadn't been besieged by people every time he left his house. His station manager had said he was just a regular guy in real life, so maybe that was why he didn't do the whole celebrity thing.

"Do you and Alex think it was an angry fan who killed him, Poppy?"

I shook my head as what we'd learned about his murder so far ran through my brain. "No, not as of now. So far, all we have is a guy in his forties who may have angered a lot of people but no real evidence to show any of them moved past being angry to actually killing him."

"That's too young to be taken from the world, no matter what I thought of the opinions he gave on the radio."

If Lee Reynolds was too young, what did that make Jessica Reynolds, who was barely my age?

"Did you ever meet his wife?"

"No. I know from talk around town he married two times and his second wife was pretty young compared to him. I think he was single when I had dinner with him that night."

I remembered how briefly Lee had been single between wife number one and wife number two. "That would be almost impossible since he was only legally single for a couple weeks between divorcing his first wife and marrying Jessica."

A slow grin spread across my father's mouth. "Ah. You don't have to be a detective to figure that out. Sounds like Mrs. Reynolds number two was the mistress when he was married to Mrs. Reynolds number one."

"Any idea what the first Mrs. Reynolds looked like? Did you ever see her around town?"

"No, but I remember hearing that his first marriage ended on bad terms and he had to pay her a substantial amount in the divorce."

Unsure of how true that rumor was, I asked, "How likely is it he'd return to the first wife for an affair then?"

My father shook his head definitively. "That seems unlikely, don't you think? A man has to give a woman half in a divorce after he possibly cheated on her, and then he goes back to her? Something doesn't fit there."

Standing from the liquor case, I walked over to the door and poked my head out of the storeroom to see McGuire's was all but empty, except for a few stragglers at the other end of the bar. Urging my father to join me, I walked out with him following and poured myself a glass of scotch.

"I think you're right, Dad. That idea doesn't work if they had a bad breakup."

My father looked around and leaned toward me to whisper, "I still think you're missing a golden opportunity with Alex, Poppy."

"I see you're not going to give up on this, so let me set your mind at ease, Dad." I took a swig of my drink and let it slide down my throat before I continued. "I admire Alex because I think he's a great detective, and I do admit we work well together. There's nothing romantic between us, though, and I think it will likely stay that way."

I looked away, unsure I could control my expression as I said that. I didn't want things to remain purely platonic with Alex forever, but too much about him and about us together made me confused. My father didn't need to know that, though.

"He likes you, Poppy. I think he may like you for the same reason you admire him. He likes your mind."

A chuckle bubbled up from inside, and I turned back toward my father. "There's nothing a woman likes to hear more than a man likes her for her mind. At least you didn't go with the idea of me having a great personality."

"You know what I meant. Of course you're beautiful and have a great personality. Those things are a given. But not every man wants a woman who challenges him. I think he does, though."

It was useless to spend time trying to convince my father of the reality of how much Alex likely didn't see me as a woman he wanted. All this talk about him was moot anyway. If I knew anything, it was this. Alex was still in love with a ghost, even if he was seeing Bethany from time to time.

And I wanted no part of being in love with a man who couldn't leave his past.

I tipped my glass to swallow the last of the scotch and set it back down on the bar. Patting my father on the shoulder, I leaned in and kissed him on the cheek. "Thanks, Dad. I know you're always in my corner."

"You know, Alex has come in a few times in the past couple weeks, and although he's never said anything, I had a feeling he was looking for you."

God bless him, he never gave up. "Dad, he knows where I live. He could just as easily come over. I think you're reading into things like a teenage girl."

"Maybe. Maybe not. Time will tell, I guess."

"Yeah, go with that. For now, I'm going to do my clean up and then head home."

"If you're not willing to believe me about Alex, then will you believe me about the guy sitting at a table in the corner who's checked you out at least four times since we came out of the storeroom?"

I looked at my father, confused as to whether he'd been taken over by the spirit of one of my friends hell bent on setting me up with a man. "What?"

He moved his head to indicate where the guy sat, and I looked around him to see a very attractive man with slightly tousled dirty blond hair and great cheekbones staring at me. He smiled and raised his glass, so I smiled back. Maybe my father wasn't wrong about this one.

The man's gaze never wavered from mine, and after a few long moments of staring at one another, he smiled and waved me over. For a second, I stood frozen to the floor, as if I couldn't move toward him or away from him. Then something inside me said I should at least walk over and say hi. It was the polite thing to do, and he was very easy on the eyes.

He stood as I approached him, and I saw he was tall, at least six foot, and lean. He had a sexy way about him that made him look more comfortable in his skin than anyone I'd ever met before. I instantly liked that about this man.

Extending my hand to introduce myself, he took it in his and I felt his strength touch me. Before I could say a word, he spoke and his voice felt like silk sliding over my skin.

Oh, I liked this man. At least I knew Alex wasn't the only cute guy in town.

Chapter Four

AFTER TOSSING AND turning all night, I awoke before sunrise and immediately began hectoring myself about how lame I was. I'd had the chance to talk to a good looking man who was obviously interested in me, and what did I do? I ran away.

Really.

He began to speak to me and I made some weak excuse about having to clean the bar and bolted from the scene.

His name was Jack. The most recent man I'd succeeded in avoiding any chance with. I liked knowing his name. It added a certain realness to the story of my pathetic romantic life.

I cringed at my behavior and rolled over to cover my head with a pillow. A perfectly good man approached me and I fled like a scared chicken. That was me. Scared chicken. I felt embarrassed and ridiculous at the same time.

This wasn't always who I'd been. In high school, I dated lots of guys. Rarely did I have a Friday or Saturday night without plans with some boyfriend. Then I went off to college and my romantic life rolled on just as it always had. Dates were never in short supply, and life was good.

Then came Jared. Nothing like finding out the man you think you're going to spend the rest of your life with is cheating on you with the mousy grocery checkout girl at Savings King everyone was sure would be an old maid. Then there's nothing like calling off your engagement to said man of your dreams who turned into a nightmare, cancelling the wedding that you'd proudly invited nearly two hundred guests to so they could share the biggest day of your life, and finally watching that same man run off not five days later to marry that shrew.

Even at that moment, I hated the mere thought of going to that store, and all that had happened almost five years ago. Since then, not only had I shunned Savings King, but I also had shunned men.

Not that I really wanted to. Well, at first I had. During those days right after my life fell apart, it was all I could do to get out of bed. I not only shunned men but the entire world. Never before or since had I so wished my mother had been there to show me how to move through all that with the kind of grace she displayed every day of her life.

But she wasn't there, so I retreated into my own private misery and stayed there for far too long. When I finally came out, I wasn't the same person I'd been before Jared broke my heart. I was suspicious and untrusting. In time, I returned more to my old self, but that scarred Poppy still lived and thrived in the two places inside me that couldn't believe things would ever work out for me again.

My heart and my head.

Normally, they worked against one another in other people, but not me. Since all that happened, both of them were all but sure I was destined to be what the gossips in Sunset Ridge whispered about me behind my back. Old maid. A woman who had her chance at true love and happiness but by choosing to stay in this small town with its boredom and safety under the guise of taking care of her father had sealed her fate.

Old maid.

I pushed the pillow down over my face and screamed into the room around me as the sun began to creep up over the horizon. I didn't want to think about those horrible days when I was sure life would never get better. It had. Now I had purpose to my life with my work at *The Eagle* and with Alex.

And there was no way I wanted to return to that time when all I did was hide out in bed, afraid of facing life. I may not have overcome all my fears, especially the ones about love, but I wasn't that broken, betrayed woman anymore.

At least that wasn't all I was.

Tossing the pillow aside, I grabbed my phone off the nightstand and called my partner. Today called for a change of scenery. That was for sure. His phone rang as I hoped it wouldn't go to voicemail. I didn't want to talk to a machine or type out my words this morning. Today called for the closeness a person's voice could provide, even if they had no idea they were giving someone that.

"Poppy, it's not even seven in the morning. Is everything okay?" Alex said in a groggy voice.

"Did I wake you up? I'm sorry. I just wanted to tell you I'd like to go to the Madison instead of The Grounds this morning."

"Feeling like a change today, huh? Fine with me. We were probably getting in a rut at The Grounds anyway."

Curious, I asked, "How did you know I wanted to change things up a little and wasn't just in the mood for pancakes instead of my usual danish?"

The phone fell silent for a moment, and I wondered if Alex had fallen asleep on me, but then he said, "I can hear it in your voice. You sound different this morning. Is everything okay?"

Choking up, I smiled. "Yeah. I'm fine. See you at nine at the Madison Diner?"

"I'll be there. If you get there before me, get me a coffee. I'm going to need it this morning."

Even though I knew I shouldn't care, my heart sank at the thought that he was exhausted because he'd spent the night with Bethany. Before I could stop myself, I asked, "Rough night?"

I heard a rustling noise in the background and then he slowly blew the air out of his lungs. "Derek lectured me until nearly one AM about finding Lee Reynolds' killer. He's worried about the town looking incompetent on a national scale because he's already begun getting calls from outside of Sunset Ridge about it."

Feeling defensive about our work and protective of Alex at the same time, I swung my legs out of bed and threw up the window shade. "It's only been a couple days, for God's sake. What's wrong with him? Why is he acting like Lee Reynolds was anything but a small town radio guy? I swear since he became chief, Derek has become a real politician."

"Yeah, well, I didn't get home until almost two and then I had to deal with…"

Alex's voice trailed off, leaving me hanging about what he'd had to deal with. Was Bethany camped out on his doorstep wearing nothing but a smile? Had wild dogs found her waiting naked for him and torn her into a million pieces which he'd found scattered all over his front porch? Had he left the water in the kitchen sink running all day and returned home to a flooded house?

What the hell had he had to deal with in the middle of the night?

My brain and my heart, working together to do their damnedest to my happiness this morning, made my mouth their co-conspirator and I blurted out, my voice on full panic mode, "What did you have to deal with? Was Bethany there? Oh my God, is she still there and I'm interrupting?"

I stood in the middle of my bedroom holding my breath as a combination of dread and embarrassment washed over me. This was what happened when a person avoided men for years. I was barely better at social relations than those wild dogs.

"No, Poppy, it's okay. She wasn't here last night and she isn't here now. We rarely see each other anymore. I just meant I had to deal with having a hard time getting to sleep."

My dread faded away to allow the feeling of foolishness to join my embarrassment. They were close friends, so they'd keep each other company. Quietly, I said, "I'm sorry. I didn't sleep well last night, so clearly I'm leaning toward crazy today. I swear I'll be normal by nine."

For the first time that morning, I heard a smile in Alex's voice. "It's okay, Poppy. This is what partners do—we're there when the rest of the world thinks you're nuts. I'll see you at nine."

I ended the call and threw my phone into my blankets as a feeling of calm came over me. Alex had that way that no matter what mania was tearing through me, just a few words from him and I didn't feel so crazy anymore. I liked that. Hopefully, he got something similar from me.

PUSHING OPEN THE door to the Madison Diner at five before nine, I saw the place was packed and practically standing room only. Perhaps a change of scenery wouldn't be happening after all. I pushed past the crowd hovering around the hostess station and scanned the restaurant for any sign of Alex. Waitresses buzzed up and down the aisles between tables, making it hard to see anyone for more than a second or two, but from the back I saw him wave toward me, so I made my way to where he sat back near the restrooms.

"Choice seats, I see," I teased as I sat down in the booth across from him.

"The cop uniform doesn't carry much weight when there's only two seats left. It was this or right next to the kitchen, and I wanted to avoid what happened last time."

Remembering the mess of having a waitress dump an entire tray of drinks as she passed me on the way to her table when we were last at the Madison, I cringed as I nodded. "Yeah, I don't feel like having to go home to change this morning."

I'd worn my favorite pale pink sweater with the three-quarter length sleeves. It was meant to make me feel more attractive, and the last thing I wanted to do was get it drenched by a tray full of coffee and tea.

"I'm happy you wanted to change things up, Poppy. Don't want us to get into a rut."

Alex's smile traveled all the way up to his eyes, lighting them up, so even though he sounded like he was joking with me, I knew he approved of the change. We'd return to The Grounds tomorrow, in all likelihood, but for today, we'd begin work on the case right there in that booth with the shiny red vinyl seats.

Candy, a pretty blonde with a black and white Madison Diner uniform that never had enough buttons closed, walked up to the table and immediately began flirting with him instead of taking our order. Between her need to punctuate every sentence she uttered with a touch on his shoulder and my hunger, it didn't take long for me to resent that she seemed to be incapable of doing one of the few tasks her job entailed.

After a minute or so of her fawning over Alex, I tapped on the table in front of me and said loudly, "Excuse me, Candy? I'd like a coffee and an order of French toast. Please bring me extra butter too. Oh, and can you bring over more milk?"

A look of surprise crossed her face, as if my telling her my order was something so strange she didn't know how to react. She looked back at Alex, who smiled at her, and then at me before taking out her pencil and order pad.

"A coffee and French toast. What would you like, hon?"

I opened my mouth to remind her how about the extra butter and fresh container of milk, but Alex began to speak before I could say a word. "Candy, don't forget about Poppy's extra butter, okay?"

She smiled sweetly and touched him on the shoulder again. "Of course, hon. I never forget what you tell me. You don't want the milk, though, do you? You always get your coffee black from me."

"I think I'm going soft this morning, so be sure to bring enough for both of us. I'll also have two eggs scrambled with American cheese and breakfast potatoes."

With a final touch to his shoulder, she gathered up the menus and trotted off toward the kitchen to put in our order. I looked at Alex and asked, "Why are you coming off your black coffee routine of late, and if you don't mind me asking, how do you stand her touching you like that?"

Grinning, he winked at me. "I'm not, but I didn't want you to have to ask her for milk again later. As for her touching me, my shirt's so starched I can't feel a thing when she does it."

I couldn't help but laugh, but his way of using his sexuality made me wish I was that comfortable with my own. I would have been happy with being able to talk to a man I liked. Thinking he might be the perfect subject to practice on, I asked, "Alex, what do you do when you're not working? I've known you for nearly six months, and all I know is that you like watching sports on TV."

With a smile only for Alex, Candy set our coffees down and the container of extra milk right in front of him and walked away. He pushed it toward me and asked, "Is this that you don't know anything about me business again?"

Disappointed I'd already failed at even making small talk with him, I poured milk and sugar into my coffee and said, "No, but it's okay. I was just wondering. Nothing big."

He took a drink of his coffee and after a few minutes

of us saying nothing, he answered my question. "Normally, I would have stayed home and watched the baseball game last night, for example, but Derek was busy reading me the riot act about this case. Why do you want to know?"

"Just wondering. Do you watch a lot of sports?"

Alex nodded. "Every season has one. Right now, baseball is ending and football is in full swing. Soon basketball will join football until after the new year, when football will end and then it's just basketball until baseball returns."

"And that's what you do when you're not working? Nothing else?"

"That's about it. I'm a typical man, unfortunately. What about you? What do you do when you aren't working cases with me or asking what I do in my spare time?"

I thought about my life and didn't like the answer I had to give him. "Not much. I worked at the bar last night and then went home to sleep. Now I'm here with you on a bright and sunny Saturday morning."

"No plans for tonight?" he asked in a tone that made me wonder if he thought I was as pathetic as I did.

"None right now," I muttered casually, as sure as I knew my own name that I wouldn't be doing anything other than watching sad Saturday night television if I wasn't out working on the case with him.

"Well, we certainly are perfect examples of small town life, I guess."

"Nice way to say boring."

For someone like him who'd lived in Baltimore and had an exciting life as a detective, retiring to someplace like Sunset Ridge felt right. He'd lived the big city life and now wanted to relax and take it easy, assuming Derek didn't drive him crazy over our current case. But me? I'd lived in Sunset Ridge nearly all my life, never really spending any time away other than my years at college, and it wasn't like I'd lived anywhere exciting during those four years either.

I had to face the facts. My life and I were boring, and I had no one to blame but myself.

And then as I sat there hating how boring my life was, the handsome man from the corner of McGuire's the night before walked right through the front doors of the diner and laid eyes on me. As if I hadn't acted like some scared teenage virgin, he made a beeline to where we sat while my mind scrambled for a way to escape what would undoubtedly be an awkward conversation of me trying to explain why I'd acted so ridiculously when we'd first met.

It was no use, though. Before I could bolt into the ladies' room, he was standing at our table smiling down at me like he still wanted to talk to me. "Didn't I see you behind the bar last night? I hoped to get to meet you instead of just sharing longing gazes across a room, but you left in such a hurry I barely got to introduce myself. Just in case you don't remember, I'm Jack."

Taken aback at how friendly he was once again, I extended my hand to shake his. "I'm Poppy. Poppy McGuire. That was my father's bar you were in last night. Are you new in town?"

Calm down. You don't have to serve him up twenty questions as soon as you start talking.

Jack nodded, and I saw a slight frown mar his attractive and very chiseled features. "I guess you could say that. I haven't been in Sunset Ridge for a long time."

"Oh? What brought you back here to us?" I asked with as much confidence as I could muster.

Hanging his head, he said quietly, "My brother's funeral. I'd just gotten into town when I saw you last night."

Nice, Poppy. Way to be smooth. Why couldn't you just keep it light and question free?

"I'm so sorry. I didn't mean to…I never intended to pry."

Jack swallowed hard. "I always thought I'd have more time with Lee. I guess I was wrong."

Shocked to hear he was none other than our murder victim's brother, I said, "Oh, you're Lee Reynolds' brother? I'm so sorry about your brother. We're the ones working on his case."

"I'm his younger brother. Only brother. Only sibling. We were separated by a lot of years, among other things."

He turned to look at Alex but didn't address him, and then he looked back at me. "Well, Poppy McGuire, I hope I have the good fortune of seeing you again while I'm here in Sunset Ridge. It would be nice for at least one good thing to come from my being back."

Stunned at the turn of events, I smiled and mumbled some words about hoping to see him again too before he walked away to sit at the counter. I'd underestimated how good looking he was the night before. In the light of day, he was stunning.

And he was interested in me.

Jack Reynolds, the gorgeous brother of Lee Reynolds, our victim, liked me. I sat there in that booth staring at him as he got his coffee to go and strode out of the diner just a minute later and couldn't believe he'd even wanted to talk to me after my behavior the night before.

Alex cleared his throat and brought me back to reality. I turned to see him staring at me with a look that said he was definitely unhappy about something.

"What's wrong?"

He crossed his arms and leveled his gaze on my face. "I've never seen you act like that."

"Act like what?" I asked.

"Like a lovestruck girl," Alex said, a strange tone echoing in his words.

I pooh-poohed his statement. "You're nuts. I was just being friendly to someone in their time of need."

"You didn't know he was in need until well after that lovestruck thing took over."

Candy brought our order to the table and did her touching thing on Alex's shoulder, but he didn't even look up at her. Instead, he continued to just stare at me like he disapproved. I didn't like that look.

"Maybe we should talk about the case so we can get it solved before Derek has a breakdown?" I asked, changing the topic.

"I think that's a great idea, but I wonder if you're able to focus or is your head filled with fantasies of Jack Reynolds."

I looked across the table and saw he was serious. "That's ridiculous! Maybe we should just eat and then after we can talk about our case, okay?"

He grumbled something about being able to talk about the case now and began to eat his eggs. I couldn't understand what had gotten into him. While it was true that Jack had been a little rude in not introducing himself to Alex, and I hadn't done much better, I didn't think that was any reason to be so surly with me. In truth, the chance to introduce him to Jack hadn't come up, and anyway, why would he care?

We sat in silence eating our breakfasts as an iciness set in between us. Of all the people I had in my life, and there weren't many, Alex was the only one other than my father I didn't want to fight with, so I needed to fix whatever had happened before it snowballed into a problem.

I pushed my plate of syrup into the middle of the table and took a deep breath. Whatever the issue was, we could work through it. With a smile, I said, "Thanks again for nudging Candy about the milk. I appreciate it."

Alex looked up from his eggs and nodded. "My pleasure."

Suddenly, he sounded like the man I met that first day in Derek's office, that cold and unfeeling person who had taken a dislike to me from the instant he was introduced to me. Had my liking Jack Reynolds' attention made me into someone he couldn't respect anymore? What had happened to that man who had warmed up enough with me that I considered him a dear friend?

Whatever it was, if it had to do with Jack, I had to take the bull by the horns and show him I was still the person he admired because of her mind and how she helped him solve cases. Sitting straighter in my seat, I said, "Alex, if this is about you thinking how I acted was unprofessional, I swear that wasn't my intention."

He didn't speak for a long moment and then finally said, "Well, now that you mention it, I don't think it's right for you to be so friendly with our victim's brother, who may very well turn out to be a suspect."

So that was it. I hadn't even considered the idea that Jack would logically have to be considered as at least a possible suspect. We didn't know anything about him or his relationship to his brother, so Alex had a valid point.

"I didn't think about that. I'm sorry. It was wrong of me to act that way once I knew who he was."

Alex's hard expression he'd held since Jack had walked away softened into a smile, but I noticed it didn't go all the way up to his eyes. But he seemed satisfied with my answer and said, "It's okay, Poppy. I just didn't want to see you disappointed if he becomes a suspect at some point."

"That's what partners do, right? They look out for each other. Thanks. I appreciate it."

I didn't know why, but he didn't seem happy with my agreeing with him about Jack. I wasn't really happy either. The one man who liked me in town and even seemed to be okay with my bizarre running away from him was the one man I shouldn't want to see again. Sometimes life didn't seem fair.

Chapter Five

THE SATURDAY MORNING crowd slowly left, emptying out the Madison Diner until the only people left were us and a small family a few tables away. Alex and I hadn't said much since we finished our breakfasts, other than my awkward apology about how I'd acted with Jack and Alex's equally as awkward acceptance of it.

But now that the din around us had calmed down, I wanted to start the day fresh again and forget what had happened. Whatever change I was looking for when I called him that morning hadn't turned out the way I'd hoped, but I could change that too.

Candy refilled our coffees and as she walked away sashaying her hips for Alex's benefit, I joked, "I wonder if that thing she does gets her more tips."

He looked over at her for a moment before turning back to look at me. "You mean that touching thing? I bet it does. Many men love that kind of thing."

"No, I meant the way she walks so it looks like there are two squirrels under her uniform having a brawl."

A slow smile crept into Alex's expression, and he shook his head. "You really do have a way of putting things sometimes, Poppy. I don't think I'm ever going to be able to look at her the same way again."

"Then my job here is done," I joked, happy to see him finally lighten up. "Now onto our case. How would you sum it up so far?"

His smile slid into a frown. "Not much. We have no suspects. That's how I'd sum it up so far."

"Well, don't get down. Let's just talk it out and then we can decide what our next move is. First up is Jessica, the wife. What do you think of her?"

"She has an alibi and seems genuine when she says they were blissfully happy."

I twisted my face into a dissatisfied grimace. Things weren't starting off well, but I wasn't convinced Jessica was one hundred percent innocent. Not yet, at least.

"I think we can agree she either wasn't seeing what was going on in her marriage or she was lying. She thought Lee was working late every Thursday, yet we've found no evidence that he ever did that. And then there are the red silk panties and the note from Cherise. I'm just not getting a happily married man vibe from all of that, Alex."

Alex sat back and threw his arm over the back of his side of the booth. "Okay, I'll grant you she may not have been seeing her husband as he truly was. So what was our victim doing when he claimed to be working late every Thursday?"

I grabbed a pen out of my purse and wrote the word CHEATING on a napkin. I slid it across the Formica table toward him and tapped on the word for emphasis. "That's what he was doing. Trust me. I know about these things."

Arching a single eyebrow, he looked at me for a moment before saying, "Cheating with the ex-wife? I don't know many men who go back to the one they left."

"Especially if it was for the woman he's currently married to," I thought aloud. "I mentioned this all to my father, and he said the same thing you just said. He didn't think Lee would go back to his first wife since it seems like he was cheating on his first wife with Jessica."

I stopped for a moment to catch my breath as a brief spike of rage tore through me. "But then again, since he was a cheating bastard to begin with, what would make him a stand-up husband the second time around?"

My words came out with a lot more venom attached than I wanted to show Alex, so I quickly forced a smile on my face. "Then again, who knows, right?"

After all that, Alex didn't seem to have anything else to add. "It sounds like you've thought about that a lot. Okay, let's leave what he was doing on the back burner, along with Jessica's part in this, if there was any, for later. I think we should focus on the first wife for now."

Happy for the change in topic, I asked, "What do you have in mind? We don't even know where she lives."

"Detective. I have her address ready to go. Your friend Keri was very helpful when I talked to her yesterday afternoon. She seemed very interested in how you're doing, though. Any idea why she's so worried?"

I knew full well why Keri thought she should be concerned about me. To her and everyone else who knew me when that whole thing with Jared happened, I hadn't moved on because I hadn't hooked up with a new man since then. If I knew Keri, she already suspected Alex and I were together, or at least she hoped we would be.

Brushing off the worry he'd seen from her, I said, "You know how people get sometimes. It's nothing. I'm glad she was so helpful, though. Where does Mrs. Reynolds number one live?"

"Just over the border in Pennsylvania in Waynesboro. It's about an hour away. Up for a road trip this beautiful October morning?"

At that moment with memories of Jared marching through my mind, the idea of getting out of Sunset Ridge sounded perfect. Grabbing the check, I waved it in front of Alex and said, "Since you're doing the driving, I'll get breakfast. Sound good?"

He drank the last of his black coffee and slid out of the booth to stand next to me. "I think the gentleman in me should have a problem with that, but since I'm getting to perform the manly job of driving, I guess I can live with it."

I rolled my eyes at his talk of manly duties. As Candy approached us, I whispered to him, "I'll meet you at the car. Careful or she might actually touch somewhere that's not starched."

While I paid the check, Alex practiced the fine manly art of avoidance and walked out to the car. I saw Candy pout for a moment as he escaped her clutches, but she wouldn't be sad for long. There were potential shoulders to touch on the four men who walked through the door as I passed them on my way out, and for women like Candy, one shoulder was as good as another.

WE PULLED UP to what looked like an abandoned farmhouse nearly an hour later, and the two of us looked at each other with confused expressions. I'd expected something better for the ex-wife of a man who had been rumored to have paid a hefty sum to divorce her.

"Are you sure this is the right address?" I asked, leaning forward toward the windshield to get a closer look.

Alex took out his notepad and checked the information Keri had given him. Showing me the address, he said, "That's what it says. Let's get out and check around. Maybe she moved since signing the divorce papers."

We walked toward the house as a brisk October wind whipped past us. Just an hour north, Waynesboro with its far more open spaces had a distinctly rural feel to it compared to Sunset Ridge. Looking down the road, the closest house to the one we thought was Cherise's appeared to be at least three hundred yards away.

The house itself sat back about ten yards off the road like some forgotten place that had meant the world to someone long ago. White paint, faded from years of neglect, peeled back from the wood beneath it, and the black shutters framing each window looked as worn as the paint. The black front door looked newer, though, as did the tiny windows in the door frame that surrounded it. Fireplace chimneys flanked both ends of the house, something I wished I had in my own home.

"Two fireplaces," I remarked as I pointed to the partially intact brick chimneys. "I'd love that."

Alex stopped in front of the home and gazed up at it like he was looking at the Taj Mahal. I'd never seen him so in awe of anything, and to see him so struck by this rundown mess surprised me.

"You okay?" I asked, suddenly wondering if this place brought back memories from his life before coming to Sunset Ridge.

"I'd love to have a house like this. Something I could fix up and really make it shine," he answered in a faraway voice.

I looked at him and then back at the old farmhouse he so longingly stared at. "Really? I had no idea you were handy with this kind of thing. I didn't peg you for a construction kind of guy."

He laughed and held up his hands for me to look at. Strong and big, I could imagine him building something impressive with them.

"I can make great things with these hands, Poppy. Just need to find the right project."

As I began to walk toward the front door, I joked, "Maybe you can take this one on if nobody's grabbed it yet."

He caught up with me and still wearing the smile he'd had as he admired the place knocked on the front door. While we waited for someone to answer, I had to admit his enthusiasm for the right project, as he called it, made me see him in a different light. This was basically how I learned things about Alex. While I told him things about myself, he tended to show who he was through the most random and unplanned actions. It made finding out who he really was a slow process but not an unexciting one.

To my surprise, the black door opened and in front of us stood a woman with red hair, blue eyes, and alabaster pale skin. Thinner than Jessica Reynolds, she looked to be about the right size for those red silk panties. She wore jeans and a thick cream colored sweater, but she didn't look like the type of woman who normally dressed in either piece of clothing. Something about her screamed beaded cocktail gown instead of jeans.

Alex held up his badge and explained who he was, and in return she gave him a big toothy smile. Whoever she was, she didn't seem unhappy to see us.

"Officer Montero, what can I do for you today?"

"Is your name Cherise Reynolds, ma'am?" he asked far more politely than I expected.

Her smile shrunk a bit and she nodded. "I am, but I can't imagine I'm that much older than you are for you to call me ma'am. I hope this is a southern gentleman thing since you're from Maryland."

He apologized as I tried to assess just how old she might be. My father hadn't said anything about her age, but I'd gotten the feeling she was closer to Lee's forty-something than mine or Alex's age. As I looked at her now, I guessed her to be on the better end of forty by the wrinkles near the outside corners of her eyes and above her lips. She wore enough makeup that they weren't obvious, and the makeup was definitely the expensive kind that didn't settle into the nooks and crannies of her face, but the telltale signs of age were there if someone was looking close enough.

"Ms. Reynolds, we'd like to speak to you about your ex-husband, Lee Reynolds. May we come in?"

I sensed the eagerness in Alex's voice was more about seeing the work Cherise was doing to the farmhouse and less about actually finding out about what she knew, if anything, about our victim's murder. Not that I blamed him. If a project like this was a dream of his, who was I to say he shouldn't love seeing one up close and personal, even if it was in the course of doing his duty?

Cherise stepped back to let us in, and we walked past

her into a newly remodeled room that looked like a sitting room. Painted in Wedgewood blue with pristine white crown molding at the ceiling and around the doorway into the kitchen ahead of us, it was a pleasant surprise after seeing the outside of the home. A white couch and navy blue wingback chair sat arranged around a dark wood rectangular coffee table and on top of new cherry wood flooring, all of which gave the effect that Cherise had spent not only a lot of time designing this room but a lot of money too.

"I only have two rooms and my bedroom with an attached bath done, but let me show you the kitchen," she said as she waved us on to follow her.

We walked behind her into the next room as the sound of hammers and saws from the back of the house filtered up toward us. Cherise explained they were working on the rest of the first floor and she hoped they'd be done before the beginning of the year.

Taking a seat at a kitchen table made of a similar dark wood to the sitting room's coffee table, we stared in amazement at how impressive her newly remodeled kitchen looked, our heads swiveling left and right to take in all the work. Almost completely white, except for the stainless steel appliances and what looked to be teak floor, the room had a clean look I couldn't help but love. A bank of windows above the large white farmhouse sink let the mid-morning sun flood in, making the room warm and welcoming despite its almost complete lack of color.

After letting my mouth hang open for nearly a minute, I said to Cherise, "I can't get over how beautiful the inside of this house looks compared to the outside. When we drove up, all I saw was a rundown farmhouse, but this is incredible."

She beamed her happiness at my compliment. "Thank you. The house is still more than half under construction with the rooms torn down to the studs in a majority of it, but these two rooms are just the beginning. I love how it's turning out."

Alex sat gazing around the room as she offered us coffee, so I told her yes for the two of us and explained, "My partner is in love with projects like this. I think I can see him quitting his job as a cop if he had a house like this to redo."

"It's life altering, but so worth it," she said as she opened a drawer and took out some pictures to show us. "Take a look at these before and after shots. The change is incredible."

We looked through the pictures and saw she hadn't exaggerated. What had been a dilapidated old house on its last legs was being transformed into a brand new home. Some rooms were still just walls and studs, but others like the one we sat in were show home level. Alex focused on each picture, staring at the details like he'd finally found the roadmap to happiness.

I pointed at him and chuckled. "See what I mean? He's in love with your house."

"Are you reluctant to let your husband take on a project like a whole house remodel because it's such a huge job?"

Another person who thought we were married simply because we were partners. I quickly corrected her. "No, no. We aren't married. We just work together."

Cherise looked at the two of us for a long moment and then smiled. "I'm sorry. I guess I just misunderstood. You look like you're a couple."

Alex put down the stack of pictures in time to hear her say she thought we were together and turned to look at me with the same confused expression I knew I wore. I didn't know why people kept thinking we were a couple. It wasn't as if we finished each other's sentences or either one of us fawned over the other in any way.

"Well, anyway, a house redo is so worth it, even if it seems like you're living in a construction zone for ages."

Now curious about the remodel, I asked, "Isn't it a strange time to be redoing a house since it's going to be the dead of winter soon?"

Cherise placed the pictures back into the drawer and brought our mugs of coffee to the table. "The entire house had to be remodeled, so at some time they'd be working in the winter. It's not too bad because they put up plastic like they use in commercial freezers, so when it gets really cold, I'll be able to keep the heat contained to the part of the house I'm using."

Interrupting our discussion of the remodel, Alex cleared his throat and quietly said, "We're here about your ex-husband's passing. Did you know Lee had been murdered?"

His choice of words struck me as intentionally shocking, but then again, maybe that's what he thought she needed since she'd treated our arrival as more of a personal visit than an official one. His tone worked, and she turned serious immediately.

"I did," she answered, her eyes filling with tears. "I found out yesterday."

"I'm sorry. Were you close?" he asked pointedly.

She sat down across from us and shook her head. "I still can't believe he's gone. We weren't really what I'd call close since the divorce and his remarriage."

Alex jotted a few words down in his notes and looked up at her. "When was the last time you saw him?"

Cherise sighed. "Not in the last year, I don't think."

"You haven't seen him anytime in the past month at all?"

She shook her head and answered without a hint of wavering in her voice. "No, I haven't."

One of the construction workers called her name from the far back of the house, so she excused herself and left us alone. While I sipped on my coffee, Alex received a text that made him smile even more than looking at the before and after pictures of Cherise's house had. Curious at what a single text could have included to make him so happy, I asked, "Get some good news?"

He looked over at me and put his phone into his pocket just as she returned from talking to the construction worker. No sooner had she sat down he began to ask her more questions.

"Cherise, did Lee have any enemies that you know of? Anyone who would want to do this to him?"

Tearing up again, she sniffled and said, "No. I can't think of anyone who would want to kill him. He just wasn't that kind of man."

I opened my mouth to ask her what kind of man she meant, but Alex asked, "I hate to have to ask, but it's not uncommon for exes to be suspects in cases like this, so where were you Thursday night."

Cherise seemed very understanding and nodded. "I get it. We weren't close, but we weren't enemies either. But to answer your question, I was here. The workers stayed until about seven before going home."

Alex stood from the table and thanked her for being so cooperative, a clear sign he had no more questions for her at the moment, and although I'd normally ask a few of my own, I was too curious to know what that text had said to make him so happy, so I silently followed him toward the door as Cherise walked with us.

Just as we were about to leave, he turned to face her and with a big smile asked, "By the way, do you own any guns?"

Cherise shook her head and frowned. "No. They terrify me."

Alex seemed pleased by her answer. He gently squeezed her hand and said, "Please accept my deepest sympathies."

Then he walked away, leaving me feeling like I was the only one not clued in to what was going on. I thanked Cherise for her hospitality and offered my own condolences on her loss before I jogged to catch up to Alex, who was already behind the wheel of the car.

Once I was in the passenger seat and my door was closed, I turned to him and gave him a glare. He looked at me with the expression of a naughty child who knew they'd misbehaved and asked, "What's that look for?"

I rolled my eyes and squeezed his arm. "Please accept my deepest sympathies. Not our deepest sympathies. *My* sympathies."

He chuckled at my disgust, irritating me more, but explained, "It was more a play on words, but I guess you wouldn't know that since I didn't tell you what that text said."

"What did it say?" I asked excitedly, willing to forgive his partner faux pas if it was indeed that interesting.

"That text was from Craig. I asked him to check if Cherise owns a gun. That was the answer. She does. A .38."

I looked back at the house where she'd all but convinced me she couldn't be the murderer. "But she said she didn't because they terrify her, and now we know she owns the exact kind of gun that killed Lee Reynolds."

Alex started the car and smiled at me. "I guess she got over her fear of guns. Am I forgiven for my misstep?"

I wrinkled my nose at him. "This time, but next time, you might not be so lucky, Officer Montero."

Throwing the car into drive, he nodded his understanding. "Then I'll have to make sure I don't make that mistake again, Ms. McGuire."

Chapter Six

WE RETURNED TO Alex's office at the station to find the coroner waiting for us. Sitting in the chair in front of the desk like he was having a meeting with an invisible person, he turned to face us when we walked in and handed Alex a folder.

"I wanted to bring you this myself. I thought you might find it very interesting."

Donny worked for the county, not the town of Sunset Ridge, so his bothering to come down to see us, especially on a Saturday, meant he found something important to our case. A little man with mousy features and a comb over, he'd worked with the dead for as long as I'd known of him. The first time I saw him at a crime scene I thought he was unwelcome there like me. He skulked around ducking in and out of shrubbery and avoiding the police, so I assumed he must be just a curious onlooker who'd been told by Dominick to stay away from his crime scenes.

Alex looked at me with curiosity in his eyes and took the folder out of Donny's hands. "What's this about?"

As he opened it, the coroner pointed at the top sheet of paper. "Take a look. This guy certainly did have people after him."

My interest piqued by Donny's claim, I sat down beside him and began to pump him for information. "What do you mean? Did you find something other than the gunshot wound that shows someone tried to kill him another way?"

"Tetrahydrozoline? What's that?" Alex asked.

I looked at him and then back at Donny for the explanation. His smug expression told me he was pleased that we had no idea what that word meant and that he'd have to enlighten us. I understood that desire to be the one in the know. Everyone wanted to feel like they could add something to the investigation.

"That was found in his stomach when I did the autopsy. Any idea what that is?"

"Something watery?" I guessed as I wished I hadn't disregarded much of high school chemistry in favor of my junior year boyfriend.

Donny turned to look at me with approval. "I'm impressed, Poppy. That's not exactly it, but it is a liquid."

Feeling particularly intelligent, I puffed out my chest and smiled at Alex. "He's impressed by my guess. You have any idea what it is?"

Amused by our back and forth, Alex shook his head and smiled. "Nope. I leave that kind of thing to the science people like Donny here, who I'm sure is going to tell us what tetrahydrozoline is any minute now."

"Your victim died from a gunshot wound from a .38 caliber gun, but someone was also poisoning him, albeit incorrectly."

"Interesting, but we still don't know what you say someone was poisoning him with," Alex said in a voice that told me he was growing tired of Donny's grandstanding.

"The tox screen found tetrahydrozoline in his system, which mean someone was making sure he ingested eye drops."

I looked at Alex to see he was as confused as I was. "Donny, why would anyone want to see Lee Reynolds drink eye drops?"

"Whoever was trying to kill your victim had read too many inaccurate news reports that said putting eye drops into someone's liquid would kill them. It just gives them nausea, high blood pressure, and diarrhea. But Mr. Reynolds definitely would have been feeling bad for a while. I'm just guessing here, but I'd say he's been being dosed for a while, at least a few weeks."

Eye drops in someone's liquid? I'd never heard of this before. "Is this a thing now?" I asked, looking back and forth from him to Alex to see if I was the only person who was completely baffled by this.

"It is," Donny said with a chuckle. "At least for people who have no real idea about chemical compounds and how they affect the human body. Eye drops won't kill anyone, but someone around your victim thought they would."

Alex closed the folder and looked over at me. "Now we just have to find out who and why."

Behind us, Derek cleared his throat and stepped into the office. His handsome face wore a stern look that told me finding out about someone attempting to kill Lee Reynolds added to the fact that someone already had wasn't making his day any better.

Before Derek could say a word, Donny made some excuse why he had to leave and quickly got out of the office. For a second, I considered doing the same since I wasn't technically one of Derek's employees and would have a hard time keeping my mouth shut if he began to ride Alex about the case. I didn't leave, though, because he was my partner, and even if I wasn't really a cop, I knew about this case.

"What's this I hear from him about someone trying to poison Lee Reynolds?" Derek asked, crossing his arms in a clear sign that was the last thing he wanted to hear about this case.

Alex stayed relaxed in an effort to offset the emotions practically flowing off his chief. "He just told us. We'll check into it and see if who was trying to kill him is the same person who actually shot him."

A look of disgust I'd rarely seen from Derek settled into his face, making him look years older than his early thirties. "I want this case solved fast and hearing there's another crime associated with our victim doesn't make me happy."

"Then how about hearing that the victim's ex-wife owns the exact caliber weapon that shot him?" Alex asked in a hopeful voice.

"How likely is it that the ex-wife was poisoning him, though?" Derek asked in return, making all the hope I shared with Alex dissolve.

Neither of us said anything. It wasn't likely at all that Cherise would have the opportunity to poison her ex-husband for weeks on end. Unless we found there were other gaps in his time with his wife or at work other than one afternoon each week, Cherise just wouldn't have the chance often enough.

"I didn't think so," Derek said with a sigh. "Find out who was behind the messy poisoning of the victim before you go blaming his ex-wife. It sounds like the current wife had an ax to grind."

With that, Derek left us with our case no clearer than it had been as the morning began. After that trip out to Waynesboro, I really thought we'd made headway and finally had a lead that meant something. Now with Donny's eye drop report, everything about the case of who killed Lee Reynolds seemed muddled once again.

We sat silently, the two of us lost in thought until an idea came to me. Excited, I blurted out, "What if the wife and the ex-wife were in it together?"

I knew it sounded more like something from a Lifetime movie than a real theory, but Alex's eyebrows moving north up his forehead told me he thought it was pretty ridiculous.

"Really? Why?"

At least he was willing to entertain my outlandish idea, so I ran it through my mind a moment and then explained it all to him. "Say Jessica found out he was seeing Cherise every Thursday afternoon for a quickie out at her farmhouse with her in those red silk panties. She confronts Cherise and they have it out."

He interrupted me and shook his head. "This doesn't sound very promising, Poppy. Now if one of them had killed the other, this theory might work."

"Wait, it gets better. So now Jessica decides she wants Lee dead for being a two-timing cheating bastard. She doesn't know how to do it, but she sees one of those inaccurate news reports about how eye drops killing someone if they drink them and figures there's her answer. She begins putting them in her husband's orange juice every morning and waits."

Still skeptical, he leveled his gaze on me and asked, "And then when it didn't seem to be working, she went to the woman her husband was cheating on her with and asked her to shoot him, which of course Cherise said yes to?"

I opened my mouth to continue explaining my theory, but his question had just shot it full of holes. Crestfallen, I slouched in my chair and sighed. "Okay, you're right. That doesn't make sense."

"Nice try, though. I think we have to approach these two crimes as separate. I don't think whoever was dosing Lee Reynolds with eye drops was involved in his murder. I do want to know why the eye drop poison person wanted Lee dead, though."

"So let me see if I have this straight. Someone shot him and left a bullseye around the wound before leaving him there to die in the woods. The guy was widely popular for his controversial opinions he voiced on air, but he also had enemies because of these opinions. However, we haven't spoken to anyone who can say a bad word about him in his personal life, and we have no sense that this murder was committed by an angry fan. Am I right so far?"

Alex nodded somberly. "All that fan mail has been checked and there were no threats to kill Lee Reynolds. For all his bluster, his audience wasn't exactly full of raving lunatics, it seems. But you just brought up an important point. I haven't heard anything about that chalk used to draw that bullseye on the victim's back."

He picked up his office phone and pressed Craig's number. After waiting a few seconds, he said, "Craig, did you find that piece of chalk at the murder scene?"

I couldn't hear his answer, but Alex's frown told me it was no. He hung up the phone and stood from his desk. "We need to find that chalk before it rains and it's washed away."

"But what if the murderer took it with him?" I asked as I stood to leave with him.

"Then we don't find it, but I can't see someone keeping it on their person. For now, though, we have other things to keep us busy. Derek likely will give me a hard time getting a search warrant for Cherise's place to look for that gun before we check out this eye drop business, so it looks like we need to go visit Jessica Reynolds again."

"Off to Jessica's again," I said with a chuckle. "I have to admit I have a hard time imagining her trying to poison her husband, though, Alex."

He stopped to look at me as we walked out to get back into the squad car again. "Too much in love with him?"

His mocking tone telegraphed how unlikely he thought that possibility was. Shaking my head, I answered, "No, actually. I think she did love him, but I can't imagine her doing that for the simple reason that I just don't see her as someone who would kill anyone. She just doesn't have that kind of passion in her."

"This may not have been a crime of passion, Poppy. It might have had nothing to do with love."

"I didn't say it did, but I still can't see her as a murderer."

As usual when I made my proclamations, he merely smiled and walked away. Whether he believed me or not, I couldn't put my finger on it, but my gut said Jessica Reynolds could never kill anyone.

HALFWAY THERE, MY cell phone rang with a call from

my father. Since he rarely called during the day, I quickly answered it, afraid something bad had happened.

"Hey, Dad. What's up?"

"Why do you always sound frightened when I call you? I would think a call from your father would make you happy."

He was right, and I was happy to hear from him whenever he called me, but usually the first emotion I felt was dread. Pure, unadulterated dread at the mere thought that something had happened to him. I knew it stemmed from losing my mother and I had to get a handle on it, but that didn't change the fact that I worried about him.

"I'm always happy to hear from you, Dad. What's going on with you today? Having a good Saturday?"

"I am, but not as good as you, I think."

His singsong voice made me wonder what he was up to. "You sound particularly happy this morning. What's going on, Dad?"

"I just got a delivery at the bar a few minutes ago. For you."

Why would someone send me anything to the bar?

"What are you talking about? No one would send me a package to your place. I'm sure it's just a mistake by the mailman. You know how he is. He figures since we're related, he can take shortcuts. Do you remember that one time he decided to deliver my magazines to your house for a whole month because he had to get to his part-time job at the packaging plant a few years ago?"

I felt Alex's gaze on my left cheek and turned to see him staring at me with a strange look on his face.

Shrugging, I covered the phone and said, "Sorry. My father got something for me at his house. I'll end the call and talk to him later."

He waved off my concern. "No need. We still have at least a couple minutes before we get to the Reynolds' house, so you're fine."

Putting the phone to my ear again, I said, "Dad, I have to go. Alex and I are working on a case right now. I'll come by and see you later after we're done, okay?"

"Poppy, this isn't some mistake by the postman. The delivery is from Carson's."

"The flower shop?" I asked, even more confused. Someone had sent me flowers?

"Yep. So who is Jack the guy from the corner?"

A giggle escaped from my lips. "Is that what it says on the card? Jack the guy from the corner?"

"So you know this mystery man," my father said with a tone of approval. "Who is he?"

I felt my cheeks warm from a blush and admitted who Jack was. "Remember the guy you said was checking me out at the bar last night? His name is Jack. I actually saw him this morning, but he didn't mention anything about sending me any flowers."

"Well, well. And here I was worried about you being too afraid to make a move. You must have made quite an impression on him last night."

"I don't know how. I didn't even talk to him. We didn't have our first real conversation until this morning when I saw him at the Madison Diner."

Out of the corner of my eye, I saw Alex's expression morph into a frown that drew his entire face downward. I knew how he felt about my having any contact with Jack since he could be a potential suspect in our current case and didn't want to go against his wishes on this.

"Dad, I have to go. I'll drop by later to get the flowers. Thanks for letting me know."

For a moment, the phone fell silent and then my father asked, "Is everything okay, Poppy? I thought you'd be happy to hear about the delivery. It's a dozen red roses and pretty nice. He seems like someone who's interested in you."

I looked over at Alex, who had transformed his face into a true grimace. "Oh, I am. Thanks for calling, Dad. I just have work to do, but thanks. I'll talk to you later, okay?"

My father said something else about how beautiful the flowers were, but I ended the call as soon as I could. Stuffing the phone into my purse, I avoided looking at Alex and instead just stared out the window at the brilliantly colored leaves and pumpkins decorating the homes we passed in the car.

Finally, he spoke and I knew for sure Jack's flowers had made him unhappy again about him. In a voice barely more than a growl, he said, "It's nice that you still help her father out at the bar even though you have a full-time job and work cases with me."

I had a feeling what he really wanted to say was that he didn't like how I was acting concerning Jack Reynolds, but he didn't say those words so I didn't say anything about it either.

Still staring out the window, I said, "I do it to spend time with him because I know he's lonely since my mother died. She was his whole life, and now all he has is me."

Alex said nothing, and when I turned to look at him, I saw he still wore a deep frown. I didn't know why he didn't tell me what he really felt. That no matter how flattered I was to get flowers from Jack, I couldn't encourage him to show me any more attention because he very well could be a suspect at some point in our case. I didn't want to hear that, but I knew it was probably the truth.

What I didn't know was why everything about Jack Reynolds seemed to create such tension between Alex and me.

Chapter Seven

JUST AS WE had the first time, we parked in front of the Reynolds' upscale townhouse on Colonial Drive and knocked on the door, expecting to speak to our victim's widow. The person who we encountered was nothing like the Jessica Reynolds we met just two days earlier.

She opened the door and immediately began sobbing. One look at her told me she'd spent the day crying. Her jet black mascara that made her blue eyes stand out sat on the bags under those pretty eyes and her nose looked raw and red. I half expected her to confess right there before we even got inside the house, but she didn't. Instead, she sobbed almost uncontrollably so neither Alex nor I could understand what she was saying.

"Mrs. Reynolds, has something happened?" Alex asked in his authoritative policeman voice. "Are you okay?"

She mumbled something through her tears and shook her head. Then inexplicably, she began to cry harder, although nothing he'd said warranted the explosion of her emotions. Then again, she was dealing with the sudden death of her husband.

Alex leaned forward to peek inside the house and

asked, "May we come in? My partner and I don't want to leave you here alone like this."

I saw Jessica's eyes fly open in terror at Alex's suggestion. She moved to block his view, and for a moment I didn't think she'd let us into the house. Alex sensed something was wrong, but he asked again if she was okay and she just nodded.

Reluctantly, she opened the door wider to allow us in and we saw she wasn't alone. There standing near the large brick fireplace on the far wall of the living room was her brother-in-law and the man who'd sent me flowers that afternoon.

Jack wore black pants and a gunmetal grey dress shirt under a black leather jacket. Looking like he belonged in the townhouse, he casually leaned on his elbow against the fireplace mantle wearing a confident look on his face.

"Jack? What are you doing here?" I asked before my brain could stop my mouth.

He smiled and walked toward me. "I came over to see if Jessica wanted anything in her time of need. We're both just trying to find a way to deal with the loss of Lee."

Feeling stupid for asking such an obvious question, I waved away his answer. "Of course. I'm sorry. I should have known that."

From behind me, Alex said in that authoritative voice he'd just used on Jessica outside, "Mr. Reynolds, we need to speak to your sister-in-law alone, if you don't mind."

I spun around to see him glaring at Jack with a look that could kill in his eyes. For his part, Jack didn't seem upset about Alex's order to leave. He took Jessica's hand

and kissed it, telling her to call him if she needed anything before he said to me, "I'll leave her in your very capable hands then."

Pleased he was being so good about things, especially since Alex had been so rude, I smiled as he passed. "Thank you. I'm sure you understand. We have to do our job to find your brother's killer."

"Of course. I'll get out of your way. I hope to see you again soon, Poppy."

Jack thanked me and left without another word as Jessica began sobbing uncontrollably again at my mention of Lee's murder. I was a little surprised he didn't stop to comfort her, but since Alex had all but told him to get out, he likely didn't feel he could stay to help.

Taking her hand in mine, I guided her to the couch to try to make her feel better. The tears continued to come fast and hard, even as I sensed my soothing words were having some good effect.

"We're here, Jessica. I understand. Both Alex and I do. We've both lost people we loved, so we know how hard this is for you."

She dried her eyes and blew her nose into a tissue she pulled from her pants' pocket. "I don't know what I'm going to do without him. He was the love of my life. My soulmate. What am I supposed to do rambling around in this empty townhouse with all its memories of the good times we shared?"

I nodded my understanding, genuine in my attempts to help her. "I remember when my mother died. My father was inconsolable. He didn't feel like he could go on. He did, though, but it was hard. He had to take it one day at a time."

Jessica gave me a tiny smile and wiped her eyes

again. "It is hard. Lee and I have been in love since the minute we met. Even his brother saw it."

As I opened my mouth to ask her exactly when that was, Alex interrupted me with his own question. "The coroner found some strange anomalies when he did Lee's autopsy, Jessica. I'd like to ask you some questions about that."

"Autopsy?" She repeated the word in horror and then buried her face in her hands as she began to sob again. "Oh my God! My poor Lee! I can't bear to think of him laid out on a cold coroner's table."

I shot Alex a nasty glance meant to let him know how unfeeling I thought he was being with her. He returned my look with one of disgust I knew meant he thought I was coddling Jessica too much. As I gently rubbed her arm, I whispered, "There, there." What I really wanted to say was, "My partner is an insensitive jerk, so don't listen to him."

While she sat on the couch crying, I excused myself and quickly pulled him into the dining room. Leaning close to him, I whispered, "I have no idea what you're trying to do here, but being such a heartless ass to a woman who's just lost her husband isn't going to get you whatever you think it will."

His face filled with frustration before it twisted into a grimace. "You can't see those are crocodile tears? You're smarter than that, Poppy."

I had thought her crying was a tad much, but then I remembered back to when my mother died and how my father and I had cried for what seemed like weeks on end. It had only been a couple days since she'd gotten the news that her husband had been murdered, so I thought it was possible the reality of never seeing the man she loved had finally set in.

Not that I wanted to say anything of that to Alex at that moment as he waited for me to answer him about my ability to see someone lying directly to my face. "Of course I can see that. I'm not an idiot. I may not wear a badge, but I can tell when someone's emotions are forced, Alex. I still don't think you're going to get anywhere with her acting like you are."

"Then what do you suggest?" he asked in that clipped way that told me he was even angrier than his expression indicated.

"Let me talk to her. Just back off a little and let me see if I can get her to answer some questions."

He thought about my suggestion for a moment and nodded. "Okay, I'll head off to the bathroom to see if there's anything that would indicate she was the one poisoning him."

I looked back at Jessica still sobbing on the couch and then back at him. "We don't have a warrant, though. Won't that mean anything you find will be inadmissible in court?"

A look of amusement flashed in his dark eyes. "Now it's my turn to tell you I'm not an idiot. I didn't say I was going to do anything but look. I'll save the touching for when I get a warrant."

Jessica's crying grew louder for some unknown reason and I whispered to him as he began to walk back into the living room, "I think our being here is upsetting her."

He shook his head. "I think she's playacting, so feel free to ask her any questions you want, and I'll do what I do best."

Alex walked past her to stand with his arms folded

across his chest in the corner of the living room while I did my part to find out anything I could between her sobs. Taking my place next to her on the couch again, I lightly touched her arm and smiled, hoping she wouldn't sense I had doubts about her misery.

"Can I get you anything? A glass of water? More tissues?" I offered.

She took a deep breath in and let it out in a shudder that shook her entire body. "No, I'm okay. I don't mean to be so useless with your investigation. I really don't. It's just that I can't stop thinking of all the things we had planned that aren't going to happen now."

Tears welled in her eyes for the future taken from her and her husband. Maybe she wasn't completely forcing them.

"Mrs. Reynolds, can I use your bathroom?" Alex asked abruptly.

I'd planned to provide him a way to ease into asking, but apparently, he couldn't wait. I turned to look at him and squinted my eyes in anger. I got that he didn't think she was all that broken up about losing her husband, but why did he have to come in like a wrecking ball just as I was getting her calm again?

His request caught her off guard and pointing toward the hallway in front of him, she said, "It's down there. Third door on the left."

I saw a flash of something in her eyes when she looked back at me. Was it fear? Guilt? Had she been poisoning her husband and left the proof of it in the bathroom?

"How are you feeling now? A little better?"

She took another deep breath and didn't shudder when she let it out this time. "A little. Thank you for being so nice. I think I'd be a weeping mess if I had to deal with just your partner."

I fought the urge to roll my eyes at how that partner was acting. "He's very much a man about things like this. Men don't understand emotion. I think it's the testosterone that dulls their ability to truly comprehend sadness."

"Lee did. He understood when someone was sad and always knew the right thing to say."

Nodding, I pressed a smile onto my face and wondered if Lee Reynolds could be as wonderful as his wife continued to claim he was. Loving, attentive, and sincere? Did such a man indeed exist, or were her memories tainted by sadness, or even worse, guilt?

As curious as I was about that, I needed to ask her about the case so I gingerly introduced the idea of his work into our conversation. "Jessica, can you think of anyone at Lee's job who might want to hurt him? We talked to some people there, and either they didn't know him or they loved him. It's odd for someone to not have at least one enemy at the workplace. Can you think of anything he might have told you about any problems he had?"

Jessica stopped crying and looked off in the distance toward the picture window that faced out to the street. After a few seconds, she looked back at me and said, "There was someone. Yes. I didn't think about it the last time you were here, but there was. I remembered him saying something when I was going through some of Lee's things last night."

She began to cry again and through the tears said, "I found a picture from our honeymoon to the Bahamas. We looked so happy. Who could know that just a short time later he'd be gone? If I'd known we'd have so little time together…"

As she buried her face in her hands once again, I worried I was losing her to the wash of memories that came when someone realized the one they loved was never coming back. Pressing her to focus, I asked, "What did he say about this co-worker? What problems did they have?"

Sniffling, she dabbed the tissue under her nose. "Lee told me about this one fellow DJ at work who was very jealous. Jay. Maybe his first name began with a J. Or the last name? I don't know. I wish I could remember."

"When did this problem first come about? Do you remember?"

She thought about my question and nodded. "I think it was pretty recent because Lee told me about it about a month ago."

Just then, out of the corner of my eye I saw Alex return to the living room. The happy look on his face said he'd found something in the bathroom, but that would have to wait until we were alone again. For now, I wanted Jessica to tell him about the problem Lee had at work.

"Alex, Jessica remembered an issue her husband had with a fellow employee at the radio station recently. Would you tell him what you told me, Jessica?"

She looked at Alex with fear, probably wondering if he was still going to be doing his best ice man act. His trip to the bathroom appeared to improve his mood a bit, though, and he smiled at her for the first time since we arrived.

"Yes, please do, Jessica. Anything you can remember will be helpful to us solving this case."

Now there was the Alex who knew how to charm a lady. Why it had taken him so long to let that part of him out was beyond me. I was just glad he'd finally shown up. Any more of his frostiness and I may have started to sob out of frustration.

Jessica responded to his warmth and charm and explained what she remembered about Lee and his problem with the fellow DJ.

"Lee told me one evening at dinner about a month ago that he was having some issue with one of the other DJs. He hadn't said anything to me, but I knew my husband and that long face he wore when he was worried hadn't left him for days, so one night I asked him what was wrong and he told me. He said the man was very jealous."

"Do you remember what he was jealous of?" Alex asked.

Shaking her head, she answered, "No, but now that I'm talking about it I do remember him telling me it was the DJ who did the classical music on the overnight shift. He'd see him in the mornings when they were switching shifts. And one time the DJ threatened Lee as they passed in the hall."

Before Alex could ask another question, I said, "That's great, Jessica. Thank you. Do you remember what the man said to him?"

"No. I'm sorry. I just remember Lee saying he wasn't worried about it. He didn't take the threat seriously and considered it bluster from a lesser person. Men will be men, you know?"

Alex didn't respond to her swipe at the male ego, but I knew exactly what she meant. My partner may not have been the typical macho male, but his behavior with

Jack told me that part of him did exist somewhere inside him.

Alex finished writing down notes about what she'd said and came around the couch to stand in front of us. For a moment, I thought he was going to arrest her right then and there by the intense look on his face, but whatever he was feeling passed and he simply gave her a gentle smile as he handed her his card.

"Please, if you remember anything else you think might help, don't hesitate to call. I wrote my personal number on there, so no matter what time day or night, you can find me. Oh, one more thing. Was your husband complaining of headaches or nausea recently?"

She shook her head and said no, but then she seemed to remember something. "He was sick with the flu a few weeks ago, but Lee wasn't like other men. He didn't complain when he was sick. He just went to work as usual."

Jessica and I stood to walk to the door, and as we left, I hugged her. It wasn't professional and it wasn't anything a near perfect stranger like myself should do with her, but I did it anyway. As I pulled away, I reminded her that we could come back if she needed us to, and she began to sob again.

This time her tears were clearly forced, though. Why, however, was the question.

She closed the door behind us, and as we walked to the car, Alex nudged my side with his elbow. "Nice touch there."

"It wasn't meant as anything phony, but I guess her fake tears sort of ruined whatever I was trying to do to help."

Alex chuckled. "She'll be fine. Something tells me

she has a tendency to land on her feet no matter what happens. I wonder if Jessica was an actress before she married our victim. She sure can cry on cue."

Stopping at the car, I opened the passenger side door and leaned against the roof to shoot him another glare. "Back to being the heartless bastard again? She did just lose her husband, Alex."

We got in and closed the doors as he started the car. "I know, Poppy, and I know how bad it hurts to lose a loved one. You know too. You also know a lot of those tears weren't real."

"I wonder why she was doing that," I thought out loud.

Alex turned to me and grinned like the cat that had just eaten the canary. "Maybe it was the five full bottles of eye drops and two in the garbage she was afraid I'd find when I went into the bathroom."

"Really?" I asked in amazement. In all the talk about someone poisoning Lee Reynolds, I'd never truly believed his wife had been any part of that.

"Yeah. Maybe that's why she was turning on the water works so much so she could explain why she'd need that many bottles of eye drops."

I had to laugh. Even from Alex, that sounded silly. "So just to recap, are we thinking Jessica was trying to kill her husband but for some reason decided to stop waiting for him to die and shot him in the back in the woods outside of town? I'm not sure what to think of this."

Alex shook his head and shrugged. "I don't know if we should consider her a suspect in the shooting, but I definitely think she was part of why Donny found the eye drops in Lee's system. So was she trying to kill him and got impatient? And if so and she didn't pull the trigger, then who did? And why?"

I sighed in frustration. "Every time we take a step forward in this case, it feels like we take a step back right after," I said as he pulled away from the curb.

"Two steps is what it feels like to me."

I heard the frustration in his voice too. How did a guy who so many people said they loved or didn't even know end up dead with a bullet in his back? Who hated him so much to shoot him and leave him for dead? And why hadn't we found anyone who even showed a hint of that level of hatred?

"What I don't understand is what would have been her motive? Are we still thinking he was cheating on her with another woman, maybe his first wife? I'm not feeling that, Alex."

He pursed his lips and nodded as he stared straight ahead. "I don't know, Poppy. All I know is I can connect her to the attempted poisoning of her husband. That's it for now."

"Are you going to get a warrant for Jessica and Lee's townhouse?" I asked, figuring it was just a matter of time before he accused her of some part in her husband's murder.

Alex didn't answer me while we drove back to town, appearing to be lost in thought. I watched his expression change from his usual placid look he wore when he was around me to one dominated by a frown and didn't want to ask why.

Was it the case or something that had happened at the Reynolds' townhouse that weighed so heavily on his mind?

Chapter Eight

MY FATHER'S FACE lit up as I stepped into his bar, a look of surprise in his eyes at seeing me two nights in a row. He hadn't called me to fill in for an absent bartender tonight, though. No, I was at McGuire's for purely recreational reasons.

"Poppy! I didn't think I'd see you again today after you came by for the flowers. Any chance you're here to say thanks to the sender of those flowers?" my father asked with a twinkle in his eye.

The usuals who sat at the end of the bar tore their attention away from the televisions on the wall above the shelves of liquor and began teasing me like a bunch of schoolgirls about having a new boyfriend. I ignored their sing-song taunts I knew meant no harm and walked behind the bar to pour myself a drink.

"See what you started?" I joked with my father as I walked away to sit at a nearby table.

He followed me and sat down in the seat opposite me. "You know I always like seeing you when I don't have to ask you to fill in for one of my bartenders, don't you?"

I took a sip of my beer and smiled. "I know, Dad. This isn't a big deal, so don't make it something it isn't.

I'm just hanging out on a Saturday night."

He gave me one of his charming Irish grins and put his hands up in surrender. "No problem. Whatever brings you in you know I'm happy to see you. Are you meeting Alex here to talk about the case? Any breaks yet?"

Shaking my head, I admitted the truth of the situation. "No, and Alex has Derek on his back day and night to get it solved before some national media outlet gets their hands on the story and the police department looks like a group of Keystone cops who can't solve a crossword puzzle, much less a murder case."

"It has only been a couple of days. Maybe someone needs to remind Derek of that."

"He's the chief now, Dad," I said, reminding him of Derek's new important status in town. "That means he has to answer to the mayor and the town council. I get that. He's got a lot more pressure now that he's the big guy in charge. It's just that his worries are becoming Alex's worries and it's affecting him too."

My father gave my hand a sympathetic pat. "He's a strong guy. He can handle it. I wouldn't worry about him."

"I guess, but I think Derek's pressuring him to solve the case quickly is making him have trouble sleeping. He said something about it yesterday, and he's been particularly miserable for the second day in a row."

"That doesn't sound like him," my father said, knitting his brows like he did whenever he was concerned about something. "He's usually a pretty easygoing guy."

I thought back to how he'd reacted to my father's call about the flowers and nodded. "I know. I've gotten used to that guy with such an even-keeled personality, but a couple times yesterday and today he's actually snapped at me and his face seems to be in a permanent grimace lately."

My father's look of worry deepened into a frown. "Well, you're his partner. Do you think it's a lack of sleep that's getting to him?"

Mentally, I walked through everything we'd gone through since finding Lee Reynolds' body in the woods Thursday night and nothing stood out except for his complaining about Derek hovering over him to get the case solved and off to the DA as soon as possible.

"I can't think of anything else that would explain his crankiness about so many different things. For both our sakes, we need to solve this case so we can get back to being the partners we're supposed to be."

Leaning forward, he said eagerly, "So let's talk about those flowers."

With a wink, I said, "Mind your own business."

"You know I'm all for the idea of you getting out more, Poppy, but isn't it a little maudlin to start a romance because he's back in town for his brother's funeral?"

"I love you, Dad, even though you intrude on my life, like you are now. We're just two people who happen to be interested in one another. Let's not make a big deal out of it, okay?"

My father simply smiled and patted my hand again. "I'm going back up to the bar, but let me know if you need anything."

"No need, Dad. I know my way around the bar as well as you do, so if I need anything, I'll just grab it myself."

He rolled his eyes and shook his head. "So independent and so like your mother."

As he walked away, I yelled to him, "I'll take that as a compliment."

Turning back to look at me, he gave me a wink. "You should. It was one of the most attractive things about your mother."

Alone again, I thought about what he said about her and remembered the time when I was a little girl and wanted so badly to be a part of the popular girl clique at elementary school. Every day, I would come home crying because I'd been left out again at recess. I was only eight years old and nothing was more important to me than fitting in with that group of girls who all looked so perfect with their long hair in pretty barrettes and ribbons and adorable dresses they wore every day.

So much the opposite of me with my long hair that never seemed to obey a brush and my tomboy ways that made me hate dresses. I would have worn one of them, though, if it meant those popular girls would have accepted me into their group.

One night as she was tucking me into bed, I told my mother I wanted her to buy me new clothes different from what I'd always worn and put my hair in a pretty ponytail. She sat down with me on my twin bed and asked me why I wanted to change how I looked. I told her the truth—that I wanted them to like me and that's how I'd get them to play with me. The look on her face wasn't disappointment or sadness but strength. She cradled my face in her hands and smiled as she said, "We can get you new clothes but not for that reason. People have to accept you for who you are, Poppy. There's no other way to live life. You can change the outside all you want, but I suspect that what makes you different from them isn't how you look but how you think and feel."

Then she placed her hand on my heart and said softly, "Don't ever change for others. Change because you want to for you, not for anyone else. Nobody is worth that."

I'd never forgotten how her telling that made me feel. As I lay there looking up at her smiling down at me like I was the most beautiful thing in the world, I wanted to be just like her. She never needed dresses or ponytails to make her the person my father adored and everyone in town loved. I didn't get those new clothes or wear my hair in pretty barrettes. Instead, I got a new ten-speed bike I ended up riding until the wheels practically fell off. And those girls never asked me to play with them at recess.

It didn't matter, though. Years later, in high school after the days of recess on the playground were over and I'd grown out of most of my tomboy ways, I became friends with some of those same girls. Much to my surprise, it wasn't life changing like I'd been so sure it would be when I was that eight year old girl so hungry for acceptance. My mother had been right all along.

I wore my independence proudly as she had hers, but the way people viewed me wasn't the same as the way they saw her. My mother had been loved by everyone who met her. I tended to elicit a different response. I liked to tell myself that was because of their small minded ideas about how a woman in her early thirties should be living her life, but maybe it was something else.

Maybe my independence didn't fit me as well as my

mother's had fit her.

Lost in thought as I remembered that strength even in her last days, I didn't see the bar begin to fill up around me. When I finally focused on the present again, there stood Jack Reynolds just a few feet away from my table staring at me.

"You looked like you were a million miles away. I hope I'm not interrupting," he said in that same silky voice I'd heard the first time we'd met in the bar.

"No, not at all," I said as my eyes scanned his frame. His clothes hung from his body like they were clinging to all the right spots. I had a feeling that blue sweater and jeans he wore hid a toned and lean body.

And I had to admit I wanted to find out more about him and the body under his clothes.

He sat down across from me and confidently leaned back in his chair. "I'd hoped to find you here tonight. I didn't know if you worked here or not, but I figured it was worth a shot."

"I don't exactly work here as much as do my father favors every so often. My day job is at *The Sunset Eagle* and with my partner solving cases."

Jack looked at me with appreciation in his eyes. "I like a busy woman. You have some varied interests there. Tending bar, writing articles for a newspaper, and solving murders. I'm impressed."

I basked in his compliment for a moment until a thought tore me out of the good feeling. How did he know I wrote for *The Eagle?* Quickly, my suspicions rose and I asked, "You seem to know a lot about me. I never said I was an article writer at the newspaper."

Without missing a beat, he leaned forward until there was barely a few inches between our faces and said in a voice full of sex, "I like knowing about the women I'm interested in."

Nearly breathless from the electricity between us, I didn't know how to respond to that, but it didn't matter because he leaned back in his chair and said with a smile, "Plus, I picked up the paper over at my sister-in-law's house and saw your name on an article from one of last week's editions."

"Oh."

"Excuse me for a minute so I can get a drink. I won't be long and we'll pick up right where we left off."

As I watched him walk up to the bar, excitement coursed through me. Jack Reynolds had a way about him that screamed seduction, and while I rarely fell for that kind of guy because they usually seemed too slick, I liked how he made me feel. His confidence made me more confident.

But what Alex had said about it being improper for me to spend time with a potential future suspect echoed in my mind. He was right. I knew that. I also knew that in all the years since I'd returned to Sunset Ridge, no other man had made me want to take a chance like Jack. Maybe it was because I knew so little about him. Maybe it was because he obviously liked me.

Or maybe it was just the pure physical attraction that existed between the two of us. Whatever it was, I found it hard to obey the rules Alex had set forth for my interactions with Jack.

And perhaps he was just the person I saw and not a potential suspect in his brother's death. I wasn't planning a life with him or anything past the next few days, after all, so what harm could come from spending a little time getting to know him?

Jack returned to the table and smiled at me like he knew what I'd been thinking about in his absence. As much as I wouldn't call myself aggressive, I wouldn't have minded him knowing what I liked about him. He had a way of making me want to go after what interested me.

"So where were we? Oh yeah, you were telling me how busy you are yet I'm lucky enough to see you here all alone. Where's the ever-present police officer who seems to be by your side all the time?"

I saw through his question to the real point he wanted to know about. "I don't know where he is tonight. We only spend time together on the job, to be honest. Maybe he's with his girlfriend."

At hearing the word girlfriend, his eyes narrowed ever so slightly and he ran his tongue along his delicious looking bottom lip. "Good to know."

The lull that came next didn't make me want to fill the dead space with useless words, so I didn't. Instead, I kept my focus on him, forcing myself to not look away when he felt too close and like he was seeing inside me to what I'd already decided I wanted from him.

"You're an interesting woman, Poppy McGuire. To hear the people in this town talk, you're the model for that woman on the Old Maid card deck, but as I sit here with you now, I see someone entirely different from her. I like what I'm seeing, don't get me wrong, but I'm wondering how you got this entire Podunk town to see you as something entirely incorrect."

His mention of the gossips of Sunset Ridge at first made me feel self-conscious, but as he continued to talk, I liked that he was able to discern a different part of me. "They think what they want to think and don't let anything that contradicts their opinion to get in the way. It's what keeps them happy in their little lives."

That came out a little sharper than I'd intended, but he'd hit a nerve with his mention of my sad reputation in town. Jack didn't seem to be bothered by my indictment of them, though, and just took a drink of his beer.

"I like you," he said with a smile that could charm the birds out of the trees. "You're smart."

I winked and asked, "Podunk smart?"

Shaking his head, his eyes flashed a seriousness I hadn't seen in him before. "Oh no. You're way smarter than anyone gives you credit for. That's for sure."

As much as I liked talking to him, I couldn't help but feel like he was studying me. That unnerved me, so I quickly moved to change the topic to him since I knew little more than his name and his relation to a dead man.

"So tell me about you, Jack Reynolds. What do you do when you aren't here?"

He swiped his tongue over his lower lip and smiled again. "What do I do? I'm a freelance photojournalist. When I'm not here, I'm a million other places in the world. Shanghai, Tibet, the Cape of Good Hope, Moscow, Lisbon. You name it, I've been there."

"Really?" I asked, enchanted by the idea of his traveling the world. I wanted to hear more about his life, which sounded more like an adventure than mere living.

"Yep. I've been everywhere and seen the world. Oh, the places we could go, Poppy. I see you in Madrid on a hot afternoon at a stadium watching bullfighting or in Paris on a spring day at an outdoor café eating something light and sweet."

Just the brief description of me in those places sounded wonderful, and I found myself joining him in the daydream of the places we could see together. I'd always fantasized traveling to faraway places, and even though I'd returned to Sunset Ridge and stayed all this time, those dreams hadn't faded away. If anything, they remained in my mind more often because the life I'd chosen wasn't exactly the life I wanted.

Gazing into his exotic green eyes that seemed perfect for someone with such a fantastic life, I said, "I could listen to you talk all night, Jack. What you do sounds so interesting. So free."

His face lit up from his broad smile that stretched ear to ear, and he pointed his finger at me. "That's the secret to a great life, Poppy. Freedom."

Freedom. That word resonated in my brain. Of all the things I had in life, freedom seemed so far down on the list that it barely made it. I lived on my own in my own house. I owned my own car. I ate what I wanted, where I wanted, and enjoyed what I loved whenever I felt like it. I chose where I went and with whom every day.

But rarely would I have considered my life one based on freedom.

"You're very lucky to have a life like that, Jack. What made you want to be a photographer?" I asked, eager to steer the conversation away from more talk of freedom.

He raised his hands as if to frame my face inside them. "I loved seeing people. I mean really seeing them and who they are. The camera doesn't lie. It purely and objectively shows what a person is. I wanted to be someone who gave that to the world."

"How long did you go to school to learn how to do that?"

He brushed off my question with a sneer. "I went to college for art, but school isn't where someone learns how to see the world. Life experience is what teaches you that."

"So you're a self-taught photographer? That's impressive."

Leaning back in his seat, he crossed his arms over his chest. "When you find something you love, it's nothing to learn everything about it. I bought myself some equipment and set out to capture what I saw."

"That sounds so great!" I said, loving how easy he made heading out into the world on his own sound. "What's your favorite place you've visited and your favorite picture you've taken?"

He closed his eyes and pressed his lips together before answering me. When he decided on his answers, he opened his eyes again and smiled. "My favorite place, hands down, has to be Fiji. The water is so perfectly turquoise and when you take a picture of it, it's so pure looking you feel like you're right there no matter where you are. And my favorite shot? That would have to be the one I took of the Cathedral of Vasily the Blessed in Moscow at night."

"I've never heard of that. Would I have seen it before?"

Nodding, he whipped out his cell phone and swiped the screen to get to his pictures. "I took a picture with my phone too so I could quickly send it to my friend. It's not the same as the one I took with my gear, but I think you'll recognize the place."

He held the phone in front of me and I instantly knew the famous building. "St. Basil's. Oh. I didn't recognize it by the name you used."

"That's the correct name of it in Russian."

I'd seen pictures of St. Basil's before and always found myself in awe at the design of the gorgeously colored domes that set the cathedral apart from every other church in the world. Never had I met anyone who'd seen such a fantastic sight in person, and there sat Jack right across from me talking about it among all the other wonderful places he'd seen in the world.

"So now I want to hear about you, Poppy McGuire. What incredible story is your life?"

I cringed at his description of what I was about to tell him. Very little of my story was incredible, unfortunately.

Quietly, I said, "I wish I could say I had a great tale to tell you, but I'm afraid I don't. I grew up in Sunset Ridge, went away to college, and right before I graduated my mother passed away. So I came back here to be with my father after her death. I started working at *The Sunset Eagle* and I've been there and here ever since."

How quickly that time had flown by and how many plans I'd had that had never come to pass. I couldn't help but wish my story was more exciting.

I waited for a look of disgust or at least disappointment from him, but it never came. He simply smiled and leaned forward to stare into my eyes. "Life is for living, not regretting, so you should begin living. It's never too late to go after everything you want in life, Poppy."

His acceptance of who I was, even though I probably wasn't like the people he usually spent time with, charmed me. I knew what I wanted, and at that moment, I wanted him.

But then suddenly, he kissed my hand and

announced, "It's been delightful talking to you, but I have to leave, unfortunately. I promised my sister-in-law I wouldn't be gone long, but I had to try to find you tonight. Would you join me for dinner Monday night?"

Enchanted by the idea of a date with Jack but curious about why we couldn't have dinner the next night, I didn't think twice and said yes immediately. "I'd love that! My house is at 138 Barn Street."

He stood and leaned down to kiss me on the cheek. The scent of his cologne filled my nose with the delightfully masculine smell, and I closed my eyes to savor it.

"I'll pick you up at seven Monday night. See you then, Poppy."

I opened my eyes as he pulled away, leaving the delicious scent lingering around me. As I watched him walk out of the bar, I told myself that it was time to go after what I wanted out of life. The first thing I'd go for was him Monday after dinner. After that, I didn't know, but I was sure of one thing.

I'd spent my last day wishing for a better life.

Chapter Nine

MY GAZE MET Alex's as soon as I walked through the door of The Grounds, and I saw the stressed out look on his face he'd worn since this case began. Committed to changing that, I plastered a smile onto my lips and hurried to our table where my second cup of morning coffee waited for me along with my partner.

"Sorry, sorry. I overslept by a few this morning, and ever since I've been playing catch up."

He studied my face for a moment and then returned my smile with one of his own. "You look like a ray of sunshine this morning, Poppy. A happy ray of sunshine. I need that after the night I had."

"Was Derek on your back again last night?" I asked before taking a sip of The Grounds' new French Roast coffee I'd recently fallen in love with.

He sighed and nodded. "Yeah, that was part of it. He's worried, so he's making sure I am too. I guess I don't blame him. Thankfully, nobody outside of Sunset Ridge seems to care about Lee Reynolds' murder."

Part of it? What else was Alex dealing with after hours that was ruining his nights? He'd told me he and Bethany didn't really see each other anymore, so was there someone else?

Knowing I was snooping but needing to find out, I asked, "What's keeping you up nights other than our good friend Derek and his broken record routine?"

Alex averted his gaze toward the opposite side of the restaurant, and I turned to follow it but didn't see anyone there that would be the answer to my question. He didn't say anything, but I sensed I'd stepped over the line and truly pried into his private life, something I strived never to do.

Feeling bad, I reached across the table and gently touched the sleeve of his uniform. "I'm sorry, Alex. I didn't mean to seem like I was intruding on your privacy."

He turned his head to look at me again, and in his dark brown eyes I saw genuine sadness that struck my heart like a fist. What was wrong? The look he gave me wasn't the kind of look someone gets from being hassled by their boss. No, this was real sadness.

But why?

I had to admit I knew next to nothing about what he did when we weren't working together. From what he'd always told me, he seemed to spend most of his off-duty time at his house. I didn't know what he did there except spend a lot of time watching sports on TV. Other than that, I knew he'd dated Bethany for a while, but he'd said that was basically over.

So what problem had been making his nights miserable and caused that terrible look of misery to fill his eyes?

"You don't pry, Poppy. I know you're like that. It's nothing important and not part of the job, so you don't have to worry about it getting in the way of what we do together."

As he spoke, that sadness disappeared, replaced by the thoughtful look I usually saw in his eyes. I wanted to ask if there was anything I could do to help, but I didn't. Whatever we were as Officer Alex Montero and Poppy McGuire working together on cases, we weren't anything as just Alex and Poppy.

"It would never even enter my mind that you'd be anything less than professional, Alex. You don't have to worry about that."

He took a sip of his coffee and changed the subject. "So what was that smile about when you walked through the door? You practically lit up the entire place."

I didn't want to tell him the real reason for my smile. He didn't approve of my spending time with Jack, and I knew if I told him I'd agreed to go on a date with him after hanging out with him last night at the bar that Alex would be unhappy.

But I didn't want to lie to him either. We may not have been close outside of work, but I considered Alex my partner and a friend, and for that, he deserved to be told the truth.

"It's nothing. Just went out last night and had a good time."

Not exactly the truth, but if we were going to have a conversation about Jack, I figured I needed to ease into it. Alex wasn't exactly his biggest fan, although I wasn't sure why.

More interested than I thought he'd be, he probed further about my generic answer of a night out. "Really? That's not like you, Poppy. You're more of a homebody. Where did you go?"

Suddenly feeling like I needed to defend myself or at least prove to him I didn't spend all my time alone sitting in my house, I said, "I go out. Well, I go out sometimes. It's nothing big. Just hung out at my father's bar."

He knew I was avoiding answering his questions. His expression grew serious, and he cleared his throat. "Poppy, I think it might be time for us to clear the air about something. You don't have to feel awkward about mentioning Bethany, if she's who you went out with. Just because things didn't work out with us doesn't mean she's going to cease to exist. Sunset Ridge is a small town, and she's a good friend of yours."

So that's why he thought I was dancing around the truth. That would have been easier than telling him about my time with Jack. I couldn't avoid this conversation any longer, so I swallowed hard and began telling him what really happened.

"Oh, it's not that, Alex. I am sorry that things didn't work out between you two, but I didn't go out with Bethany. I hung out with Jack Reynolds at McGuire's last night. I know you don't think that's right because he might be involved with the case at some point, but I had a nice time talking to him. He's very interesting, and to be honest, I don't meet that many people in this town who are like that and want to spend time with me."

He didn't look angry as much as unhappy at my explanation. Or at least that's what I thought because that same look he'd had a few minutes ago came back and turned his brown eyes sad.

"You underestimate yourself, Poppy. Any man with a brain in his head would want to spend time with you."

"But you still don't approve, do you?"

Alex shook his head. "No, I don't."

"Why? Do you truly believe Jack's going to be a focus of this investigation at some point? We've got no evidence to show he had anything to do with his brother's death. He wasn't even in Sunset Ridge when the murder occurred. I don't see what the problem with him is."

He hesitated and began to speak before stopping a few times, but then he said, "I just have a bad feeling about him. I can't explain it."

His answer made me smile and feel better about the whole thing about Jack. "Well, since you rely on me for gut feelings, I think we'll be fine since I don't get a bad vibe from him. For what it's worth, I don't intend on marrying the guy, so you don't have to worry about me. I just like spending time with him. Nothing more. And if he looks like he's going to be a person of interest in our investigation, I'll break it off with him so fast your head will spin."

For the first time since we became partners, Alex looked worried about me. Laying his hand on mine, he said, "Just promise me you're going to be careful. I don't want to see you get hurt."

"See, there's the partner I'm used to. I promise, Alex, I'll be careful, but you don't have to worry. It's not like Jack is going to stop roaming the world and settle down in this Podunk town. He'll leave after his brother's funeral and I'll just be a memory. That's okay, though. Sometimes it's nice to just get together with people for a few days."

A strange silence settled in between us, and even though I had the feeling he wanted to say something else to me about the Jack situation, he didn't. We sat there at our table in the back of The Grounds as the Sunday morning crowd filed out to begin their day and said nothing for a long time. I didn't mind that we didn't have anything to say. I just wished it wasn't because he disapproved of me spending time with Jack.

"I forgot to tell you I got the information on Jessica's financials," Alex announced, breaking the silence after about ten minutes.

"On a Sunday? How did you do that?"

"Computers work every day of the week," he said with a smile as he pulled out the information from inside his coat.

"Like us?"

He chuckled at my joke. "Yeah, like us. I actually got it yesterday, but take a look at this." He pointed to the bottom of a bank printout. "The account she and Lee had at the First National Bank branch in town is practically empty."

I studied the information he showed me and was surprised to see a bank account with so little in it. "Five hundred and twenty-nine dollars? That's not a lot of money for a guy who had to be making a good paycheck each week. Did they have other accounts?"

Alex shook his head. "No, not together. This one was opened when they got married. Lee didn't have any other ones either. She has another one, though, in her name only. That's a far healthier one."

"Really? That's interesting, don't you think?" I asked, wondering why Jessica Reynolds felt the need to have her own bank account separate from her husband.

He flipped over the top sheet of paper to show the printout from Jessica's individual account. I read down the page to see a balance of fifty thousand dollars at a bank in Waynesboro, Pennsylvania.

Surprised to see that town involved in our investigation once again, I looked up at Alex and said,

"What's with this out-of-the-way town and our case?"

"I know. I didn't expect to see anything else about it, and there it is as the place where Jessica has a bank account all to herself that's doing much better than the one she shared with her husband. Sounds like she's been hiding money away."

"Is it merely an odd coincidence that Lee Reynolds' first wife lives in that same town that Jessica has a bank account in? I mean, it's not like Waynesboro is a popular place like Baltimore or even Frederick."

With a sly grin, he said, "I don't know if it's a coincidence or not, but I'm starting to wonder if both of Lee's wives conspired to kill him. One has the right caliber gun and the other has enough eye drops to last a lifetime. Did Jessica get impatient because they weren't doing the job and used Cherise's gun?"

"We don't even know if they knew each other, though. It wouldn't be out of the ordinary for the first wife to hate the second wife," I suggested before he got ahead of what we could prove.

"True. It does seem odd that they're both connected to that small town, though, don't you think?"

"Do we know where Jessica got the fifty grand?" I asked as I nodded toward the printout.

He scanned the information and read what it said. "There were only three transactions in the past month, and none of them explain that amount. From what I can see, the account has gradually grown after an initial deposit about a year ago of thirty grand and each month she's deposited another two grand, while every so often withdrawing smaller amounts."

"Maybe her husband was giving her the two thousand dollars every month as an allowance?" I offered, knowing how unlikely that sounded. Two thousand was a sizeable amount for most husbands to give their wives, even a pseudo-celebrity like Lee Reynolds.

Alex looked as unconvinced as I was that she'd been getting that money from our victim. "I think we need to go back to Waynesboro. I want to speak to someone at that bank to find out where these deposits were coming from and where the initial thirty grand came from."

"Well, it's Sunday, so we can't do it today. I have to make an appearance at *The Eagle* bright and early tomorrow before my editor thinks I jumped ship, but I can be ready to go by ten probably. Sound good?"

I turned to stand and leave and heard him say, "You're in a pretty big hurry. Got somewhere better to be?"

The truth was I didn't have anywhere else to go. I just hadn't thought of staying there with him now that we'd decided we couldn't do anything else about this part of the case until tomorrow.

"No, not really. I just figured I'd go home and do a little work on my articles before my meeting tomorrow. Do you have something else you wanted to talk to me about regarding the case?"

I waited for him to say something, but he simply gave me a forced smile and shook his head. "No. See you tomorrow, Poppy. I'll meet you in front of the police station at ten."

"Sounds good. See you tomorrow, Alex."

I thought about telling him I hoped he enjoyed the baseball game I knew would be on that night and knew he'd be watching, but I didn't and I didn't know why.

*   *   *

BRIGHT AND AS early as I could after my editor kept me late at our meeting, I met Alex in front of the Sunset Ridge police station at nearly quarter after ten Monday morning. He stood leaning against the squad car, but I didn't notice any look of unhappiness about my being late.

"So sorry again. I swear I had the best of intentions to get here by ten, but my boss couldn't stop talking. I'm guessing it would be too much to ask that you'd have gotten me a coffee this morning, right?"

He grinned and held up a cup from The Grounds in front of him. "It's probably cold since I got it nearly twenty minutes ago, but the thought was there."

I took the cup from his hand and lifted it to my mouth for a much-needed drink of coffee. "It's the thought that counts, and this is still pretty warm, so you get credit for the thought and the action."

"Ready for a road trip?" he asked as he climbed in behind the wheel.

"I'm ready to find out where Jessica's been getting her money from," I answered as I closed the passenger side door. "I'm also ready for a break in this case, to be honest."

Alex nodded and looked over at me as he started the car. "I'll second that. Four days of Derek nagging me is more than enough."

We drove to the tiny town of Waynesboro right over the Maryland-Pennsylvania state line and chatted about the case, the weather, the baseball game from the night before, and some other meaningless topics, like we always did when we were in the car. I sensed that whatever he'd been dealing with for the past few days had passed, or at least abated, and now he was back to being the guy I was used to.

Main Street in Waynesboro looked like what most people thought of when they heard someone mention a main street in a small town. While there were a number of empty shops, most of the storefronts showcased unique little stores. As we drove down the street, I saw one dedicated exclusively to scarfs and wraps and another one that sold only hand dipped candles. In many ways, this small town reminded me of my hometown.

The Third National Bank sat on the corner of Main and Locust Streets, so we parked the squad car in the parking lot next door and walked into the old building with its large columns flanking the doorway. The white marbled floored lobby sat empty, except for us and a single bank worker at a welcome desk just inside the front doors.

Alex approached the dark haired woman whose eyeglasses hung on a chain around her neck and flashed his badge to get her attention. "I'm Officer Alex Montero from the Sunset Ridge police department. I need to speak to the bank manager. Is he or she here?"

"He's not here right now, Officer Montero," she said with wide eyes full of apprehension. "He should be in by noon, though. I can give you his card and you can call him, if you like. His name is Thomas Rubens."

Alex took the manager's business card and told the woman behind the desk that we'd return at noon to speak to him. "Maybe we should poke around town to see if anyone knows Jessica."

Walking out into the mid-morning sun, I took out

my cell phone to see if I could get us some information on a hunch I had. "Give me a second. I want to check something out."

I dialed Keri's number and asked her for Jessica Reynolds' birthplace. As I guessed, she was from Waynesboro. Thanking her, I turned to Alex and said, "Jessica was born in this town. She listed her address on the marriage certificate as 174 Chambersburg Road Waynesboro."

Alex's eyes lit up with excitement. "Interesting. Let's stop in at that bakery across the street and ask for directions. Maybe this is the break we need."

We crossed the street and headed into Martin's Bakery. The deliciously sweet smell of cakes and pastries washed over me no sooner had I stepped inside the store, and I closed my eyes to take a deep inhale of an incredible mix of sugar, flour, and cinnamon from the apple tarts on the glass case.

The elderly woman behind the counter chuckled at my reaction to the delectable baked goods all around me, and I opened my eyes to see Alex staring at me.

"You okay there?"

"The smell of fresh baked goodies is my kryptonite," I said as I scanned the glass cases in front of us for what I wanted to take home.

"What can I get you?" the woman asked me as I stood staring at those apple cinnamon squares.

Alex spoke up before I could pick my baked poison. "Can you tell us how to get to 174 Chambersburg Road Waynesboro?"

When she heard the address, she laughed and her chubby face scrunched up. Confused, he looked at me and I shrugged. Maybe there was something amusing about that address.

"What's so funny?" he asked as she looked at us like we should know what the inside joke was.

"There is no Chambersburg Road in Waynesboro. The closest Chambersburg Road I know of is in Fayetteville, over ten miles away. Back when my daughter was in high school, she and her girlfriends used to use it to get rid of boys they didn't want to date or if they got in trouble outside of Waynesboro and needed to lie to the police. You know, typical teenage stuff."

Alex still looked confused even after she explained that where we needed to go didn't exist, so I stepped in. "I'm looking for a woman I met in Baltimore one night—a woman named Jessica. She gave me that address after a fight at a club, and I just wanted to thank her because she was nice enough to give me some money to get a cab after someone stole my purse. All I know is her first name is Jessica. Could she be one of your daughter's old friends?"

The woman thought for a moment and nodded. "I think I do remember a girl named Jessica hanging around my house. A pretty girl with big eyes and long blond hair. That was about fifteen years ago, though. Her last name was Borden."

"Do you know where she lives?"

"I don't know, but my daughter might. She lives above the bakery if you want to go talk to her."

I jumped at the chance to speak to someone who may know something about Jessica outside of Sunset Ridge and grabbed Alex's arm to pull him toward where the woman walked to the back door.

"You wanted a break? Something tells me we might get one now," I whispered as we walked to the stairway at the back of the bakery.

The old woman held the door open for us and said, "My daughter's name is Christine Jeffers. Her apartment is the one to the right at the top of the stairs. Be careful because they're steep."

She walked away before I could thank her, and as Alex and I looked through the door at a staircase that seemed to be almost perfectly vertical, I nervously asked, "You have a gun with you, don't you?"

He nodded. "Yeah. Why are you asking?"

I stared up at the stairs we were about to climb and then looked at him. "I don't know. I think I saw this in a movie once. It didn't end well."

He nudged me into the stairwell and closed the door behind us. "Too late now. Time to go meet Ms. Jeffers and see what she has to say about Jessica. Don't worry, though. I've got your back."

Chapter Ten

THE DOOR TO Christine Jeffers' apartment had a
dent in it like someone had tried to shove their foot
through it sometime recently. I pointed to it and said to
Alex, "Why do I get the feeling this place has seen its
share of all kinds of action?"

Whispering to me as he rapped his knuckles on the
door, he said, "Makes me wonder what we're going to
see when this door opens."

A woman answered our knocking and to no one's
surprise, she looked like someone had tried to shove their
foot through her recently too. Rough was the only word
that popped into my mind the second she appeared in
front of us.

"Yeah? What do you want?"

So much for niceties.

Alex displayed his badge and asked, "Are you
Christine Jeffers?"

For a moment, the woman didn't answer. I had a
feeling she'd seen her fair share of cops in her lifetime by
the way she jutted her right hip out aggressively and
snapped, "Yeah. Who's asking?"

"I'm Officer Montero and this is Poppy McGuire.
We'd like to ask you some questions about a woman you

knew when you were a teenager. Her name was Jessica Borden."

Christine Jeffers squinted her eyes at us and shook her head. "So that's all you want?"

I quickly answered, pretty sure any more coming from Alex might spook her. "Yeah. That's all. Can we come in?"

She hesitated for a few more moments until Alex finally said, "I'm not interested in whatever illegal things you're up to. We just want information on Jessica Borden. That's it."

Pointing at me, she warned him, "I have a witness you said that. My lawyer will be able to get whatever you charge me with thrown out if you decide to change your mind."

"I know. I give you my word. We only want to know about Jessica."

Even after all that, I still wasn't sure she'd talk to us until she actually opened the door wide and waved us in. We walked into her apartment and the sweet smell of baked goods reached my nose first, followed by the sour smell of old cigarettes and finally another sweet scent I hadn't smelled since high school.

Turning back to look at Alex, I saw he smelled it too. "Nothing like a joint to start out your day," I said with a chuckle. "We better not stay too long or I'm going to leave here with a contact high. I never was very good with pot."

A look of surprise crossed his face. "You never cease to amaze me, Poppy. Is that where you got your nickname?"

I rolled my eyes and grimaced. I couldn't count how many times someone had asked me that question. "No.

Just focus on the case, will you?"

Christine Jeffers sat down on her couch cross-legged and lit a cigarette. "So what do you want to know about good old Jessica?"

As Alex asked her how she knew her, I took a good look at Christine. To be friends with Jessica, she had to be around the same age, but she looked far older than around thirty. Perhaps it was her short, jet black hair next to her pale skin that made her look older. I'd always found black hair and green eyes to be a striking combination on a woman, but on Christine it just looked stark. In addition to that, her skin looked like it hung off her body. Maybe it was from a recent loss of weight or sickness, but the effect in combination with the starkness above her neck made her look considerably older than Jessica.

"I last saw her a few years ago right before she got married to some bigwig guy who I thought was crazy old for her. He was in his forties, for God's sake!"

"Yes, that's her," Alex said. "Can you tell us anything else about her?"

Christine hemmed and hawed about not knowing much, but I had the sense it was the person asking her that had suddenly made her memory go bad. I gave her another minute to answer him while I looked around her apartment at the worn brown rug on the floor and the beige walls that had yellowed over time from her smoking before I stepped in and asked her a question myself.

"When we spoke to your mother downstairs, she said you knew Jessica when you two were in high school. What was she like back then?"

Alex raised his eyebrows and shot me a look of

surprise before taking a single step back away from Christine. We'd worked together long enough for me to know when he wasn't getting anywhere questioning someone and I needed to step in. He, in turn, trusted me to ask the right questions so we could find out what we needed. We worked well together, and even though he never failed to give me that look of shock when I took over, I knew he was okay with it.

"She always wanted more. It was like she thought she came from some fancy family and deserved only the best. Jessica didn't come from some silver spoon life, so I don't know why she thought she was all that."

"Was she popular?" I asked, relatively sure I already knew the answer.

"Oh yeah," Christine said with a chuckle. "She was popular alright. Teases always are, you know?"

I looked over at Alex to see him taking notes on what Christine was saying. Had he just written tease in his notes? I stifled the urge to lean over and sneak a look and continued asking my questions.

"So she had lots of boyfriends? Or did she just have a steady one?" I asked, guessing Jessica had a line of guys a mile long who wanted to date her.

Christine screwed her face into a scowl and took a drag off her cigarette. "I don't know if I'd say she had lots of boyfriends. Jessica had goals, if you know what I mean. She wanted things from the guys she dated."

Not sure what she meant by goals, I shook my head. "No, I'm not following."

She rubbed her thumb across her fingertips on her forefinger and middle finger. "Money. She refused to date poor guys, which around here is a pretty hard thing to do. There aren't a ton of rich guys in Waynesboro."

"Was she successful in finding a rich guy?"

Shrugging, Christine said, "Sometimes. It never lasted with her, though. She was always on the lookout for her next guy. It was a thing with her. We weren't really close because she was like that with friends too. If you couldn't give her stuff, she wanted nothing to do with you."

"Do you remember if she was with anyone when you graduated from high school?" I asked, hoping to hear she had been serious with someone who maybe she never stopped seeing, even after she married Lee Reynolds.

Unfortunately, Christine didn't remember things that way.

"No, she was wild and free and took off when we left school," she said with a grin. "No one wanted to be tied down once we could do whatever we wanted."

"Do you know where she went?"

"Nah. I just know she left like most everyone else after they gave us those diplomas. I would have left too if it wasn't for my mother and that damn bakery of hers. So I've been stuck here ever since. What did good old Jessica do to get you two looking for her?"

Alex stepped forward and interrupted me just as I was about to give Christine a vague answer to her question. "Thank you, Ms. Jeffers. One more question. Have you seen Jessica since high school?"

"Yeah, a couple times. She used to come back every so often to see her parents. I'd see her in town. They lived in a house over on Charles Street. I saw her once last year when her mother died and she came to clean out the house and sell it within a week of her death."

I thanked Christine and followed Alex down the

steep stairs back into the bakery, curious to know what he thought of her answers. Rather than talking to me, he walked directly to her mother behind the counter and instead of asking her any questions ordered a powdered sugar doughnut to go for himself and one of those apple cinnamon tarts for me. When we finally stepped out onto the sidewalk to head back to the bank, I couldn't help myself. A cop ordering a doughnut? It was too good not to tease him.

Taking my pastry, I chuckled. "A doughnut, Alex? You don't think that's a bit stereotypical, you being a cop and all?"

He said nothing but rolled his eyes as we made our way up the street to the Third National Bank. But when we got there, he continued on to the car instead of going in.

"We aren't going to speak to the bank manager?" I asked, confused since he hadn't said a word to me since leaving Christine Jeffers' apartment.

Finishing his doughnut, he tossed the napkin the elderly woman had given him in a trash can and shook his head. "Not yet. I want to find out more about that house over on Charles Street. The bank manager won't be there for another thirty minutes or so anyway, so I thought we'd take a drive to the county courthouse. I don't think it's far from here."

I opened the door to the car and looked across the roof at him. "You could tell your partner this. Maybe if you weren't scarfing down that doughnut you could have mentioned your plans."

He smiled and got into the car. Turning over the engine, he laughed. "I didn't know if you were impaired from our time at her apartment. By the way, if that's not how you got the nickname Poppy, how did you get it?"

A little powdered sugar sat above his lip, so I reached over and wiped it off before explaining the origin of my nickname. "I got it from not being able to pronounce words correctly when I was a little girl. When I couldn't say a word right, I would just say poppy. So my father began calling me Poppy, and it stuck."

Alex stopped the car at the parking lot exit and turned to look at me. "That's adorable. Much better than the idea of you being a pothead in high school."

"I'd say so. While I definitely had some wild times as a teenager, I wouldn't say I was a pothead. Now Derek, I could tell you stories that would make your hair curl. That boy was wild!"

Without saying a word, I saw Alex didn't want to know any more about his police chief's past, so I didn't go any further with my tales of Derek. We drove the ten minutes it took to get to the county courthouse saying little as I enjoyed my delicious pastry, but I thought about what we'd learned. Until we knew the details about the sale of Jessica's childhood home, all we'd found out about her from Christine Jeffers was she was a gold digger, even as a young girl, and didn't spend much time in Waynesboro once she didn't have to.

The county records clerk added to that information, though, so by the time we were once again in the car driving back toward Waynesboro we did have information to discuss. Although it wasn't his usual way, Alex seemed downright excited by what we'd learned.

"I had a feeling that was where the thirty grand had come from, but I find it most interesting that Jessica used her maiden name to sell that house and take the proceeds."

I'd noted that immediately when the clerk had told him what name she'd used for the transaction. "Was she trying to keep that money away from her husband?"

"I have no idea about that, but I think we can fairly say Jessica Borden Reynolds is a liar," he said as we turned onto Main Street once again. "She lied on her marriage certificate and then used her maiden name on the sale of the house. This makes me wonder what else she told us that was a lie."

"Add to that the eye drops and what Donny told us about how some people think that's a way to kill someone and she's looking pretty guilty of a bunch of things," I said as we parked the car in the Third National Bank parking lot.

Alex opened his door and nodded. "Let's see what the bank manager can tell us about those smaller deposits."

THOMAS RUBENS SAT behind the welcome desk in the bank lobby with a smile for us as we approached him. He wore a finely made grey three piece suit that fit his rotund body snugly, causing the buttons on his suit vest to tug uncomfortably. As I scanned his person, I wasn't surprised to see a bare ring finger on his left hand. No wife, even one who didn't love her husband anymore, would have her husband dress so badly for so much money.

He stood to greet us and escorted us to his office in the back of the bank. We sat down in front of his desk, and he folded his hands on top of the desk blotter as he asked, "What can I do for you today, Officer Montero?"

"I'm conducting an investigation that involves one of

your customers. I want to know about deposits she made into an account here."

"What is the customer's name?" Mr. Rubens asked as he turned slowly in his desk chair to face his computer.

"Jessica Borden Reynolds. I believe her account is in her maiden name, however."

He turned his head and nodded his recognition of her name. "Oh yes, we know her from a long time ago. She's been a customer at this branch for years. I do hope she's okay."

Alex didn't offer the bank manager any information on Jessica, much to the man's chagrin as he waited a few seconds before turning back to look at his computer. He tapped his fingers on a bunch of keys and her information came up in green on the screen.

Leaning forward to look at it, Alex said, "I want to know about the deposits she makes each month. What can you tell me about them?"

Thomas Rubens read what was on the screen and shook his head. "Not much. She makes the deposits in cash. They always come on the tenth of the month, or the day closest if the tenth lands on a Sunday. We're open on Saturdays, so when the tenth is a Sunday, she's deposited on a weekend. Other than that, I don't have any other information."

Alex jotted down the word CASH in his notes and looked up at the bank manager. "Nothing else? Are you sure it's her who deposits the money in person each time?"

Thomas Rubens closed his laptop and turned his chair so he once again faced us. "I wouldn't know that from the records. All it says is the money is deposited in cash into her account."

Looking frustrated, Alex closed his notebook and put it back into his pocket. I didn't know why he didn't ask anything else, so for the first time I spoke up. "What about your tellers? Would they know since she's been a customer here for so long? Surely one of them would know if she's been in here recently."

The bank manager thought about what I'd said for a moment and then asked us to wait as he checked with the two tellers on duty. As he walked out, Alex turned to me and smiled. "You didn't think I was going to ask that, did you?"

I narrowed my eyes to slivers and asked, "Were you?"

"I would have eventually," he answered in tone I knew meant he hadn't thought of it.

Waving his claim off, I sat back in the upholstered office chair. "This is what partners do, right? We complement each other."

Just then, Thomas Rubens returned and I saw by the disappointed look on his face that his tellers hadn't helped us. Taking his seat behind his desk, he said, "Neither teller can say for sure if it was actually Jessica who deposits the money or someone else. All we know is the deposits come in cash each month and are deposited in person right here at this branch. I wish I could help more."

"What about cameras?" I asked before Alex could open his mouth to ask another question. "I saw them in the lobby when we walked in."

The manager fidgeted in his seat and after a few moments nodded. "Well, they are there..." He stopped for a long pause and then continued. "I think you'd need a court order before I could let you see them, though."

Alex shook his hand and smiled. "You've been very helpful. Thank you, Mr. Rubens. If we have any more questions, I'll let you know."

The bank manager smiled at me as we left basically empty-handed. We'd already known the amounts of the deposits and when they came in each month. What we needed to know was where she got the two grand each month, something we still were in the dark about.

As we walked through the bank doors, I grabbed Alex's sleeve to stop him. "Are you going to get a court order to see the tapes? Do you think you'll have a difficult time getting one?"

Alex smiled but shook his head. "Probably not, but my guess is that Mr. Rubens got uncomfortable when you asked about them because they aren't working."

"Not working?"

"Nope. Or there's some other problem with them. He wouldn't have been so awkward if there wasn't an issue with the cameras."

Frustrated, I sighed. "We can't seem to catch a break with this case, can we?"

Stopping at the car, Alex gently touched my shoulder. "Don't get discouraged. We'll figure out what's going on with Jessica and who killed Lee."

On our drive back to Sunset Ridge, I tried to imagine where Jessica Reynolds could be getting two thousand dollars each month. She didn't work even part-time, so if she wasn't making the money, someone had to be giving it to her.

But who?

"You're uncharacteristically quiet, Poppy. You okay?" Alex asked as we rolled down the two-lane highway toward home.

Turning to face him, I adjusted my seat belt and explained what I'd been thinking about. "Where is she getting the money each month? I've gone through it, and all I can think of is someone's giving it to her. The question is who and why?"

Alex slowly shook his head as he stared out the front window of the car. "I don't know. I do know people don't give money away for nothing, so that makes me think Jessica has been up to something in her spare time."

"Do you think it's another man giving her the money? Or maybe it's Cherise who was paying her to poison Lee."

Turning to look at me, Alex looked confused. "That's a lot of money over time to kill someone who ended up dying of a gunshot wound last week. I'm not sure that makes sense."

As he turned back to look at the road, I had to admit he was right. "Okay. So sometimes my theories don't work out. Don't I get credit for trying?"

He pulled his cell phone and notepad out and handed them to me. "I've got something of my own I'd like to try. Do me a favor and find Kevin Nash's number and call him. Put the call on speaker so I can ask him a question."

I did as he asked and held the phone near him as he continued to drive. Kevin Nash answered quickly and Alex said, "Mr. Nash, it's Alex Montero from the Sunset Ridge police. I had a question about when the station pays its employees."

"We pay every other Friday."

That didn't help to explain why Jessica had two

thousand dollars to deposit on the tenth of each month. Disappointed, Alex thanked him for his help once again.

"My pleasure. I wanted to tell you that we here at the station have started a fund for Lee's widow."

"That's nice to hear," Alex said flatly, looking over at me and raising his eyebrows to show his amusement at more people giving Jessica money.

"We feel terrible for her since he had no life insurance or anything to leave her taken care of. He was part of our WXSN family, so we want to do whatever we can to help her. Please let me know if you need any more information to solve this terrible murder."

I pressed END on the call and set Alex's notebook and phone on the seat next to him. "I guess we can cross off the motive of killing him for the insurance money from our list since there was none to have."

"I never had the feeling this was a murder for money. No, this has always been a personal attack, a murder of one human being by another for reasons far deeper than just money."

"Like?" I asked, wondering where he was going with this. He'd never said anything about his theory of the case.

He turned to look at me and then back at the road as we entered Sunset Ridge. "Revenge for a broken heart. Revenge for a betrayal. A crime of passion."

"That sounds a lot more like wife number one than wife number two, don't you think?"

He pulled up in front of the Sunset Ridge police station and turned off the car. His two hands still on the steering wheel, he looked over at me and grinned. "I'd say so, and as soon as I can convince Derek that I need a search warrant for Cherise Reynolds' house, I'm going to see what I can do about proving my theory. Until then, I've got some ideas about this case I want to look into."

"Care to share with your partner, or do you plan to keep her in the dark for the second time today?"

I waited as he stared straight ahead and said nothing, knowing that I'd have to find a way of bowing out of any more road trips he wanted to take that day. I had a few hours before my date with Jack Reynolds, but since I hadn't actually had a real date in ages, I'd planned to spring for the works—mani/pedi, facial, and maybe even a massage.

And I was certain hearing me chose those over whatever work he wanted to do on the case was the last thing Alex wanted to hear.

Chapter Eleven

A LEX CLOSED THE car door and looked over at me. "I'm going to head out to the crime scene. Craig still hasn't had any luck finding that piece of chalk, and I want to scour the place myself. Would you grab a couple coffees from The Grounds and I'll meet you back here in say ten? Twenty if Derek's waiting for me."

Part of me wanted to join him and go out to the woods to look for evidence. However, another part of me wanted to go home and take a long, luxurious bubble bath and fantasize about my date with Jack in a few hours.

That part had all but stifled the other part of me on the drive back, but now as I saw the eager look in Alex's eyes as he talked about us working together out there in the woods to find some lost sliver of evidence, I couldn't help feel bad about what I was about to tell him. I felt guilty, even though I wasn't sure why.

"I wish I could. I do. I have to take care of a few things this afternoon, though, so I'll have to take a rain check. I'll be back around tomorrow, though."

The words came out like someone was yanking each syllable out of my throat with pliers.

"Your boss at *The Eagle* on your back like mine?" he

joked with a sense of camaraderie at that moment I wished was the case.

For a moment, I considered lying. He told me nothing about his personal life, so why should I have any problem keeping mine under wraps? We were just work partners. That was it. Nothing more. Well, we were friends too. At least I thought of him as my friend.

That was the problem. Alex was more than just some guy I spent time with tracking down bad guys. He was my friend, and lying to a friend, even about my going out with someone he didn't approve of, felt wrong.

So I told the truth.

"Jack's picking me up at seven and I wanted to spend the afternoon getting my nails done and other girly stuff you probably think is stupid." Shrugging my shoulders, I added, "It's a female thing. No biggie."

With each word he heard, his face morphed into a look of pure unhappiness. In fact, I didn't think I'd ever seen him look so miserable. He wasn't so much sad as much as disgusted, or at least that's what his expression told me. He said nothing in response to my explanation and simply nodded before walking into the police station, leaving me standing at the car with a hollow feeling inside.

I thought about following him into his office, but what good would that serve? Alex clearly didn't approve of my seeing Jack, and more talking about it wasn't going to change that fact. He had a right to his opinion, and I had a right to date anyone I chose to. So without another word between us, I left and headed back to my house to get my car.

Five minutes later, I was at Candy's Cuts ready to splurge on a mani/pedi, something I did once in every blue moon. I hadn't been there since my visit to investigate what she knew about Geneva Woodward's murder over six months ago, so I was in dire need of some beauty help.

Only one woman sat under a dryer off to the side of the shop, and Candy stood next to one of the stylist chairs sweeping away hair that had fallen to the floor during her last haircut. Wearing jeans and a brown sweater with practically no makeup on her face and her hair simply hanging down the sides of her head, she looked as plain as she ever did.

She saw me as soon as she heard the front door close. "Poppy McGuire, are you here to talk to me about murder again?"

Her smile told me she was teasing me, so I laughed and shook my head. "No. This is a desperate-woman-needing-help visit."

Quickly, her eyes scanned me from head to toe. "You don't look so bad. What's the problem?"

"I'm going out tonight and want to look my best," I admitted, realizing I'd just opened myself up to a slew of questions about who I was going with and what we were going to be doing.

"Oooooooh, going out?" she cooed. "Anyone I know? Could it be that sexy cop you're always hanging out with? What's his name again?"

I rolled my eyes but felt my cheeks warm. "Alex is my partner, and no, he's not the person I'm going out with tonight. Can you fit me in for a mani/pedi and maybe a trim?"

"Going with the upsweep again like last time?" she asked, taking me back to that night I'd gone to dinner with Alex at Diamanti's.

"No, I thought I'd go with my hair down tonight. I'm hoping for a less sophisticated look, if you know what I mean."

Candy set her broom aside and waved me up to sit in the chair. "Less sophisticated, huh? So you want to look sexy and wild instead of sexy and demure. I think we can do that for you."

Sexy and wild. Was that what I was going to attempt to be that night? Even though Candy knew nothing of my plans or who I had them with, she'd hit the nail right on the head. Jack had awoken a desire in me to be free and go after what I wanted, and wild was definitely a good word to describe what I planned to do.

Never before in my life had I set out to seduce a man. Not that I didn't know how to. Well, technically I knew how since I'd read every article available on the subject since women's magazines featured that topic in every issue. Clearly, I wasn't the only woman in the world who wanted to be wilder but just never felt right doing it.

But tonight I would be that seductress every magazine claimed I had inside me. Tonight I would show Jack that I didn't care about anything else but having him in my bed.

I looked in the mirror as Candy talked about something concerning the split ends in my hair and blushed a deep red just thinking about wanting a man solely for sex. I was no prude, but for me, sex had always involved some level of togetherness, some sense of commitment from the man to me and vice versa.

I didn't want that from Jack Reynolds, though. From him, I wanted the far baser act of sex. I knew he wouldn't be around for much longer, and I didn't mind that. He'd ignited a fire inside me to be with a man sexually but not romantically, so his leaving worked perfectly. I didn't love him or want to spend the rest of my life with him.

I just wanted to sleep with him.

Candy jabbed my shoulder with her fingertip. "Did you hear what I asked you, Poppy?"

Looking behind me, I saw her staring back at me with frustration in her eyes. "I'm sorry. I was lost in a daydream there for a second. What did you say?"

"I asked you if you were going to just get a trim or did you want something more?"

Hair stylists always seemed to want to do more. I guessed they were like artists, in a way, and got tired of doing paint by number when they knew they had it in them to create something far more wonderful. I didn't want one of her creations, though, so I politely begged off a completely new look and stuck with the trim to get rid of the split ends.

She was silent while she washed my hair in the sink, but it didn't take long after I sat back in her stylist's chair for her to mention the Lee Reynolds' murder. Since she wasn't a potential suspect in this case, she was far freer with her ideas on this one.

"I can't believe what happened to Lee Reynolds. What's this town becoming when a man like him is killed like that?"

Her tone sounded genuine. I didn't know how well she knew our victim, but maybe through gossiping with her I might find out something useful to our investigation. So despite the fact that I knew talking about the case wasn't what Alex would want me to do, I took Candy's bait and answered her.

"From everything I hear, he was a nice man who everyone seemed to love."

I watched her face for any reaction, but all I saw was a frown as she nodded her agreement.

"I only knew him through his wife, but she never said a bad word about him, and trust me, wives come in here all the time to bitch about their husbands. Never once with her, though."

Even though I was relatively sure she was referring to Jessica, I played dumb and asked, "Do you mean his first wife or his second?"

For a moment, Candy seemed surprised by my question, stopping the scissors as they cut the ends of my hair, but then she resumed her work and said, "His second, Jessica. I didn't know his first wife."

Hoping that I wasn't giving out important information, I said, "Well, even she's sad about what happened. For an ex-wife, she's awfully fond of him. I wonder how that made Jessica feel."

Candy quickly jumped to her defense. "Oh, she had no problems with the first wife. I know that for a fact. She isn't that type of person."

"Were they friends?" I asked, intrigued by the idea that it was obviously common knowledge that Jessica and Cherise weren't enemies. But how close were they?

Once again, Candy stopped cutting my hair. She thought about my very simple question and then answered, "I don't know if they were friends, but it wasn't like it is with many ex and current wives. I have a feeling they were very civil whenever they met."

For the first time in our investigation, Jessica and Cherise actually spending time around each other had been mentioned. Working to keep my interest tamped down, I merely nodded at her comment and told myself to remember it for later to tell Alex.

Candy finished cutting my hair and explained she was going to let it air dry as she worked on my nails. I followed her over to the manicure area, and as I sat down in front of her, she said, "I feel so bad for Jessica. She's a young woman left with nothing. No life insurance at all."

Curious as to how she knew this, I asked as she began her work on my fingernails, "Oh? How do you know?"

"She mentioned it in passing once a few months ago. I told her she needed to change Lee's mind about getting some, but she said he'd be around for a long time and she didn't have to worry. If only he'd changed his mind."

I couldn't help feel bad for Jessica Reynolds. If she wasn't trying to poison her husband through the ill-advised method of using eye drops, she was just as Candy thought—a young widow left with little. Not that she was as poor as most people thought. That fifty thousand dollars in that Pennsylvania bank would help. In truth, though, fifty grand couldn't replace a loving husband, which by all accounts Lee Reynolds truly was.

"Did she come into the shop often?"

Candy finished painting the nails on my right hand a color she said was sinful pink and focused her attention on my left hand. "More often than you," she said looking up at me. With a smile, she continued, "She used to say that she liked to look pretty for Lee. He adored her too. He did everything for Jessica. She was practically helpless without him."

I thought about that statement and had a hard time

imagining Jessica helpless. It was true that I had only seen her in grief, but even then she hadn't looked helpless as much as distraught. Candy seemed to know her better, though, so perhaps she wasn't the woman I'd made her out to be in my mind.

"I remember one time last year when Lee had to go out of town he had his brother come stay with Jessica because he didn't want her left alone even for a few days. That was the kind of man Lee Reynolds was. Always taking care of his wife."

"His brother Jack?" I asked, happy to hear something so noble about the man I was about to sleep with tonight.

She looked up from my ring finger nail and nodded. "Yeah. He had him come stay with her so she wouldn't have to stay in that townhouse of theirs alone. I remember Jessica telling me she didn't think it was necessary and wanted Lee to tell Jack not to come, but I told her she deserved to be treated like a queen and to let Lee do this for her."

"That was very nice of his brother to do that. I don't know Jack well, but he seems like a good man," I said more for my own benefit than to further the conversation.

Candy looked up at me as she swiped the last coat of nail polish on my left pinky finger and arched her eyebrow. "I don't know how good he is, but he's certainly good looking. I can't help but wonder sometimes why Jessica never got together with him since he's closer to her in age, but it was Lee she loved."

Unsure what to say as I suspected by the sparkle in her eye that I wasn't the only woman in her shop who liked Jack Reynolds, I mumbled, "The heart wants what the heart wants." It wasn't particularly insightful and added nothing to our conversation, but Candy didn't seem to mind my less-than-stellar gossiping skills. She was more than adept at them all on her own.

She moved to work on my toes, choosing a fire engine red for those nails and explaining that a woman could go a little racier on them since they weren't seen as often during this time of year. I rarely painted my toenails any color, so I was fine with whatever she chose. The reality was that even though Candy usually didn't do much of anything with her own appearance, she had remarkable skill at helping others with theirs. So if she suggested red for my toenails, then red they would be.

A half hour later, after all my nails had been painted and my hair had been styled in a sexy, wavy look that framed my face quite nicely, I was off to my house for that bubble bath I'd planned and a relaxing couple of hours before I had to dress for my date. As I slid into the water, careful not to ruin my hair after pinning it to the top of my head, I let the scent of the bubbles and the vanilla candles scattered around my bathroom ease me into complete relaxation. I couldn't remember the last time I took a day just for me and treated myself to the works as I had this afternoon. It was long overdue.

Ten minutes into my bath, my phone vibrated on the small tiled table I kept beside the tub. After drying my hand on a towel, I reached for it and saw a text from Alex.

Heading out to the scene. Can wait if you want to still go. Let me know.

A twinge of regret pinched at me for a moment, but

I didn't answer his text. I'd message him later before Jack arrived to let him know I wanted to hear all the details bright and early tomorrow morning. Setting the phone down again, I closed my eyes and let a daydream of how I hoped my night would end fill my mind.

JUST BEFORE SEVEN, I heard a knock on my front door and opened it to see Jack standing there dressed in a dark grey suit and stunning royal blue shirt that made his eyes pop. His dirty blond hair still looked like it usually did, like someone had just run their hands through it, but the overall look was simply gorgeous.

His eyes drifted from my face down my body and back up again before he said anything. And when he spoke, I knew all the effort I'd made that afternoon had paid off.

"You look incredible, Poppy."

He wasn't wrong. I did. My little black dress hugged every curve of my body and was meant to impress, as were my black stiletto heels. And my hair, makeup, and nails all added to the effect.

I was a seductress on the hunt for my prey, and tonight, that prey was Jack Reynolds.

Running my hand up the front of his dress shirt, I complimented him on his look. "I love this color on you. Great choice!"

By the way he was looking at me with eyes filled with desire, I wasn't sure we would make it to dinner. Not that I cared. All that afternoon's preparation wasn't for the people who would see us at Diamanti's, so if we never left my house, that would be fine. Dinner was merely going to be foreplay anyway.

"Are you hungry?" he asked as I locked my front door and joined him to walk to his car.

"I am," I said with a little giggle, finding the double entendre echoing in my head amusing.

We arrived at the restaurant and were seated immediately, and it didn't take long to see we were the talk of Diamanti's that night. Not that it was a surprise. He was a good looking man, and I had cleaned up nicely. He sat with his back to the door, so patrons first saw me sitting at the table near the entrance and then saw him. One after another, couples entered and looked at me with wide eyes before seeing him and immediately whispering to one another as they were shown to their tables.

A small part of me liked the effect we had on everyone there. Maybe they wouldn't be so quick to condemn me to old maid status from now on.

As we waited for our meals, we talked about his life as a photojournalist. Every place and every assignment sounded so exciting. I listened with eager anticipation to hear one story after another, never minding that he was doing all the talking. All the better since my stories were either boring or crime related, and no one other than Alex enjoyed those.

Jack lifted his wine glass to make a toast. "To us, Poppy McGuire, and all the busybodies in this town who can't take their eyes off us."

I clinked my glass against his and smiled. "You saw that? I wasn't sure you noticed how interested everyone in here is in us. We're going to be the talk of the town, you know."

He took a sip of his wine and winked at me. "Good. I hope they let their imaginations run wild with what we're going to be doing after dinner."

Even the seductress that lived inside me couldn't help but blush as he said that, and I took a sip of my wine as I averted my eyes from his intense gaze that threatened to make me feel too exposed right there in the middle of Diamanti's. It wasn't that I didn't want what he wanted. It just hadn't occurred to me in all my daydreaming about it that he'd thought about it too.

"So tell me, is it true you used to work as an investigative journalist?"

I nodded, silently wishing that job had been half as exciting as his. "I did. I worked for an online magazine that basically snooped on celebrities' lives." I stopped for a moment and then said, "God, that sounds so incredibly boring, and the truth is even worse. I didn't write for them, I only did research."

He knitted his brows like he disapproved and shook his head. "Not at all. There's nothing boring about that. And research is just what I can see a smart woman like you doing."

Waving off his compliment, I said, "I'm not that smart. No smarter than most people."

"You're right. You're astute. That's what you are. I see it in those sharp blue eyes whenever you talk. Nothing gets by you."

At that moment, as he sat there gazing into my eyes and looking so incredibly gorgeous, I couldn't think of anything better than hearing him say that to me. I'd always wanted to be seen as astute, and there he was, this worldly and accomplished man, telling me that's exactly what he saw me as.

And then I looked up and saw Alex walk through the front door of Diamanti's. As he walked behind the hostess, I watched for Bethany or someone else, but no one joined him. Our eyes met just before he was led into the side room of the restaurant, and all I saw in his was that same look of unhappiness I'd seen earlier in them. I smiled and moved my arm to wave hello to him, but he turned away when he realized I'd seen him.

Even though I had no reason to be upset, I was hurt that he didn't even wave hello, much less come over to make small talk with us. I knew he didn't think I should be spending time with Jack, but I was his friend and he'd snubbed me like I was nobody to him. I quickly pushed my hurt feelings down so Jack didn't see them, reminding myself that he wanted to spend time with me even if my partner and friend didn't, but a twinge of sadness pinched at me.

We sat there for over an hour talking and drinking wine as we enjoyed a fine meal and each other's company. When we left, I looked over toward where Alex had been sitting and saw he was gone already. He hadn't said hello or goodbye.

By the time we got back to my house, I'd forced myself to forget Alex's slight, at least for the time being. Jack sensed something was wrong and as we stood on my front porch, he asked, "Everything okay?"

It wasn't in other parts of my world, but in the part that included him, everything was going great. "Dinner was wonderful. Thank you. Would you like to come in for a drink?"

Jack ran his tongue across that beautiful lower lip of his and smiled. "I'd love to. The night's still young."

Yes, it was, and this woman intended on letting her inner seductress out to play for the first time ever.

Chapter Twelve

I SLOWLY OPENED my eyes and immediately squinted from the morning light streaming in through my bedroom windows. Rolling over in my full size bed, I saw the other side next to me empty. Confused, I scrubbed the sleep away and tried to remember what had happened. Jack and I came back here after dinner at Diamanti's. We had a glass of wine and then…

I lifted the sheets to see my body naked under them. I wasn't losing my mind. Jack had spent the night. So where was he now?

As the events of the previous hours flowed through my mind, I stretched my limbs and felt the night gradually ease out of them. A few minutes later and as awake as I was going to be without my morning coffee, I rolled over and felt something under my hand where Jack had been just a few hours earlier. Looking down at the bed, I saw a piece of paper and lifted it up to read the words in the morning sunlight.

Poppy,

I hated that I had to leave, but Jessica is having a hard time dealing with the loss of Lee and nights are the worst times for her. Thank you for a wonderful date, and I hope we can have another night like this again before I leave.

Until next time,
Jack

When a man leaves after sleeping with a woman, it usually isn't an occasion to smile, but I couldn't help it. His note was so sweet. How could I be angry with a man who left to take care of his sister-in-law in her time of need?

I folded his letter neatly and slid it under my pillow before turning over to check my phone. Panic raced through me at the sight of the spot where it usually sat empty, but then I remembered I hadn't taken it out of my purse when we returned from the restaurant.

Not that I got many calls and texts. As I rolled out of bed and made my way to the bathroom, Alex's text flashed through my mind. Oh my God! I'd never answered it. Was that why he was so cold at Diamanti's?

Immediately after my shower, I called him but after two rings it went directly to voicemail. I knew what that meant. Either he was too busy to answer his phone, which had never happened before, or he was avoiding me.

Unsure which it was and what to do if he was avoiding me, I dressed and made my face presentable before taking a nice walk to The Grounds. A slight chill in the air nipped lightly at my cheeks as I made my way to where I'd get my first coffee of the day, and I was thankful the line at the coffee shop wasn't too long when I arrived at just around nine AM like we always did.

Alex was nowhere to be found, though. Needing caffeine before I even began to consider what was happening between us, I sat at our table at the back of The Grounds and sipped on my French Roast made just right by Jennie. A cherry danish sat on the table in front of me waiting for me to dig in, but I didn't want to begin eating until Alex arrived.

By quarter after nine, I had a sinking feeling he wouldn't be showing up for what had become our everyday routine. I tried to keep my mind preoccupied with people watching The Grounds' customers as they came in for their morning fuel. The former mayor came in without the First Lady and quickly changed his order to go when he saw me sitting nearby. Clearly, he hadn't gotten past what Alex and I had found out in the Geneva Woodward case because that was the fourth time since we solved that case that he practically ran in the opposite direction the second he saw me somewhere in town. Oh well. The guilty had to find ways to live with what they'd done, and if bolting every time he saw me was how the former mayor Girard lived with his guilt, so be it.

At nine-thirty, my danish remained untouched and my coffee was empty, so I gathered up my things and threw my breakfast in the garbage. Usually, I couldn't pass up a cherry danish from The Grounds, but this morning my stomach just couldn't tolerate it with all the knots it had tied itself into.

I bought Alex a black coffee and began the short walk across the street to the police station, the whole time wondering why he was acting like this. When he and Bethany began dating, I didn't ignore him. I didn't love the idea of them together, but I accepted it. Why couldn't he accept Jack and me? We weren't any different from them.

Well, that wasn't entirely true. In a few days, Jack would be gone from Sunset Ridge and there would be no Jack and Poppy, but Bethany still lived here and she and Alex could get back together at any time. Still, I didn't freeze him out, so why was he doing exactly that to me? Or maybe I was misreading the entire situation. Maybe he was kept at the police station by Derek and his silly worrying about the Lee Reynolds case.

One step into his office and I knew my gut feeling had been correct. Alex was avoiding me. Seated behind his desk and staring at his computer, he had a coffee cup from The Grounds beside him. He'd gone to where we met every day and hadn't bothered to wait for me. My heart sank at the sight of that paper cup with the letter B scribbled on it in black marker just like the one I held in my hand.

"Hey, partner. Why didn't you come to The Grounds like always?" I asked as I placed the coffee I'd bought him down on his desk.

Alex looked at the cup and then up at me. "I didn't want to intrude on anything."

He sounded odd, like he felt nothing for the words he was saying. Something was definitely wrong. Had his voice caught on the word intrude? He looked like the same old Alex I knew, and I didn't even see that look of sadness in his eyes I'd seen so often lately.

I wanted to believe whatever was going on was all in my mind. Yes, he didn't approve of me spending time with Jack, but maybe he was just trying to give me space to have a personal life. That would explain why he wouldn't come over to our table the night before at Diamanti's and why he might think Jack and I would be having breakfast together this morning.

With all this swirling around in my head, I sat down in front of his desk and waited for him to begin talking about our case. He'd gone out to the crime scene, at least he'd planned to according to his text, so I was sure he had some news to tell me.

But he said nothing, instead just staring at the screen in front of him like I wasn't even there.

Finally, unable to stand the silence between us anymore, I asked, "So how did the trip to the scene go? Find anything good?"

Still silent and staring at that damn computer screen, he opened the top right drawer of his desk and pulled out a large plastic baggie containing a phone. He placed it in front of me, and I saw the phone looked damaged beyond repair.

"What's this?"

For the first time since he said he hadn't wanted to intrude, Alex spoke to me. "I found it at the scene. It's been stomped on and thrown into a tiny pond near where the body was found, but I think it might be the victim's."

The words *the victim* instead of our victim seemed to echo throughout his tiny office.

"Do you think you're going to be able to get some information off it? It looks pretty beat up," I asked as I examined the phone through the baggie.

"I'm going to stop by Jessica's house to ask her if it was Lee's and then I'm going to head down to Baltimore to meet my friend St. Clair. He says he knows a tech who might be able to retrieve information from the SD card."

He didn't ask me to join him, but then again, he never really asked. Something in his voice made me feel excluded, though—a coldness different from his usual quiet way and even different from the way he was when he was angry with me. I didn't know exactly what had changed in him, but I heard it when he referred to only him going out to investigate instead of the two of us.

For the first time, I felt like an intruder on his case. I wanted to be the person he looked to as a partner, not just someone he looked through as she sat as his desk with him.

Quietly, I asked, "Do you mind if I come with you?"

He nodded and merely said, "That's fine."

Suddenly, as if everything inside me threatened to tumble out of my mouth if I didn't say something, I began to explain why I'd asked. "It's just that I wasn't sure since you didn't ask. I mean, I know you don't usually ask, but it just seemed like you didn't want me to go with you."

In a voice barely above a whisper, he said, "I never had to ask before, but I didn't want to assume you were coming just in case you had something better to do with your day."

Before I could say this was what I did with my days, except when I had to be at *The Eagle*, and that I didn't want to do anything else with my days, he picked up the phone and walked out to the car. I hurried behind him to catch up, unsure if I didn't that he wouldn't simply leave without me.

Never since the first minute we began working together had I felt so unwanted and unwelcome in his world. As I closed the passenger door and turned to see him starting the car, I wanted to say something to fix whatever was wrong so we could get back to being Poppy and Alex like we'd been for months, but I didn't know what to say.

He said nothing in the car as we drove to Colonial Drive and Jessica Reynolds' townhouse, but I sensed a growing chasm between us, even though I couldn't honestly say he was acting out of character. Alex never talked much when we were in the car together.

I spent the entire ride rationalizing and justifying his actions because I hated not understanding what was happening between us. I didn't know what to do or how to fix what we'd become, but I knew I had to if I ever wanted things to be right again.

We walked silently to Jessica's front door and waited without a word for her to answer it. She barely got the door open before she began crying upon the sight of the smashed phone in pieces. I escorted her inside to the living room couch and tried to soothe her so she could tell us what she knew about what was obviously Lee's phone.

When she finally calmed down after five minutes of continual sobbing, Alex sat down in a chair across from her and held the baggie up in front of her. Far nicer than he'd ever been with her, he gently asked, "Jessica, can you tell me if this is definitely your husband's cell phone?"

She wiped her eyes and nodded. "Yes, that's Lee's phone. He got a brand new phone two months ago. I made fun of him because I thought it looked like he was holding a tablet up to his head when he made calls because the phone was so big. I teased him about it all the time."

I braced myself for more crying, but she took a deep breath and merely sniffled. "Where did you find it?"

"Near the crime scene," Alex answered as he stood to leave. "Thank you for your help, Jessica."

I smiled at her and gave her hand a sympathetic squeeze. "Are you going to be okay here alone?"

She tried to smile and then just nodded. "I'm fine. I know I must be the worst person to ask questions of since I'm constantly crying, but I do want to help you find Lee's killer."

"You're doing fine. If you think of anything that might help us, you still have Alex's card, right?"

"I do. If I think of anything, I'll call."

I smiled, hoping she'd be okay and then remembered that Jack was likely there with her now. As I followed Alex out of the townhouse, I scanned for where Jack might be but didn't see him. All the better since it would likely make things worse between Alex and me.

By the time I reached the car, Alex had it in gear and was ready to go. I didn't look forward to the ride to Baltimore in complete silence, so even though I wasn't sure how he'd react, I decided I needed to make the first move to get this partnership back on track.

"Do you think Jessica's tears were for real this time?" I wondered aloud, hoping he'd take the bait and join me for our first real conversation of the day.

Unfortunately, he didn't. All he did was make some quiet humming noise for a second or two. Then he returned to staring silently out the front window and driving.

"I mean, she likely was trying to kill him by eye drop

poisoning. Even if it was destined to be unsuccessful, she didn't know that."

"I wish more people believed nonsense like that so fewer people would end up dead."

It wasn't much, but at least he was talking, so I continued. "I guess that would be a good thing, but aren't you thinking Jessica could have ended up shooting Lee? Maybe she got impatient?"

He shook his head and frowned, and for a moment I worried I'd said something to derail what little talking I'd succeeded in getting him to do. Then he said, "It's possible, but I'm not thinking she was the shooter. Neither she nor Lee own a gun, and we have someone related to the victim who does own a .38, the gun used to kill him."

Cherise, wife number one.

"Why haven't you gotten a search warrant for Cherise's house then? Aren't you worried she might try to get rid of the gun before you can get there to find it?"

He turned right off the highway, and at the bottom of the exit, he looked over at me for the first time since we got into the car. "I will today. First I want to find out what I can about this phone. As for Cherise Reynolds getting rid of the gun, I'm not really worried about that. Derek's had someone watching her around the clock, and Craig is there today. If she goes anywhere, he'll be right there with her. When I'm ready, I'll go out to her house and execute the search myself."

More I'll instead of we'll talk. Whatever progress I'd thought I'd made, his use of the singular showed me we hadn't gotten very far.

After leaving the car in a parking garage and walking no less than five blocks in complete silence, we stopped at a tiny store with a sign that merely said Computers Fixed Here. Alex opened the door for me, so I walked in as he followed but I immediately stopped at the sight of around a billion gadgets and pieces of other gadgets all around us on shelves, racks, and even on the floor. I wasn't OCD by any means, but even I felt distressed by all the things around me as I stood there.

"We need to go to the counter," Alex said as he gently nudged me forward. "We're meeting my friend from my days on the force here and the guy he goes to whenever he needs tech help."

Something touched the top of my head, and I looked up in a panic to see a million more things hanging from the ceiling not even two feet above me. As all those pieces of things began to feel like they were closing in around me, I stepped toward the counter and hoped to God I didn't dislodge anything and cause an avalanche of stuff to bury us.

"Montero, how the hell have you been?" a deep voice I didn't recognize called out.

I looked beyond the counter to see a huge man with dark skin and short black hair smiling at me like we were long lost friends. He turned his attention to Alex right behind me and laughed.

"It looks like your friend isn't used to George's set up here."

Whoever he was, George clearly wasn't OCD either. He may have been someone we needed to rescue from a hoarding situation, though.

Alex extended his hand through the cut out in the wall and shook the man's hand. "Good to see you again, St. Clair. Rick St. Clair, this is Poppy McGuire, my partner these days."

The man's attention focused on me for a long moment like he was trying to figure out something about me, and then he asked, "Partner like work or something else?"

I smiled and shook my head. "Just work. It's nice to meet you, Rick."

He grabbed my hand and gave me a strong handshake. "Call me St. Clair. Everyone else does."

I looked into the part of the store he stood in and saw it wasn't floor to ceiling pieces of gadgets everywhere. "Any chance I can come back there with you? Out here is giving me the creeps with all this stuff all over."

He pressed something under the counter and a buzzer rang to open the door. Alex and I walked into that room and my anxiety level quickly dropped in proportion to the amount of things and doodads surrounding me.

"George will be right back. He got an emergency call, but he said he'd be back soon. In the meantime, you can bring me up to speed with what's been going on in your life, Montero. Still living out there in the sticks?"

I turned to see Alex smile. "Still there."

"I was surprised when you called and said you were on the job again. Happy to hear it but surprised."

Tapping me on the shoulder, Alex said, "I can thank Poppy here for that."

As I smiled at the first sign of defrosting from Alex, St. Clair settled his gaze on me and folded his arms across his chest. "I'm intrigued. I didn't think there would ever be another soul who could convince you to be a cop again. Who are you, Poppy McGuire, and how did you do it?"

I shrugged as I tried to think of a cool way to explain how Alex and I had become partners. I wasn't a real detective, so I felt a little embarrassed to tell him that. "He tells the story better than I do, I think."

Alex chucked St. Clair on the shoulder and laughed. "She's got a sixth sense for crime I haven't seen since you and I worked together in those beginning days on the force. Don't let her modesty fool you. She's got that gut thing you always said a cop should have."

"I'm not a cop, though," I said in a rush, not wanting him to think I was pretending to be something I wasn't and disrespect him.

"I'm even more intrigued. What are you then?" he asked as he stared at me.

This time Alex didn't speak up for me, so I had no choice but to admit the truth. In a small voice, I said, "I'm a reporter. Sort of."

A look of surprise came over him, and after a few seconds he gave me a big smile. "Well, you must be something pretty fantastic to get this guy back to being a cop. Whatever it is you did, I'm glad to see him back doing what he's good at."

Right then, the man we waited for came through the back door of the shop. George was the only person St. Clair trusted when it came to tech issues, even more than the force's tech guys. As St. Clair told us about how he'd helped him solve a case involving some stolen laptop ring, I took stock of the person he thought so highly of.

George looked like every computer guy I'd ever met. Short with disheveled brown hair and a nondescript face, he wore thick black glasses and clothes that didn't exactly work together with the blue stripes in his shirt not at all matching the brown pants he wore. He had a mousy look, but by the way St. Clair talked about him, he sounded like some kind of superman with anything involving computers, including cell phones.

He made the introductions, and then Alex set the baggie with Lee's phone on his work bench. "I'm hoping you'll be able to help me find out whatever I can from this phone. It was our victim's, and I think whoever killed him did this to it."

George lifted the bag and looked in at the damaged phone. "It looks like a herd of elephants trampled it," he joked. "But I have a feeling we might be able to find something on it. Let me take a look."

He slid on the kind of gloves Alex and I wore when we went to crime scenes and began to gingerly lift the pieces of Lee Reynolds' phone out of the bag. He placed each one onto a stainless steel tray and began picking at them with a pair of tweezers like a bird pecking at a feeder.

Within seconds, he held up a tiny square chip and smiled at Alex. "I love the older phones with SD cards."

I looked over at him and shook my head. Lee's phone was only two months old. Why would George call it an older phone? Alex said nothing as the tech slipped the card into another phone he had nearby and began looking through the pictures he found on it.

"Pretty lady," he said as he showed us all a picture of Jessica. Scrolling to the next pictures, he said, "Niagara Falls last summer with pretty lady. Pretty lady with younger guy not at Niagara Falls before that."

On the phone I saw a picture of Jessica and Jack in a room that looked a lot like her living room at the townhouse. Curious how George knew when the picture had been taken, I asked, "How do you know when that picture's from?"

He smiled and pushed his glasses up the bridge of his nose. "It's all on the card. Lots of data most people don't even think of when they take pictures. Like when, where, what phone number they're associated with."

Alex knitted his eyebrows and asked, "How did pictures that old get on a new phone he bought two months ago?"

"When you're talking SD cards, it's just a matter of taking it out of one phone and putting it into another. Your guy didn't get a new phone two months ago, if this is the phone you're talking about, though. New phones don't have SD cards."

I turned to face Alex. "But Jessica just identified that phone as Lee's new one."

He raised his eyebrows and answered, "She might have been mistaken in her grief, but it's just as possible she lied. Again."

"So now we need to find another phone too?" I asked in exasperation.

Alex just nodded. "One step forward and two steps back."

George packed up the phone pieces and SD card in the plastic baggie and handed it back to Alex. "Don't forget to check the guy's voicemail and text messages. Texts might be really useful, and if your vic was like 99% of the world, he never checked his voicemail and there's likely a wealth of information there."

St. Clair slapped the tech on the back and grinned. "Told you he was good. This is why I come to George when I need help with any of this tech stuff. The guys on the force who do this would still be asking me about the details of where I found the damn thing while George cuts to the chase."

We thanked George for his help and then St. Clair, Alex, and I left the shop. St. Clair needed to get back to work, but as he was saying his goodbyes, he leaned in and whispered in my ear as he hugged me, "Thanks for getting this guy back where he belongs."

He stepped back and shook Alex's hand. "You know you can call sometimes when it doesn't involve some poor bastard's death. Bryer's going to be angry he didn't get to see you, but I'll make sure to tell him you look good.

Happier than I'd seen him in days, Alex smiled broadly and chucked his friend on the shoulder again. "Tell him I'll call one of these days, and next time you hear from me I swear it won't be because I need help with anything involving a dead body."

"Good," St. Clair said with a smile. "Poppy, it was a pleasure. Don't you be a stranger either. Next time we'll get some beers and talk about how a reporter gets partnered up with Montero out in small town America. I have a feeling that's a story best told over drinks."

I smiled, liking the way St. Clair thought. "It's a deal."

He left to return to his precinct, and we made our way back to the parking garage. It had been a short but productive road trip, but even more than that, it had changed Alex's mood for the better more than I'd expected. As much as I considered him right at home in Sunset Ridge, he looked like he belonged in Baltimore too.

As he started the engine, Alex turned to me in the passenger seat and asked, "So what do you say we head back home so we can get those voicemails and try to figure out which wife offed poor Lee Reynolds?"

I laughed at his attempt at gallows humor. "So you've zeroed in on the wives of Lee Reynolds as our murderer?"

"I don't know if I'd say zeroed in, but all the evidence we have points to one of them. I'm hoping what we find in the texts and voicemail messages will tell us which one."

Poor Lee. I couldn't help but feel bad for the guy. Two wives and it seemed neither marriage was ultimately successful. He definitely hadn't lucked out in the marriage department.

Chapter Thirteen

AS I WAITED, Alex called Judge Dardon to get a warrant for Lee's phone records. Dardon was known locally as the most cop-friendly judge, and even though the warrant Alex wanted wasn't anything out of the ordinary, he wanted it quickly. The judge's willingness to sign just about anything for the police meant he'd get it and get it fast.

His secretary put him on hold, so I took the chance to ask what I hoped wasn't a dumb question. "Why do you need a warrant to search a dead man's records?"

Cupping the phone receiver, he answered, "Because the phone was in both Lee and Jessica's names. He's dead, but she isn't."

"Ahhh, okay. I didn't know that. I learn something new every day working with you," I said with a chuckle.

The judge began speaking and in less than a minute, Alex had his warrant. Without even hanging up the phone, he contacted the cell phone company and an hour later, we had the records of Lee's text messages.

Alex handed me a copy of the faxed pages and I asked, "What about the voicemails? They can't give us transcripts of those?"

"The voicemails are going to take longer because

there was some kind of system-wide blackout with his cell phone carrier a few hours ago and things are a mess," he explained as he began to read through the documents. "All we can have are the texts for now."

I thumbed through my stack of Lee Reynolds' texts and couldn't help but notice he didn't text a lot. "I guess he was more of a phone call guy?"

Alex gave me a look of resignation, as if he had hoped the text messages would have been a bit more plentiful too. "You never know. We might find the key to the entire case in one of these texts."

"Maybe," I said as I began to read a text from Lee to Jessica from right after he got his new phone.

I felt awkward, like I was intruding on their private life. Looking up from the perfectly benign text about what time dinner would be that night, I watched Alex scour another of Lee's text for any clue.

"Can you imagine what it would be like if someone sifted through your texts like this? I'm not sure I'd be okay with it if it were happening to me."

Alex smiled. "That's what the warrant's for—to make it okay."

That didn't make me feel better about what I was doing. "I'm not kidding. What do you think someone would think if they read your messages? I don't think mine give the correct impression of who I am. It's so easy to take things out of context."

He stopped and looked across the desk at me for a moment before smiling. "I think if someone read my texts they'd think I spent a lot of time with you, and they'd be right."

"Are you telling me you don't get texts from anyone else other than me?"

He thought for a second and shrugged. "A few from other people, but most of my messages are from you. You text me a lot."

I had to smile at the mention of how frequently I texted him. At least four or five times a week, I woke him up with some message about the case we were working on. I couldn't help it that I had brainstorms first thing in the morning. Then I'd text him practically every day to let him know I was running late for coffee. And then I often texted him late at night right before I went to bed with more ideas about our current case.

"Well, I'm the kind of partner who likes to share my ideas. I could be like you and only write OK in all my texts," I said, teasing him about his all-too-common habit of sending me back that one tiny word in response to my much longer messages.

Alex reached into his jacket hung on the back of his chair and pulled out his notepad. He flipped to the beginning of the tablet and placed it in front of me on the desk. There on the pages of the notes he took on each case were my texts written out in his handwriting.

I looked up from reading my words I sent at all hours of the day and night and saw him smiling at me. "You handwrite all my texts to you? Why?"

"Because you have good instincts, for the most part."

"Why not just keep the texts in your phone?" I asked as I flipped through page after page of my ideas on a case from months ago.

"I do, but I like to write them in my notes too so I can have all our notes on a case in one place."

Handing him the notepad, I was struck by how he called them our notes. Never before had he referred to all those ideas he carried around in his pocket as anything that included me. Not that I ever expected him to. It was his way of keeping the facts of the case, not mine, but it felt nice to be included nonetheless.

"If I were you, though, I'd probably be more worried if someone was reading my texts. With how much you text me, and I'm just one person in your life, I can only imagine the volume of messages an officer would have to sift through if they got a hold of your phone records."

I tapped on the stack of papers in front of him and twisted my face into a fake grimace. "Just get reading there and never you mind my messaging habits. I know better than to put anything incriminating into writing. Any intelligent female who remembers high school back before cell phones knows that."

He laughed at my teasing and shook his head. "As you command, boss. All I'm seeing is what amounts to a grocery list in this second text. Lee messaged Jessica about wanting to make her a special meal and she asked what she could pick up from the store so he'd have the ingredients ready when he got home."

I read the same message on my page and had to admit they sounded pretty happy. "He seemed like a nice guy, didn't he? She seems to love him too. I don't understand why she was trying to kill him with those eye drops then, though. The guy dotes on her and she tries to murder him."

"You never know, though, Poppy. These texts may not be the whole context, like you said before. What if he beat the hell out of her that morning and when he was messaging about wanting to make a nice meal that was his way of trying to make up for what he'd done to her before work that day? These aren't the whole picture."

I hadn't thought of that, but I had a hard time imagining Lee Reynolds as a wife beater. "I guess, but these along with everything else we've learned about the guy tells me he was one of the good ones. Even you have to admit that."

"Even me?" Alex asked as he looked up from the page of messages.

"Yeah. Even you." I saw by the confused, almost hurt look on his face that I needed to explain, so I added, "You are a pretty suspicious person, Alex. You can't deny that."

"I don't deny it at all. People are rarely what they seem to be, Poppy. You know that as well as I do. Until you spend hours upon hours around someone, you can't think you know another person. It's just not how it works."

The intense look in his eyes told me he wasn't talking about Lee Reynolds being a nice guy anymore. A strange feeling settled in between us, and for a moment I thought he might come right out and tell me how he felt about me spending time with Jack. He didn't, though, and after a few awkward moments of us looking at each other across the desk, he lowered his eyes and returned to reading Lee's loving messages to his second wife.

I did the same and began reading one of his texts regarding his working late on a Thursday afternoon. Flipping through the pages, I saw he sent a text to Jessica every Thursday to remind her he was working late.

"Did you notice he never lets her forget he'll be home late on Thursdays?"

Alex nodded. "Yeah. And every time he tells her he loves her. Then she messages back every time to tell him she'll have dinner ready for him at eight instead of six."

"And to tell him she loves him too. They seem perfectly blissful in these texts."

Leaning back in his chair, Alex folded his arms behind his head and stretched. "What was Lee doing every Thursday if he wasn't with his ex-wife? I get no sense that he was cheating on Jessica, so what was he doing since we know he wasn't working late?"

"I don't know, but I feel like we need to know to know what happened to him. Every Thursday he works late, and then on one of those Thursdays he's murdered in the woods outside of town and nowhere near where he works. Not a coincidence in my mind."

Finished with his brief break from reading the texts, he returned to them as he mumbled, "I can't shake the feeling it has something to do with his marriage."

I scanned the rest of the texts transcript and found nothing to indicate he had even spoken to his ex-wife through messages in the entire time since he bought his new phone. "Alex, I can't find anything in these that shows he and Cherise talked this way even once. If they were having an affair, we've got no proof here."

Alex nodded. "I must be wrong then. It's just that a man who takes that much care to tell his wife he's going to be working late every Thursday when she already knows is reminding her that he's going to be away so he doesn't have to deal with her calling while he's busy."

A memory of how Jared accused me of cheating on him right around the time he took up with that grocery tart he'd leave me for just months later floated through my mind. Guilty people often projected their guilt onto others, but what if Lee was the opposite and suspected Jessica of cheating?

"Here's a wild idea. What if Lee thought Jessica was

cheating on him and the whole Thursday working late thing wasn't about him making sure she didn't call him but was to make sure he let her know the coast was clear? What if he was reminding her to make sure she felt comfortable to do whatever she was up to in those hours when he was supposedly at work so he could catch her?"

For a moment, Alex looked skeptical. It was a twist on what we'd been thinking all along, but it certainly wasn't impossible. He thought it through and nodded as he opened up his notepad to jot down what I'd said. "I hadn't thought about it that way, to be honest, but she was a younger, beautiful woman so maybe Lee worried she was up to something."

"I know we have no proof of her ever cheating on him, but that would explain why she would try to kill him."

Alex sighed. "Except now we're two steps back again. If Jessica was cheating on him, we need to figure out who the other man was."

I hung my head as the excitement of my theory faded away, leaving only more questions about Lee Reynolds' murder. "Maybe we'll get lucky and find a message from him to the other man," I joked.

He smiled but said nothing else as he finished writing his note and returned to reading Lee's texts. Page after page of what were basically love letters between him and Jessica took up the next few minutes, in addition to messages between Lee and his boss, Kevin Nash, and those he sent to a guy named Phil he named The Plumber.

"A jetted bathtub in the master bedroom for Jessica's birthday in February?" Alex said under his breath.

"Maybe all that crying was real," I said. "I'd probably cry my eyes out if I lost such a great guy too. That's a nice gift."

We read on to see messages back and forth between Lee and some guy from the radio station named Anthony about meeting up at a bar named Ridgeways a couple Saturdays in a row to watch college football. More and more, it seemed like his text messages weren't going to help us at all.

Then suddenly the tone of Lee's messages changed when someone named Drake came into the picture. I looked up to see Alex's eyes light up as he began reading them too.

"You must be reading the Lee and Drake messages."

"Listen to this. There are only three messages, but these aren't like any of the others. The first one was sent by Lee to Drake in mid-September on the 15th at 8pm and says: NEXT TIME I SEE YOU DOING THAT AT WORK I WON'T KEEP MY MOUTH SHUT. Drake's response just a few minutes later says: DO IT AND YOU'LL PAY. Lee answered back around eleven PM that night. I GAVE YOU FAIR WARNING."

Now we had something to go on other than the possible baiting of Jessica and Lee making plans for home improvement and guys' afternoons out at the bar. Alex excitedly flipped through the pages of information Kevin Nash had given him about the employees at WXSN.

Looking up, he said, "There's nobody named Drake in the list of people who work at the radio station."

"Maybe it had to do with something else? Maybe he saw someone at their job doing something wrong?" I suggested.

"Then how would he get their number? No, I think this has to do with someone who worked with Lee." Reaching for the phone, he dialed a number. "I'm going to call the station manager to see who this Drake might be."

Alex placed the call on speaker so I could hear and asked Nash who Drake could be at the station. He explained there had been someone who worked there named Jason Drake, but he was let go two weeks ago. As far as he knew, the man still lived in the area. While he looked for his address, I hoped this would be the lead we'd wanted for days to find.

"Up for a visit to 798 Cressly Lane to talk to Jason Drake?" Alex asked as he slipped into his jacket and stuffed his gun into its holster at his hip.

I stood from my chair and eagerly waited for him to be ready to leave. "Of course! This is the first new piece of evidence we've had in days. I'm dying to hear what this Drake guy has to say about those texts."

"Let's go and find out what he was up to that made Lee so upset."

THE DRAKE HOUSE sat at the end of a tree-lined street in west Sunset Ridge, about five blocks from downtown. Made up of mostly older homes, this area of town had recently seen many young families buy homes here so it had a far different look with its toys scattered across front lawns and swing sets in the back yards.

Jason Drake lived in a modest red brick Cape Cod style home. Kevin Nash had told Alex he hated to let him go since he was recently married with a newborn, but he didn't have a choice due to the station owners' decision to cut back on payroll even after a successful year. Drake had left unhappily, according to his former boss, but Nash had never known of any problems between him and Lee Reynolds.

With all that information and the texts sent between the two men a few weeks ago, we knocked on his front door to get some answers and see just how angry he'd been at his former co-worker. There had only been three messages back and forth, but he had threatened our victim, so I wondered if the combination of that problem and losing his job had sent Jason Drake over the edge last Thursday.

A pretty brunette woman answered the door dressed in grey sweatpants and a pink t-shirt. In her arms she held an infant wrapped up in matching pink baby clothes. At the sight of Alex dressed in his police officer's uniform standing at her front door, she stepped back.

"Can I help you officer?" she asked in a shaky voice.

"Good afternoon, ma'am. I'm sorry to bother you. I'm looking for a Jason Drake who lives at this residence."

Her expression morphed into one of pure concern, and with a frown she said, "That's my husband. Is something wrong?"

Alex put on his best smile and shook his head. "We just need to speak to him. Is he here?"

A man appeared behind her and kissed the baby on the forehead. "They're here to speak to me about a fender-bender I saw yesterday, honey. I gave the cop my address since I was a witness. Take Katie into her room and I'll be there in a few minutes."

His wife believed what I was certain was a lie told for her benefit and gave us a tiny smile before leaving him alone with us. A large man with unkempt hair desperately in need of a trim and a five o'clock shadow, Jason Drake wore sweatpants similar to his wife's and a black t-shirt. I guessed the combination of a new baby in the house and losing his job had taken a toll on his appearance since his wife clearly was far too attractive to date a man who looked that bad, much less agree to marry him and give him children.

He stepped out of his house onto the front porch and asked in a worried voice, "What's wrong, officer?"

"We need to ask you some questions about the problem between you and Lee Reynolds," Alex answered flatly in that official tone he sometimes used with suspects.

Folding his arms across his chest, Drake quickly answered, "There was no problem."

Alex read him the transcript of the messages between him and our victim and asked, "Do you still want to go with the answer that there was no problem between you and Lee Reynolds?"

After hearing his own words coming back to haunt him, Jason Drake hung his head and quietly said, "Yes, okay, there was a problem. Lee knew I wasn't being the man I should be."

"We're going to need a little more than that, Mr. Drake. Can you elaborate?"

He looked at each of us sheepishly and then back into the house before admitting the truth. "I was seeing the secretary at the station and Lee saw us together. He told me he wouldn't ruin Mercedes' reputation at work, but he had no problem doing it to me since I was the one cheating on my wife who'd just given birth to our daughter. He sent me that first text a few hours after seeing us coming out of a closet at work. I knew he'd seen us because when I turned around after closing the door and Mercedes hurried back to her desk, I saw Lee standing there with that disapproving look on his face."

"You must have been pretty angry with Lee Reynolds for threatening to tell people what you were up to," Alex said, practically accusing Drake of wanting to hurt our victim.

"I was. I mean, you saw the text I sent him, but I didn't do anything. I stopped what I was doing with Mercedes even before I left the station. Lee knew that. I saw him at work before I was let go and thanked him for showing me what a bastard I was being. I was wrong and I felt terrible."

Alex nodded like he understood how a man with a beautiful wife and an adorable newborn little girl could be such a cheating bastard and then asked, "Where were you late last Thursday afternoon, Mr. Drake?"

He hesitated for a moment and then answered, "I went out for a drive while my wife and Katie took a nap."

"Were you with anyone who can vouch for you?"

Drake shook his head. "No, I was alone. I didn't kill Lee Reynolds, if that's what you think."

"Do you own a .38 caliber gun, Mr. Drake?"

His face hardened, as did his tone. "I think I should contact a lawyer, and if you want to speak to me again, you'll have to do it with my attorney at my side."

And with that, he slammed the door in our faces, leaving us with the obvious conclusion that Mr. Jason Drake had something to hide.

"Well, I think we have a new suspect," Alex said as he turned to walk back to the car. "What do you think?"

"I think that guy is damn lucky to have a wife and a beautiful daughter like that and his cheating on her right after she just gave birth makes him a dirtbag. I also think he could be our guy."

Alex stopped at the front of the car and nodded. "I agree. What do you say to an early dinner and we can talk about this case? My shift is ending and I'm starving."

I felt my phone vibrate in my purse to let me know I was getting a text, so I pulled it out and saw Jack had messaged me. I quickly scanned the text and saw he wanted to get together again. I didn't want to smile, but my face had a different idea and the corners of my mouth hitched up as I closed out the message.

"It's okay. Forget it," Alex said, shaking his head.

"No. I mean, why forget it?" I asked, but Alex was already in the car and couldn't hear me.

I got in and he began to drive toward my house instead of the police station, so I grabbed his arm. "You don't have to drop me off at my house, Alex. I just checked my phone because I wanted to make sure my father hadn't called. I think dinner would be great."

The part about my father was a lie, but I didn't want things to go back to being bad between us. If a little fib could prevent that, then I wasn't above lying.

And just as much, even though I hadn't told Alex, I wanted to give Jack some much needed closure by solving his brother's murder. I'd seen the familiar look of real sadness in his eyes when we talked about it the night before, and if I could be the one to make some of that sadness go away, I wanted to try to do that.

"Are you sure you don't have something else to do?" Alex asked as he turned toward the police station.

"I'd love to have dinner. Thank you. Do you think we can get in at Diamanti's or will it have to be fast food?"

He parked the squad car and turned to look at me with a broad smile. "How does a home cooked meal sound instead? While I'm making dinner, we can talk about the case and try to figure out who killed poor Lee Reynolds."

I said yes, jumping at the chance for a home cooked meal. It had been far too long since I'd had much of anything for a meal other than restaurant food. But even though many of my meals and the majority of my breakfasts had been shared with Alex in the past few months, this was the first time he'd ever invited me to his house to eat with him.

And all I could think was how much I looked forward to whatever he'd make. "Let me go get my car and I'll meet you there!"

ALEX STOOD ON the opposite side of the massive island in the center of his kitchen stirring a pot of what he called his world famous winter risotto. I wanted to mention that October wasn't exactly what I'd call winter, but I figured maybe the name was meant to be taken less literally.

I'd never seen him so relaxed. With each ladle of chicken broth he added to the recipe, he closed his eyes and breathed in the scent of the delicious dish. This was truly a side of him I'd never seen, and compared to the silent guy he usually was or the surly one he had been so often recently, this version of Alex was definitely one of my favorites.

"I'm curious. What's the difference between winter risotto and risotto at any other time of the year?" I asked playfully, not knowing the answer and unsure there really was any difference.

He chuckled and said, "It's heavier. Meant to fill the belly and stick to the ribs to keep you warm. Oh, and no lemon."

"Not to be too much of a stickler here, but I think the high today was somewhere in the mid-sixties. Not exactly stick to the ribs kind of weather."

He dismissed the details about the temperature outside and took another deep inhale of his concoction. "I've wanted to make this for months. It might be a little early, but that's okay. It'll be great."

Before I could tell him I was looking forward to tasting it for the first time, he poured me a glass of red wine and placed it in front of me. I had to admit this Alex was not only someone I liked to be around but very sexy too. His dark brown eyes sparkled as he added another cup of broth to the rice and stirred, taking that same deep breath to appreciate the delicious scent of it as it mixed with the squash, carrots, onion, garlic, white wine, and thyme.

I took a sip of my drink and couldn't help but love how it tasted surrounded by the smell of that risotto cooking right in front of me. The entire scene of Alex happily cooking a home cooked meal for me combined with the delicious scents and the sound of his laughter made for a feeling of sensory overload that nearly overwhelmed me.

"Do you usually have all the ingredients required to make such a special meal?" I asked since I often had little more in my refrigerator than a wedge of cheese and a variety of drinks to wash it down with.

He smiled and shook his head. "No. Since I live alone I usually don't, but I got them this morning instead of going to breakfast with you."

His answer struck me like a bolt of lightning. As he turned his focus back to adding the final ladle of chicken broth, I realized while he probably thought I was lying in bed in Jack's arms, Alex was shopping for the things needed to make a special meal to impress me.

And that was a problem. I couldn't deny my interest in Jack, but the friendship I'd had with Alex had changed to something else without my even knowing it. I saw it now in his dark eyes, and it frightened me because it was so real and intense.

Like him.

"Did you hear me, Poppy? I said dinner was ready."

I shook myself from my thoughts and smiled. "Sorry. I was thinking of something there for a minute. It smells great!"

We sat down at his small kitchen table in the corner of the room, and as we ate his world famous winter risotto that tasted like heaven on earth, I had to admit I'd never been so comfortable with a man in my life. All we talked about was the case, but it felt like we'd known each other all our lives.

"So who do you think our killer is?" he asked as he finished the final bite of his meal.

I savored the taste of the risotto on my tongue for the last time and set my fork down onto my plate. "I honestly don't know. I thought Cherise for a while, but something about that always felt wrong. She didn't sound guilty when we talked to her, but then again, hell hath no fury like a woman scorned or thrown over for a younger woman."

He smiled. "She waited a long time to exact her revenge, if that's what this was."

"Then there's Jessica, who very likely was poisoning her husband or trying to, but for what reason? Their messages make them seem to be in love, and she truly seems unhappy he's gone. Plus, she gets nothing upon his death."

"All true."

"Then there's Jason Drake, the cheating husband who might be willing to kill to keep his wife from finding out about his afternoon delights. He did lawyer up pretty quickly, but I don't know if he's really the killer type. He barely looks able to get himself dressed."

Alex sighed. "People do strange things to protect their way of life and even stranger things for love. I'm inclined to say right now Jason Drake is our best suspect. I'll check to see if any guns are registered to him, but I'm still bothered by what Lee Reynolds was doing every Thursday when he told his wife he was working late. Is there another woman out there we haven't found out about yet?"

I took a sip of wine and tried to wrap my brain around the idea of Lee Reynolds cheating on his wife. He had remarried quickly after his divorce from Cherise, but if he'd been a cheater then, I still couldn't see him doing that to Jessica. Nothing we'd found out so far pointed to that, especially with his texts.

"Wouldn't we have found messages on his phone if that were the case?"

With a frown, Alex explained, "Cheating men make a point of being careful about letting their mistresses leave careless messages that can be found by their wives.

No, she wouldn't leave a text, but she very well might leave a voicemail."

"When did the phone company say you'd get the voicemail transcripts?" I asked, eager to see those details.

Alex stood from the table and gathered up our plates to take to the sink. "They had some outage problem, but I hope to have them tomorrow. In them might be the key to the entire case and where we'll find the guilty party."

I lifted my glass to take one last drink of wine as my phone rang. Alex stopped dead at the sound, and I saw in his expression who he thought it was. I didn't reach for my phone, but I knew too.

"Answer it. I'm sure he's thinking you're avoiding him and no man wants that after spending the night with a woman."

Every ring echoed around us until my phone finally fell silent and we stared awkwardly at each other. Alex continued to the sink as I sat there unsure what to do.

"I guess I should go. It's getting late and my father might need me to cover a bartender shift."

The two of us knew that wasn't the reason why I was leaving. Alex said nothing and continued clearing the table as I felt the compunction to fill the silence with words. I placed my wine glass on the counter in front of him and quietly said, "Thank you for a great meal, Alex."

For a long moment, he stared into my eyes and I thought to myself that if things were different and we were more than partners, the next thing that would happen would be us leaning in to kiss one another sweetly and softly like two people whose worlds were so intertwined they couldn't imagine living without one another.

We didn't, though. He nodded and gave me a forced smile, and I thanked him for the risotto again. Worried that the phone call had harmed what I'd worked so hard to repair, I asked, "I'll see you tomorrow bright and early at The Grounds, right?"

He smiled and even though I had a feeling he wanted to say something else, all he said was, "I'll see you tomorrow, Poppy. Be careful driving home."

I checked my phone when I got to my car and it had been Jack calling. As I drove away to meet him, all I could think of was how much I'd enjoyed dinner with Alex, though.

Chapter Fourteen

Jack's voice sounded full of anticipation. "I was hoping we could get together again tonight. I've had a long day and could really go for spending time with you."

As I sat in my car there in my driveway, a tiny part of me didn't want to see him now. I liked him and thought I'd jump at any chance to have a repeat of our night together, but something had changed for me.

"I know what you mean about it being a long day," I said in a forced weary voice. "It's been a rough one."

"So we both need some down time and what better way to do that than together?" he said with a chuckle.

The part of me that had lost interest grew slowly but steadily with every word uttered between us. I wasn't in the mood to listen to more stories about his world travels tonight. I'd had a terrific home cooked meal and now I just wanted to light the fireplace in my living room and curl up on the couch. All I wanted to hear was the crackling of the fire and my own thoughts, which at the moment were focused on someone other than Jack.

"I don't know, Jack. I think all I'm good for is relaxing and then going to bed."

Damn! That didn't come out like it should have. I

wasn't interested in sleeping with him again, but the way I said that made it seem like I was all about the sex between us.

"I mean, I'm just really tired. Can I take a rain check?"

The phone fell silent for a long moment and then he finally said, "I really need someone to talk to, Poppy. I've been dealing with Jessica and Cherise since I came back to town, and what I want more than anything now is to just talk to someone who isn't grieving. I know that probably sounds terrible and I know everyone handles death in their own way, but…"

His words simply drifted off, like the strain of losing his brother and then comforting both of Lee's wives had gotten to him. I understood how death could be stressful. That had been one of the most surprising things about losing my mother. The sadness from missing her I'd expected, but I'd never expected her death to make me angry one minute and depressed the next.

I couldn't be heartless to Jack, no matter how I felt about him. If he needed a shoulder to cry on or just to lay his head on for a while, I could be that for him.

"I understand. I'll be home all night, so come on over."

"Thanks, Poppy. I knew you'd be there for me."

The relief in his voice couldn't have been clearer, and even though my mind was miles away at another house and with another man, I wanted to help Jack in his time of need.

"See you in a little bit, Jack."

I pressed END on my screen and saw a message had come in while I'd been talking to him. A quick swipe and I saw it. A message from Alex that began with the words

I wanted to tell you how. What did he want to tell me about? My heart pounding against my chest, I tapped my phone's screen to open up the text and read his message.

> **I wanted to tell you how much I enjoyed dinner tonight. I know you're busy so you don't have to answer this text. I just wanted to thank you for coming over. It felt good to cook my risotto again after so long. See you in the morning.**

My eyes scanned the words over and over as my brain teased out the sadness woven into them. I didn't know how I could have been so blind. All this time he didn't dislike Jack. He wasn't the problem. The problem was Alex liked me as something more than a partner.

And what made things even more complicated was I'd realized I had feelings for him months ago. I'd forced myself to stuff them down deep inside where he'd never see them and accept that we'd only be work partners because he didn't feel the same for me.

Now he did, but should that change anything? If we acted on how we felt, would we endanger what we were as friends and partners and possibly ruin what we had now? Even before he began dating Bethany, that fear of losing the great relationship that had grown between us had always stopped me from letting him know how much more I cared for him.

I didn't know what to do. As much as I loved the idea of having more with Alex, the mere thought of losing what we were already made my chest hurt.

My phone went dark, so I turned it on again and read his text one more time. I didn't want to leave him sitting there wondering if I received it, so I typed out a message to him as I admitted to myself I wasn't sure about much of anything with him except that other than my father, nobody else in the world made me feel safe like he did.

> **Just got home and saw your message. Thank you for making me your world famous risotto. I see now why it has that name. See you tomorrow!**

I clicked SEND and wished my words didn't have such a sterility to them. If he only knew how much I cared for him.

JACK'S SILHOUETTE APPEARED in the window of my front door less than a half hour later. In that period of time, I'd thought of nothing but Alex, which made inviting a different man into my house feel odd. I couldn't turn him away at my door, though, so I let Jack in and hoped I could be the sympathetic ear he needed tonight.

He kissed me on the cheek as he came through the door, and I forced a smile even as I hoped that would be the extent of our romance for the next few hours. His dirty blond hair and blue eyes were still as sexy as they'd been the night before, and his body in jeans and a t-shirt made me think of how incredible he'd felt next to me as we lay together in my bed. None of that had changed, but I wasn't as interested anymore.

"You are such a sight for sore eyes," he said with a sexy grin that told me my hopes were very likely going to run headlong into his far different hopes for our night.

As I closed the door, he headed into the living room. I followed and joked, "That's quite a compliment coming from a photographer, I think."

Already seated on my couch, he held his hand out for me take it. "I mean it. I can't tell you how happy I am to see you, Poppy."

I accepted his silent invitation and sat next to him even as I was thinking of someone else. I didn't want to be that kind of person—a woman who toyed with someone's feelings because she didn't know what to do instead. I'd always hated those kind of people, accusing them of being liars. All they had to do was tell the truth, I'd say to myself, but now that I was up to my ears in just the kind of situation that I'd so often condemned in the past, I saw that the truth wasn't exactly as easy as I'd thought.

"I'm sorry you're having such a hard time with Lee's death, Jack. I know how bad it can be. I wasn't right for a long time after my mother died."

I expected him to nod with a sad look and then tell me how bad the last few days had been, just like everyone who'd lost a loved one had ever acted, including myself. I'd given him carte blanche to consider me that sympathetic ear and intended to listen for as long as he needed me to.

His reaction was surprising, to say the least. No frown at the mention of his brother's death. No tear in his eye. Instead of the sad look, what I saw was one of irritation.

In a voice filled with anger, he said, "I can deal with Lee being gone. What's much harder is dealing with Jessica and Cherise."

For a moment, I disliked Jack intensely. Both women were struggling with the death of a man they loved, and he didn't like dealing with them? How selfish! Then I remembered that not everyone grieves the same, and whatever he was feeling he had a right to. Anger was part of the steps to acceptance. Even selfish anger that made someone look like a jackass.

"I'm sure it's very hard for them. They both cared for him, I know."

He hung his head and looked away. "You must think I'm a monster, don't you?"

That I had for a moment made me feel like I was just as terrible as I thought he was. I took his hand in mine and gently squeezed it. "No, no. Don't think that way. Grieving a loved one's death is a very individual thing. Nobody expects you to be crying and sobbing all over the place."

He turned to face me and smiled. "Thank you for being so understanding. I loved my brother. I did. The world's not going to be the same without him, and maybe if it was just me getting to think back on all the good times we had together…"

Jack stopped talking and sighed. I squeezed his hand to let him know I understood. "I remember when my mother died. I felt like I had to take care of my father in addition to taking care of myself. It was hard for a while there. He was lost without her, so he needed me to hold him up while he fell apart."

"You do understand. I don't want you to think I'm unfeeling, but between Cherise and Jessica, I feel like I'm drowning in a sea of tears. That's why I wanted to come over here tonight. I just need to be around someone who isn't mourning Lee."

"It's only been a few days, Jack. They'll likely be sad for a long time. They only got a few years with him. You got a lifetime."

He looked into my eyes and smiled. "I'd never thought of it that way. Lee and I were never as close as other brothers were, but you're right. He's been in my life since the day I was born. My big brother showing me how things were done and setting the bar for me."

Before I could continue talking, he leaned in toward me and softly pressed his lips to mine. It was a kiss filled with the expectation that there would be much more to come, and although I couldn't deny the feelings Jack stirred inside me, I also couldn't let go of how much I wished it was a different man sitting next to me on my living room couch.

His tip of his tongue teased mine for a moment, and then he slid his arm around me to firmly hold the back of my head. He wanted what I'd so willingly given him the night before, but I didn't.

Then as all these thoughts about him and Alex jumbled in my brain, my nose caught a faint scent of something on Jack. Light and floral, it was women's perfume. I recognized it, but I couldn't remember from where. Different from the scent I wore, it made me wonder what he'd been up to that day and with whom.

I pushed my head against his hand to pull away and looked up at him. I wasn't foolish enough to believe I was the only woman in his life, but the idea that he'd been with someone recently enough that her perfume still lingered on him made me feel way less special.

Even more, I couldn't help but compare how I felt at that moment as I wondered who she was to how I'd felt a short time before as I sat in Alex's kitchen while he made me homemade risotto.

"Is something wrong, Poppy? I thought since we were together last night that you liked me as much as I like you."

I wasn't sure if the tone that clung to each word meant he was hurt by my rejection or offended by it. Not wanting to make things worse, I smiled and quickly said, "Oh, I do like you, Jack. I just had a long day. I was just hoping we could hang out and talk for a bit."

He forced a smile and said, "Okay, I know what you mean. I've been with Cherise all day, and I can tell you it's been a long one."

The memory of Cherise and her house raced through my mind, but it wasn't on her that I'd smelled that perfume. Instantly, my brain switched to investigative mode. Hoping to be supportive while possibly learning something that could help the case, I asked, "How's she holding up? I imagine she's doing better than Jessica since she and Lee weren't really close anymore."

A frown settled into his features as he sighed. "I feel so badly for her. First, she gets tossed aside by my brother for a younger, more beautiful woman. Now, she has to deal with the fact that she never got closure from him. That's a hard thing to handle."

"What do you mean never got closure?" I asked, curious what she would need that for since they divorced years ago.

"My brother and Cherise were happily married. He told her every day he loved her and treated her like a queen. Then one day he just left her. No warning. No reason. Just that he'd met someone new and had fallen in love with her. Cherise never saw it coming, and it devastated her."

"Really?"

I had a hard time reconciling that Lee Reynolds with

the one who was so doting on Jessica in their text messages over the past few months. But then again, it sounded like Lee had been the same way with his first wife, and he'd discarded her like yesterday's newspaper out on the curb.

Jack shook his head. "I never agreed with how he did that. Cherise was a great wife to Lee, and he knew it. He even told me when he first introduced me to Jessica that he wished he didn't have to leave Cherise because she'd always been so wonderful to him."

"Then why did he leave her? What did Jessica have that Cherise didn't?"

For a moment, Jack said nothing, but then his expression morphed into a sneer and he answered, "Youth. He liked how young she was. I told him he should be with a woman his own age instead of stepping out with a woman my age. Don't get me wrong. I liked Jessica from the minute I met her. She's beautiful and sexy and I know what my brother saw in her. I just didn't think it was right."

I mentally filed all that he said away, but his attention had turned to romance once again. He cupped my cheeks and kissed me harder than before with an insistency that made it clear talking wasn't what he'd come for.

"When I'm with you, I don't want to think of any of that," he whispered against my lips. "I just want to think of how perfect you feel against me and how great we are together."

Just twenty-four hours ago, I would have swooned to hear him say that, but now his words fell flat. The problem was I didn't know how to rebuff him without hurting his feelings. On top of that, he had intimate knowledge of people Alex and I still considered possible suspects. If I could get him talking, maybe I could learn something important to solving the case.

So even though I didn't feel much for him anymore, I pretended I did to hopefully find out more about Lee's two wives. Jack's hands roamed over my back and down to just above my waist, his desire for me evident against my leg, but something in the way he sighed made me think his heart wasn't in it.

Leaning away from him, I looked up into his face. Had he sensed that I wasn't really into him anymore, or worse, that another man was on my mind as I kissed him?

Unsure I wanted to know the answer, I asked, "Is everything okay, Jack?"

He sat back against the couch cushion and sighed again. "I'm sorry, Poppy. I want to be here with you, but something Cherise said to me today has me preoccupied."

"Oh? What happened?" I asked, intensely curious about what she could have said to rattle him so much.

"I'm sure it's nothing, but during one of her unusually emotional moments this afternoon she said she was relieved. I stood there in her kitchen stunned like someone had just slapped me across the face and then I asked what she meant, but she began crying and said it's all been so hard on her to hear that the man she still loved was murdered."

Cherise had said she was relieved that Lee was dead? Why would she say that?

Trying to appear as casual as possible so he wouldn't think I was digging for information, I said, "Would you like a drink? I have beer and wine in the fridge."

Nodding, he followed me into the kitchen. Reaching into the refrigerator, I grabbed us both a beer and popped the tops off. Taking my usual seat at my kitchen table, I watched with relief as he chose to stand and lean against the counter.

I took a sip of my beer and then picked up where we left off in the living room. "People often say things when they're upset that they don't mean, Jack. It is strange that she would say she's relieved, though."

He jumped at the chance to continue the conversation. "It was strange. That's exactly what I thought right after she said it, but when I asked, she gave that excuse that it's been hard knowing he was murdered."

"Is it possible you misheard her or misunderstood what she meant?"

Jack thought about it and nodded. "I must have, right? I know Cherise had every reason to hate Lee, but she would never do anything like murder."

"Did she hate him, though? She seemed to think very highly of him when we went out to her house to interview her the other day."

"Hate might be too strong a word, I guess." He lifted the beer bottle to his lips and took a gulp before continuing. "She should have hated him, but I think what she really felt was hurt. Even years later, whenever I'd see her she'd have that hurt look in her eyes any time I mentioned his name."

I thought about when Alex and I had spoken to Cherise and remembered seeing a look of hurt pass over her face when she talked about Lee being murdered. But I hadn't gotten the sense that the hurt came from her anger with him so much as her still caring for her ex-husband.

Still, she was the woman he left for a younger woman, who he married very quickly after divorcing her. While it wouldn't be the nicest thing for her to feel, relief that he was gone wouldn't be that terrible either.

And it certainly wouldn't make her a murderer.

It would, however, be reason enough to encourage Alex to get that search warrant for her house. Maybe what she said to Jack was nothing. It probably was. After all, Cherise had the least to gain from Lee Reynolds' murder. No life insurance. No hefty bank account. No beautiful townhouse. Nothing but knowing the man who left her for another woman was dead.

"Well, I better get going, Poppy. I hope we'll get to see each other at least once more before I leave town."

Jack set his beer down on the counter and walked toward me. Leaning down, he kissed me softly on the lips and smiled. "I'd hate to leave without at least saying a proper goodbye."

He winked and turned to leave as I sat there replaying the highlights of our whirlwind romance. I'd been crazy about him and his fantastic stories of all the places he'd been in the world, and that free spirit in him had made me want him even more. But now I wanted something different than what he offered.

Someone different who I'd cared about for longer than anyone knew.

Chapter Fifteen

I WANTED TO show Alex whatever he thought happened with Jack the night before wasn't going to get in the way of my work with him, so I got to The Grounds early and took my seat at our usual table with coffee for both of us. Nine o'clock rolled around, but he still hadn't showed up and I began to worry that all the progress I thought I'd made the day before had vanished and for what?

Jack had given me some ideas about Cherise I wanted to share with Alex, but nothing he'd told me was worth damaging our partnership. As the minutes ticked by and our coffees grew cold, I couldn't help but regret leaving his house to meet Jack.

Not that I knew what I would have done if I stayed. Would we have kissed across the counter if I wasn't about to leave to go to another man? Would we have talked about the case more and then given in to what we both felt for each other?

The fear that whatever we did might ruin our work partnership never left my mind, so I didn't know for sure if I'd ever act on how I felt about Alex. As I looked down at my phone and saw it was nearly quarter after nine, I wondered if it was all academic anyway. Every time he thought I was with Jack he pulled further and further away from me.

I watched the steam slowly evaporate from his coffee and checked the time again as it inched toward twenty after. Was Alex across the street at the police station just sitting in his office like he'd been last time, retreating from everything that was me?

A noise startled me, and I looked up to see him standing by our table smiling down at me. "Sorry I'm late. Derek was in full panic mode this morning because of some obscure AM talk radio magazine that called right at nine. Can I get you another coffee to make up for it?"

I nodded, unsure if I spoke that all the things I'd been thinking about him, me, and us wouldn't come spilling out of my mouth before I could stop them. For twenty minutes I'd sat there worried that I'd ruined what we had together, and with just a smile and his simple explanation for being late, Alex had made me feel better about it all.

If that wasn't a clear sign that I shouldn't endanger the relationship we already had for something more, then I didn't know what was.

"You look a million miles away. You okay?" he asked as he sat down across from me.

"Yeah, I'm good. Just have a lot on my mind."

Alex shifted in his chair and looked around. "The Grounds is pretty empty for a weekday. You know, I need to stop getting here late since you always take my seat when you get here first."

The way his mouth hitched up told me he wasn't upset, so I teased him about his choice of seating. "I can understand why you like this chair so much. It offers a pretty good panoramic view of the whole place."

He swiveled his head back and forth to look behind him. "Exactly, which is why I hate this seat."

As I sat there, he stood and said, "Switch so I can see things the right way."

"You're serious, aren't you?" I asked in amazement as he stared down at me waiting to change seats.

"Yes. Switch seats."

I did as he ordered and sat down with my back to the rest of The Grounds' patrons. I never liked this seat either, even though I'd never disliked it as much as he had, obviously. Alex sat in his seat grinning like he'd just won the lottery.

"Are you happy now? I can't believe you made me change seats with you. I think those chewing-outs by Derek are starting to get to your brain, Alex."

He took a sip of his coffee and watched me with those dark eyes of his as I teased him. When I'd finished, he looked around the restaurant and then fixed his gaze back on me. "I need to sit in this spot so I can see everything going on. I can't protect you if my back is to the door."

"Protect me? From what? This is The Grounds. What do you think is going to happen? Is someone going to bean me in the head with a blueberry muffin? They do make the oversized ones exploding with blueberries here, so I can certainly see the need for some police protection from that."

Alex screwed his face into a scowl I couldn't tell was real or not. "Are you finished?"

"I could be. I just don't know what protection I need here in a coffee shop."

He looked at me and his expression changed to

deadly serious. "You need protection all the time, Poppy. You and I investigate all kinds of crime, including murder. That can be dangerous. My job isn't just to solve crimes but to make sure the citizens of Sunset Ridge are safe, and in my mind, you're the number one citizen I have to make sure I protect since you can be in danger at any time by working with me."

I opened my mouth to make a joke to alleviate the heaviness that had crept into our conversation, but it didn't seem right. He wasn't kidding about me being in danger. I guess in the back of my mind I'd always known working with him could put me in harm's way, but he made me feel so safe I didn't think much about it on most days.

"I wasn't trying to make fun of that, Alex. I don't have a reason to think about the danger I might be in working with you. I guess I just assume you'll protect me, but I forget that for you to do that, you have to have things your way, like this whole seat thing."

"I don't want you to worry, Poppy. Your safety is uppermost in my mind all the time, so if someone wants to harm you, they'll have to get through me first."

He said that like it was the most normal thing in the world for someone to say to me, but as he drank his coffee and scanned the room, I saw him differently for the first time since we'd begun working together. For me, working with him was something exciting and fun. I got to investigate crimes in our small town and helped him figure out who was likely guilty, mainly because I knew most of the players in Sunset Ridge. While he did the actual police work of filling out reports and answering to Derek, I took advantage of the opportunity to pursue my avocation, but until that moment, I hadn't thought of all he had to do for me to enjoy that chance.

"Thank you, Alex. I don't say that enough. I know I'm not a real investigator, but you welcomed me as your partner when you joined the force. I don't want you to think I don't appreciate that because I do."

He gave me a slow smile that reached his eyes and told me what I'd said made him happy, even if he didn't want to admit it. "You're as much an investigator as I am. This uniform and badge don't make me that. All they do is make it easier to get people to talk about the things they've done."

We sat there silently drinking our coffee as the people of the town he worked to protect came in and out, and I knew although he hadn't said anything about dinner last night and my leaving right afterward, what I'd done when I went home was on his mind. I didn't know how I knew, but something in the way he looked at me said he was worried. Did he think Jack and I were more serious than I'd acted like we were?

I finally broke the silence with what I thought was good news. "So I have some details on Cherise I think you might find interesting."

His response was tepid at best. As he watched a man and woman on the other side of the coffee shop argue about something, he said, "Oh yeah?"

Not even a question about what I'd heard. Just a mild expression of notice, like I'd mentioned that the weatherman had said the temperatures were set to stay the same for the next week.

"Did you hear me?" I asked, sure he must have misunderstood what I said as he focused on the couple now flailing their hands and talking loudly about some book they'd both read.

He continued to stare at them for a moment and then turned his attention back to me. "Yes, I heard you. I've never entirely eliminated Cherise from my list of suspects."

Talk about an answer that said little. Sure what Jack had told me would interest Alex once he opened his mind and ears to listen to me, I said, "Her brother-in-law told me last night that she said she was relieved Lee was dead."

"Sounds like virtually every ex-wife in America to me," he said as raised his cup to take another sip of coffee.

"You don't think that's a strange thing to say about someone she claims to have loved?" I asked, my exasperation rapidly growing at his behavior.

Shrugging, he made that face people made when they had to eat their second favorite meal instead of what they really wanted. If there had been a caption under a picture of him at that moment, it would have read meh.

"I can't believe you're not more enthusiastic about this. Cherise telling someone she's relieved her ex-husband is dead seems pretty damning to me."

"Why? Because Jack said it was so?" Alex asked, his voice sharper than usual.

So that was it. He felt fine discounting what I'd learned the night before because it had come from Jack.

I still believed this was important, even though it had come through someone he didn't like, so I defended my position. "No, because she had a real beef with Lee after he left her for a younger woman and she owns the exact caliber gun that killed him."

Alex sat motionless, not even scanning the restaurant

as he focused on me for a long moment and then nodded. "Fine. Maybe we'll take a ride out to see her after I finish my coffee."

"What if she's getting rid of the gun right now? Don't you think we should get out there as soon as possible?" I asked as he gave me his meh face again.

"There's been someone watching her twenty-four-seven, so if she's planning to do anything, we'll know about it. Derek agreed to the search warrant this morning, so it'll be ready by the time I finish my coffee. There's no hurry, Poppy. If she shot him, it's not going to hurt the investigation if we find out ten minutes later."

I couldn't believe my ears! This wasn't the man I knew and admired for being a great detective. Was he acting like this just because I'd heard it from Jack? I couldn't understand Alex disregarding a lead just because he didn't like the person who'd given it to me.

"You're behaving so strangely, Alex. Why? What is this about?"

He didn't answer, instead looking away at the table with the couple who had stopped fighting. The look on his face was one of unhappiness, but I thought I saw anger in it too.

I didn't want us to continue being like this every time Jack's name came up. Alex may have been jealous or whatever he was feeling about me being with him, but I couldn't stand seeing him shirk his responsibilities because of it. I needed to clear the air now or this would dog us every step of the way from this point on.

"You don't have to be like this, you know? He's just a guy I had a nice time with, but it's nothing serious."

Alex turned back to face me and said not a word. His stony expression gave nothing away about what he thought of what I'd said, and for one of the few times since we'd started working together, I didn't know what to say.

Then just as I was beginning to wonder if he'd even heard what I said, nevermind what he thought about it, he stood from the table and tossed his coffee cup into the garbage. "Ready for another road trip to Cherise's house?"

I stared up at him in amazement. "That's it? You don't have anything else to say?"

"Nope. Ready to go?"

So that was that. We weren't going to talk about Jack or anything having to deal with him. Alex's smile told me he had heard what I said about Jack not being someone serious in my life, and I suspected that made him happy. But whatever he felt about it, he wasn't going to share that with me.

"I'm ready. Are we okay?"

Without missing a beat, he nodded. "We're good. Let's go see if that relief Cherise felt was because she was the one who killed our victim."

He strolled past me toward the front door like nothing had happened, and as I walked with him across the street to get into the car, I had to admit I didn't want to talk about Jack with him anymore either.

ALEX KNOCKED ON Cherise Reynolds' black front door two times before she answered. Recognizing us immediately, she smiled and said, "Come back for another look to see the newest updates? Did she finally agree to a remodel, officer?"

He held up the search warrant and in that flat,

official voice he used right before he marched into someone's house to rifle through their belongings, he said, "This is a search warrant for your home, Cherise Reynolds. Please let us pass."

She looked at me and then Alex before returning her attention to me. Eyes wide, she pleaded, "This isn't necessary. I would have let you in to check for whatever you're looking for without the warrant. I have nothing to hide."

We walked into her home to the sound of saws and hammers and saw half a dozen construction workers watching us as we began our search. Cherise continued to explain that she didn't do anything and if we'd only ask, she'd tell us where to find what we were looking for. Her voice verged on frantic with every minute that passed without a word from us.

"I'll do anything to help find Lee's killer. I swear. Just tell me what you're looking for."

Finally, I couldn't stand just letting her watch in ignorance of our purpose there and said, "You told us you and Lee hadn't seen each other in ages. Do you still want to claim that?"

"Yes! I hadn't seen him in months."

Alex finished checking through the couch cushions in her living room and pointed to the rest of the house. "I know you have a legally registered .38 Smith and Wesson. If I'm going to have to check every inch of this house for that gun, you better believe this place isn't going to look like it does now when I'm finished."

Cherise reacted immediately to his threat, her expression a mixture of relief and anger. "You could have just told me that's what you were looking for."

"Didn't you say you were terrified of guns the last

time we asked you about one?" I asked, reminding her of the lie she'd told us just days earlier.

A look of terror crossed her face and she turned toward her bedroom. "I haven't shot it in months. I swear."

Alex followed her gaze and headed toward the only bedroom in the house. We followed him and stopped just inside the doorway. Cherise pointed to the nightstand next to her bed.

"It's in the bottom drawer. Check it out. You'll see I haven't used it in months. I wouldn't kill Lee. I still loved him."

"You loved him and he left you for someone younger. That could make a woman want to kill a man, even if she claimed to love him."

Cherise turned to face me with a look of confusion on her face. "I forgave Lee for breaking us up for her. Anyone who knows me can tell you that."

Alex lifted the gun out of the nightstand drawer with his pen and dangled it in front of him. Leaning toward it, he inhaled a deep breath. "This gun has been fired recently, not months ago."

Panic flashed in her eyes, and she shook her head violently. "That's not possible! I haven't fired that gun in forever. This is wrong! I didn't kill Lee. I couldn't have. I wouldn't have!"

I didn't know why, but something in me believed her, even as I watched Alex bag the gun that was the best piece of evidence to show she had killed Lee Reynolds. It was perfectly normal for a suspect to protest her innocence. They all did. It was just the way she did it that made me think Cherise wasn't our murderer.

Taking his handcuffs out, Alex slowly walked toward

her as he said, "Cherise Reynolds, you're under arrest for the murder of Lee Reynolds."

He explained her rights to her while she sobbed that she could never kill the only man she'd ever truly loved, and when he finished, he escorted her out of that beautifully remodeled bedroom through the finished front part of her farmhouse and out to the backseat of his police cruiser like every other criminal I'd seen him arrest.

"I'm not guilty. Please listen to me. I'm being framed. I couldn't have killed Lee, and I can prove it. If you'll just listen to me, I can prove to you I didn't do it."

I looked over at Alex to see if he planned to listen to any of Cherise's claims, but he didn't look into the back seat once, even as he shifted the car into reverse to turn around to drive back to Sunset Ridge. My curiosity nagged at me, so much that I barely was able to stop myself from turning around and asking her what she meant when she said someone was framing her.

"Aren't you going to at least hear her out?" I asked, hoping he'd say yes and let me hear what she had to say.

He stayed silent for miles as we rode back to Sunset Ridge. Cherise repeated her pleas of innocence the entire time, but to no avail.

Finally, when we were only about five miles from the police station, he looked up at the rearview mirror and barked back at her, "You have the right to remain silent. I'd suggest you use it."

Then looking over at me in the front seat, he said in a low voice, "I will listen to her when I get her back to the station. Until then, your curiosity will have to remain unsatisfied."

"Fine. I'll wait, but my gut tells me she didn't do it."

Out of the corner of my eye, I saw his mouth drop open and then he said, "So now you think she didn't do it? After badgering me to do this, you and your gut now think she's not the killer?"

I sheepishly looked over at him and saw the frustration on his face. I had been insistent about going out to Cherise's, but that had been more about the Jack thing than anything else. Quietly, I said, "Badgering seems a bit of a stretch, don't you think?"

As he pulled up to a stop sign, he turned his head and asked, "Does nagging work better for you? Maybe pestering?"

"I'm not going to dignify that with a response. Let's just get to the police station so we can hear what she has to say, okay?"

Alex rolled his eyes and then drove on, but I saw a tiny smile begin to form on his lips. We may not have always agreed on who the murderer was, but at least when we disagreed about this case, I still knew we were both on the same side.

Now if we could figure out who killed Lee Reynolds before another argument about his brother threatened to break up our partnership once again.

Chapter Sixteen

THE LONE ROOM assigned to questioning suspects at the Sunset Ridge police station looked more like a break room than a place to grill someone for the truth. In one corner of two beige walls sat a table with a huge stainless steel coffee urn surrounded by sugar packets and wood stirrers someone had thrown there, probably while cleaning up after the last holiday party. In another corner stood a metal rack holding the oldest microwave I'd ever seen. Enormous, it looked like the kind my grandmother had when I was little that used to terrify me with its loud humming noise when she made popcorn for me.

Alex escorted Cherise still in handcuffs to a metal folding chair on one side of the table that sat in the middle of the room. Quietly sobbing, she begged for him to release her from the cuffs, but he said nothing, instead taking his place in another folding chair across the table from her.

Leaning down, I whispered in his ear, "Can't we get her out of those things? I don't think we're in any danger."

For a moment, he looked straight ahead and I had a feeling I had stepped over some line that hadn't existed until this case, but then he merely nodded and handed me the keys. I unlocked the handcuffs and eased them off her wrists, earning a smile and her effusive thanks.

I returned to my position beside him in my own folding chair that pressed hard and cold against the backs of my thighs. Unlike usual, Alex had a large yellow legal pad in front of him instead of his own notepad. As he wrote down some initial notes, I studied Cherise to figure out if I was wrong about her being innocent.

The long red hair we'd seen the first time the three of us met now looked disheveled and her perfectly made up porcelain skin was blotchy and red from her crying all the way there in the backseat of the squad car. Even a mess like she was, Cherise still possessed a beauty I could appreciate. Her hands folded in front of her on the table, she quietly whimpered and shuddered every few seconds as she waited for Alex to begin the interrogation.

I just didn't see her shooting Lee Reynolds and then drawing a bullseye on his back in chalk before returning to her home in Pennsylvania and putting the gun back in its usual spot in her bedroom nightstand. If that were the case, she was the lamest murderer ever. She hadn't even tried to hide the weapon she was supposed to have used to kill someone, which made no sense to me. She hadn't shown a hint of nervousness when we visited her that first time either, which made her one cool customer, but I wasn't buying it. No matter what Jack had insinuated, I didn't see her as his brother's killer.

Alex cleared his throat and put the pen down next to the legal pad. "Cherise, we sent the gun to the lab, so you need to understand that if you continue to claim you didn't shoot it, that won't do you any good. We're going to find out your gun has been fired recently, so it's about time to come clean."

She took a deep breath in, and as she let the air out of her lungs, it looked like all the fight drained out of her body. "I can't tell you this any other way. I didn't kill Lee. I didn't shoot that gun either."

"And when the report from the lab says you did?"

"It will be wrong. I didn't shoot that gun. It's been in my nightstand where I put it since the last time I used it."

Alex stared across the table at her. "And when was that?"

"Months ago. During the summer. I took it to a shooting range and tried to get better at shooting so I wouldn't end up putting a bullet into my leg if I ever had to use it."

Clearly not getting anywhere on the gun issue, Alex switched topics and began asking her about her marriage to Lee. I wasn't sure he'd get anything new on that either, but at least we wouldn't hear the same answer over and over.

"Okay, Cherise. Tell me about your relationship with Lee Reynolds."

A look of complete relief washed over her, and she even smiled. "Lee was the one man I loved. I know that sounds clichéd and silly considering how old I am, but he was that man for me. I loved him from the minute I laid eyes on him that day in Psychology class in my junior year in college. He was a senior and so sweet."

She got a faraway look in her eyes and her smile grew bigger. "Long before he became the guy on the radio with all those bombastic ideas about everything under the sun, Lee was a wonderful college guy with a penchant for drinking cheap beer and laying out on a blanket at night to watch the stars with me."

"How long before you married?" Alex asked matter-of-factly as he jotted down details from her answers.

"We married three years after I graduated. Lee was twenty-six and I was a year younger. Those were wonderful days. I worked in a dentist's office in Frederick, and he wrote radio jingles for an ad agency. When we weren't working, we spent every minute together."

Too curious to hold back, I jumped in and asked, "Then what happened to you two to make the marriage break up? He sounds like the perfect husband."

All the happiness left her. Hanging her head, she said quietly, "We wanted to have children. Nothing would have made me happier than to give him a baby. It just wasn't in the cards, though. We tried everything, but nothing worked. By the time I turned thirty, it was clear we wouldn't be blessed with any children. Looking back, I guess it was just a matter of time from that point on. We hobbled on for a few more years, but I knew we wouldn't last. I couldn't give him what he wanted, so he found someone who could."

"But Lee and Jessica didn't have children, even though they were married for a few years."

Cherise nodded her head slowly. "Ironic, huh? Turns out that Jessica wasn't really interested in having kids like Lee thought she was, so it didn't happen for him with her either. At first I couldn't help but feel a sense of glee when I realized that, but then after a while I felt bad for him. All he wanted was a child to lavish love and attention on like he'd had when he was a child, but fate had different plans."

Alex lifted his head and squinted his eyes. "Lee has

only the one brother, right?"

"Yeah. Jack. He's night to Lee's day. I used to think that if only their parents had stopped after Lee…"

Suddenly, Alex appeared as interested in what she was saying as I was. "What do you mean?"

Looking up toward the ceiling, she answered, "Because the age difference between them was so big, it was like they were both only children. With Lee, his parents were strict and taught him right from wrong, but with Jack, that didn't happen. I don't know why. Maybe they were too old when he came along. I don't know. All I know is that Jack was a spoiled brat from the minute I met him. He wanted what he wanted, and if he didn't get it, he'd make your life a living hell. I think Lee was happy when he announced he wanted to travel the world. I mean, he loved Jack, but a little of him goes a long way."

Out of the corner of my eye I thought I saw Alex's head slightly bob up and down in agreement with Cherise. He made no comment about all she'd said about Jack and moved on to a slightly different line of questioning.

"So when the man you love left you, that didn't make you angry?"

Cherise closed her eyes for a few seconds and answered, "It made me furious." Opening her eyes, she continued, "But I never hated him for it. I understood, even though it tore my heart out."

"You understood that the man of your dreams who you married and planned to spend the rest of your life with left you for a younger, more beautiful woman he could have children with?" Alex asked sharply.

Tears welled in her eyes as his words did just as he

intended. "You don't have to remind me how much she had to offer compared to me, Officer Montero. I know."

Pressing for an answer, he asked again, "But you understood all that and still didn't hate him?"

"Haven't you ever loved someone so much that it wouldn't matter what they did? They could break your heart and you'd still love them? That's how I felt about Lee."

I watched Alex wince as she explained her feelings for our victim and wondered if he understood how much she loved Lee Reynolds. I did. With every word she spoke about their life together and losing him to another woman, I understood Cherise had never stopped loving her ex-husband.

"So you forgave him for abandoning you for Jessica, a woman who could give him children?" he asked, trying to force her to admit something I didn't think she ever would.

"Yes," she said quietly. "I forgave him."

"Then why did you murder him with your gun?" he bellowed so loud the words echoed off the walls of the interrogation room.

"I didn't!" she cried. "I wasn't even in town when he was murdered. Check it out. I was in Fort Myers, Florida from Monday to Thursday night. I flew out of BWI on Monday morning right after eight and flew back here from Florida on Thursday night. I didn't get home until after ten PM."

I looked at her in shock. "Why didn't you tell us this before?" I asked.

She hung her head and mumbled, "Because I was embarrassed. I met someone online and went to meet him. It didn't work out."

Alex dropped his pen onto the legal pad and asked in a voice full of frustration, "You were willing to be arrested for the murder of your ex-husband rather than admit you had a bad date with some guy in Florida?"

I knew her answer before she said a word. No woman wanted to admit that not only had she been left for someone else but now she couldn't even meet someone online, probably some guy who wasn't good looking and likely had the social skills of a hermit.

"I just wanted to meet someone nice, but he turned out to be a creep. I found out he lives with his mother. He's in his forties and he still lives with his mother!"

Pinching his nose to relieve the stress of finding out our case had just fallen apart, Alex groaned. Sounding defeated, he asked, "If the date went so badly, why didn't you return home immediately instead of staying in Florida for three more days?"

"I went to my sister's. When I decided to meet Richard, I knew he lived in the same town as she did, so I arranged it so we could have a little holiday together. After the date, I went to stay with her for a few days to cheer myself up. Check it out. Both of them can tell you I was nowhere near Sunset Ridge the day Lee was killed."

Alex scooped up the legal pad and pen and stood up from his seat. "Wait here. We'll be back after we check out your story. Give Poppy the numbers for Richard and your sister and what flights you took."

He tore off a sheet of paper and let it float down to the table before walking out without saying another word. I handed her a pen and the paper and smiled, happy she'd made it through the questioning without too much damage.

"We just need the numbers to check your story. Don't mind him. He's got a lot going on with this case."

Cherise wrote out the phone numbers of her failed date and her sister and slid the paper and pen back toward me. "I understand. I wish I could help more. You can even ask his brother. I told him I'd be at my sister's when he called last week."

I looked up from reading what she'd written. "Jack? He knew you weren't in town when the murder happened?"

"He had to. I spoke to him the week before and told him I'd be out of town until Thursday night. I had hoped to be gone for a reason different than the one it turned out to be, but he knew I was going away."

I grabbed the paper and pen and left as one question plagued my mind. If Jack knew, why would he insinuate that Cherise was the killer?

Alex sat at his desk in his office leaning back against his chair and staring up at the ceiling. As I walked in, Craig followed me and announced that the voicemail transcripts from Lee Reynolds' cell phone had finally come from the phone company.

Alex handed him the sheet of information from Cherise. "Thanks, Craig. Call these numbers to find out when Cherise Reynolds was in Florida. Then call the airline and find out if they can verify she was on those flights."

"Will do. I'll get them back to you ASAP."

Giving me the transcripts of Lee Reynolds' voicemail messages, he said in a low voice, "Tell me the bad news."

I read a few lines on the top sheet and quietly said, "It's the transcription of Cherise's voicemail to him left on the day before the murder."

The look of misery in his eyes made me wish I didn't have to be the one to give him the bad news. With a sigh, he said, "Read it."

"Lee, it's Cherise. Sorry I missed your call. I'll be home tomorrow night by ten or eleven, so feel free to stop over."

Alex sat silently as I stood there knowing the voicemail along with her sister's testimony would be enough to prove she wasn't in town to kill anyone on Thursday afternoon.

"Maybe she left this message intentionally so she could have an alibi," I offered to give him some hope that our best suspect wouldn't turn out to be innocent.

"Yeah, I'm thinking the same thing. Craig's checking out her alibi right now. If he finds out she wasn't in town, that seals the deal with Cherise and back to the drawing board we go."

I took a seat in the chair in front of his desk and wished I had better news for him, but from everything we'd found out so far, Lee's first wife wasn't his killer. But why had Alex thought her gun had been fired recently?

"Is it possible you were incorrect about Cherise's gun?"

Shaking his head, he frowned. "No. That gun was fired recently. I don't know if it's the gun that killed our victim, but someone shot that gun in the past few days."

"She does have a lot of workers in and out of that house. Maybe one of them used it."

My suggestion only made Alex more miserable. "That means ten more suspects we need to look into. Two steps back again."

We sat at his desk for a while silently commiserating over our case as it ground to a halt. Nothing either of us had to say was going to change that. Then a half hour later, Craig walked in with more bad news in his hands.

He gave Alex the two folders and shook his head. "You're going to love this."

Before he could explain, Craig got out of the office and left us to unravel what that comment meant. Alex opened the first folder and read aloud, "Cherise's .38 was the gun that killed Lee Reynolds. No prints other than hers were found on the gun."

"Then all that in there was a lie? What about her alibi of being a thousand miles away when he died?" I asked, not believing this was happening. It made no sense.

Alex opened the second folder and again read what it said. "The airline has Cherise Reynolds in seat 22C on the flight down to Ft. Myers and seat 24B on the flight back to Baltimore-Washington International. She wasn't anywhere near Sunset Ridge when Lee Reynolds died."

"How?" I asked, baffled at how her prints could be on the weapon that killed Lee Reynolds but she couldn't have been the killer. Then my mind began spinning with the idea of having to investigate all those men who worked for her six days a week.

He tossed the two folders onto his desk in disgust. "I have no idea. This damn case is like a nightmare that won't end. Now we're going to have to look into all those workmen."

"But did any of them even know Lee Reynolds? What kind of coincidence would that be?"

"I have no idea. I really don't."

I felt bad for him as we sat there grasping at straws.

Nothing in this case made any sense.

"What about Jason Drake? He seemed to have a grudge against Lee. Maybe he knew Cherise and got a hold of her gun," I said, even as my brain said the idea was ridiculous.

Like a man beaten down by circumstances, Alex slowly rose from his chair. "I guess it can't hurt to ask her. Who knows with this case?"

I walked back to the interrogation room where we found Cherise looking much better than before. Alex placed the two folders down on the table in front of him and with a deep breath began the second part of his questioning of her.

"We got the results back from the lab. Your gun is the one that killed Lee."

Tears filled her eyes as she shook her head back and forth in disbelief. "No! That's not possible. Didn't you call my sister and Richard to find out where I was? Didn't you call the airline? They can tell you I was on those flights."

Opening the folder with that exact information, he pointed to it and nodded. "And that's exactly what we found out. You were in Florida when this murder occurred. Both your alibis and the airline back you up on that."

"But my gun was used to kill Lee? I didn't have a break in while I was gone, so there must be some mistake."

Alex shook his head. "Ballistics doesn't make mistakes like that. The bullet from your .38 killed Lee Reynolds. Now our job is to find out who shot that gun. Did any of the men working in your house have a grudge against Lee?"

Cherise's face twisted with confusion. "Those workmen don't even know Lee. At least I can't imagine they would."

Leaning forward, I asked, "Is it possible any of them listened to his radio show and targeted him because of what he said on it every day?"

Cherise opened her mouth but nothing came out. I couldn't blame her. She'd hired construction workers to remodel her house, but there had never been any reason to ask them if they had any problem with her ex-husband, who she'd been divorced from for years.

Finally, she answered, "I have no idea. That wasn't anything I thought of when I hired the company."

"What's the name of the company doing the work?" Alex asked as he feverishly drew arrows between words on the legal pad.

"Shaif Construction. They're in Waynesboro."

I jumped in and asked, "Do you know a man named Jason Drake?"

Cherise shook her head. "No. Why?"

Alex crossed out Drake's name in his notes and stood from the table with the tablet and pen. As he walked away, he mumbled, "You're free to go. We'll keep the gun, but you can go home."

I watched Cherise's face as she wondered how she'd get home since we brought her there in the squad car. As she stood to leave, I said, "I can get my car and give you a ride home, if you need it."

"No, that's okay. I can get home. I'll call Jack. He's been very good these past few days. I think he may have actually grown up in his travels. Too bad Lee never got to see it."

As she walked out toward the door, I thought about

what she said about Jack. I'd only known him for a few days, so I'd never seen that spoiled brat she mentioned earlier. All I'd seen was the world traveler who seemed to enjoy life to the fullest, but never had I thought he was immature.

Happy to know she had a ride home, I found Alex in his office just as he was hanging up the phone. Taking my usual seat in front of his desk, I asked, "Find out anything?"

"The owner of Shaif Construction is faxing me over the names of all the workers on the crew from Cherise's house. I'm not hopeful, though."

I wished I could offer some magic theory that would make sense among all the odd pieces of the puzzle that this case had become. "Maybe the voicemail transcripts will give us something to go on."

Just then my phone rang and I pulled it out of my bag to see it was my father. Showing it to Alex, I said, "I'll just be a minute."

He waved me off, though. "Go see your father. I'll let you know if I find anything in the transcripts."

"Okay. If you need me, I'll either be at my house or McGuire's. See you later!"

As I left to find out what my father wanted, I hoped that I'd hear from Alex that he found the missing clue in those voicemail transcripts soon. Something had to fit so this case made sense.

Chapter Seventeen

MY FATHER'S PHONE rang until it went to voicemail and I heard his deep voice intone his usual message, so I ended the call and immediately redialed his number, worried something had happened. It wasn't like him to call and then not answer less than five minutes later.

I tore up Main Street toward the bar and hoped to God he was okay. The October wind nipped at my cheeks with every step I hurriedly took even as the late afternoon sun warmed them. Thankfully, McGuire's wasn't too far from the police station, and I made it there in less than five minutes.

Bolting in through the front door, I stopped and braced myself against the doorframe to catch my breath and looked around to see not a soul in the bar. It wasn't odd to see McGuire's empty during that time of the day, but to not see my father anywhere was distinctly out of character.

Rested enough to call out his name, I yelled, "Dad! Where are you? Dad!"

I listened for his answer, but I heard nothing. My panic quickly rising, I yelled again, "Dad! Where are you?"

My hands began to shake and tears welled in my eyes. Had he fallen somewhere in the house and lay waiting for me to find him? Had someone come into the bar and hurt him? I raced around the bar to check for him on the floor, but he wasn't there. Frantically, I scanned the bar but saw nothing out of the ordinary.

Turning on my heels, I raced up the stairs to his apartment on the second floor and stopped in his living room, my eyes darting left and right for any sight of him. I checked the bedrooms and bathroom but found nothing. Each moment that ticked by made my imagination conjure up a more awful fate for the only family I had left.

"Dad! Where are you? Call out if you can, please!"

I stood frozen to the spot in the middle of his living room, the tears rolling down my cheeks as the most terrifying thought I'd ever had settled in my brain. He'd called me for help, and now it was too late.

A faint sound stopped my heart for a brief moment, and then its pounding returned to my ears, but I'd heard something. Calling out again, I yelled, "Dad, I'm here! Where are you?"

I stood completely still and waited for an answer to my call, my hopes leaping inside my brain. Again I heard a faint noise that sounded like a voice, and then I heard the most beautiful sound in the world.

"Poppy, I'm down here," my father said in a faraway voice.

Following the sound, I took the stairs by two to the first floor and called out for him to tell me where he was again. This time I heard him more clearly. He was in the basement, the one place I hadn't thought of checking because he rarely spent any time there since moving the storeroom up to behind the bar.

I flung open the door to see him standing at the bottom of the basement stairs and smiling up at me. My emotions cascaded around me, and I began to cry knowing he was okay.

"You scared me to death, Dad. Why didn't you answer me when I called the first half dozen times?"

His smile faded as he saw how upset I was. "Why are you crying? Did something happen?"

"I thought you were hurt, Dad. You called me and then I called right back and didn't get an answer, so I ran all the way here from the police station to see if you were okay. And then when I got here I called your name but you didn't answer, so I ran upstairs to see if you were there."

Knowing I was rambling and probably not making much sense, I stopped explaining myself and took a deep breath as he began climbing the stairs toward me.

"It's okay, honey. I wasn't hurt. I was just showing Jack the basement of the house."

I looked behind him and saw Jack Reynolds following him up the stairs. Still reeling from the thought that my father had been lying hurt somewhere in his house, I stood there confused as they joined me behind the bar.

"What are you doing here, Jack?" I asked, sounding more suspicious than I intended.

"I came to get a drink and your father was nice enough to stand around and talk to me," he explained in his usual charming way.

My father wrapped his arm around my shoulders and kissed my cheek. "He's being far too nice. I've been boring him with stories about the history of this house for far too long. That's why we were down in the basement. I wanted to show him that stone wall we found when I first moved in."

He'd talked about that old wall since the day he found it, as if the names and symbols chiseled into the stone actually meant something. If I knew my father, he'd all but dragged Jack down to the basement to show him it.

"But why didn't you answer when I called?"

"I didn't hear it," my father answered and gave me another kiss. "Reception down there is terrible. I just figured I'd try again when we came back up. I thought you were working with Alex anyway. I didn't think you'd worry about it. I'm sorry."

The sadness that had crept into his eyes told me he hadn't intended to scare me half out of my wits, and even if he had, it wouldn't have mattered. He was my father, and no matter what he did, I loved him.

"It's okay, Dad. I just overreacted. That's all. I worry about things."

Jack smiled at me and winked. "We would have been back up here much sooner, but I kept asking your father to tell me stories about you when you were little. We got to talking and lost track of the time. I hope you'll forgive me."

"Anyone want a drink?" my father asked as he slipped behind the bar. "A beer, Poppy?"

I held up my hand to stop him before he began pouring me a glass. "No, I'm good."

"I'll take another, Joe," Jack said with a familiarity that rubbed me the wrong way. Joe? When did they get that close that he'd moved from calling my father Mr. McGuire to Joe?

My father didn't seem to mind how chummy he'd gotten, though, and quickly poured Jack another stout. As I stood there still struggling to calm my nerves from the fright my father had given me, the two of them joked around about types of beer like they'd known each other for all their lives. My father didn't even joke around like that with me, so what was he doing acting like that with someone he'd just met a few days ago?

I considered whether I should stay or return to the police station when I remembered Cherise had said she was going to call Jack for a ride back to her house. "Hey, don't you have to give your sister-in-law a ride back to Waynesboro?"

He and my father stopped their kidding around, and Jack looked over at me like I'd said something wrong. "She called, but I didn't answer. Is that what she needed? Why was she at the police station?"

Instantly, I sensed I shouldn't tell him much of what happened with Cherise, so I tried my best to look casual and said, "We found out she owns a .38, so Alex brought her in for questioning. We haven't found anything conclusive about the gun yet."

All of a sudden, he looked interested in what I had to say and his blue eyes opened wide. "Still? That seems to be taking a long time."

I smiled and worked my hardest to not look like I was lying. "You know how small town police forces are. They just don't have the resources big cities do. It could take a few more days to find out if her gun had anything to do with your brother's murder."

My father made a comment about how wonderful he thought the Sunset Ridge police department had always been as if he felt like he had to defend it against us.

Smiling at his loyalty to Derek and Alex, I quickly changed the subject to that stone wall in the basement before I had to explain any more about the case.

More interested in my social life, my father asked, "So, are you two kids going to do anything fun today?"

I knew my father didn't mean to allude to me having sex with Jack, but that's how it came out. He saw by the look on my face that he'd misspoken and quickly tried to rephrase his ideas, but that only made it worse. Oddly enough, Jack didn't seem to think anything of what my father had said as he drank his beer and stared off at the far wall.

My father excused himself to go to the stockroom. For a minute, I watched Jack and saw his expression change from preoccupied blankness to one that looked intense and focused. What Cherise said had nagged at me from the minute I heard it, and something about the way he was acting told me I needed to ask him about it.

I touched his sleeve to get his attention, and he turned to look at me with that same intense look in his eyes. It felt like he looked right through me for a brief moment, and then he smiled and they softened to their usual kindness.

"You looked like you were a million miles away. Everything okay with you?"

His smile spread wider across his face as he nodded and assured me he was fine. "Not a million, but a few miles away. I'm good, though."

Carefully in my mind, I crafted the question I wanted to ask and said, "You know Cherise pretty well, I think. Right?"

"Yeah. I think I might even like her more than Jessica, as far as my brother's wives go," he replied, his expression telling me he was lying.

I moved around to his other side so when he looked at me the light from the window illuminated his features better. I wanted to see his full expression when I asked him about what Cherise had said back at the station.

"Well, she told me something after Alex was finished questioning her that seemed odd."

As soon as the words left my mouth, his face grew hard. "What did she say?"

"She said she spoke to you last week and told you she'd be out of town from Monday through Thursday and wouldn't get home until late Thursday night."

My eyes trained on his to see his reaction. Other than them narrowing ever so slightly, he continued to stare at me with hardness in his eyes even as his expression softened.

"I don't know what she's talking about. She probably got confused. Ever since that house of hers became like a war zone with all that construction, she hasn't known if she was coming or going."

Forcing a laugh, I stepped behind the bar to get a drink of water, my mouth suddenly feeling like it was filled with cotton. I didn't know which one of them was lying, but I knew one thing for sure.

I didn't know Jack Reynolds well at all.

As I quenched my thirst with one glass of tap water and then a second, I wished my father would return. I couldn't put my finger on why, but suddenly I had a feeling I'd put Cherise in danger and if my father could keep Jack occupied, I could get out to her house to make sure she was okay.

"I'm going to go now, Poppy," he announced before finishing the last of his beer.

"Oh? You can't stay for a little while longer? I know my father would love to tell you more stories of this old house. He's got a million of them."

"Maybe later."

I grabbed his arm and subtly pressed my body next to his. "I thought maybe we'd spend some time together today since I know you'll be leaving soon."

His reaction startled me. In a flat voice with no emotion, he said, "So the investigation must be almost complete then if they're going to release the body for the funeral."

"I…I…I don't know," I stammered out, struck by how cold he sounded when he talked about seeing his brother for one last time.

"Well, your partner must not be telling you everything then, Poppy, because I have a sense this case is all but over."

What did he mean all but over? How did he know?

I wanted to ask, but I was afraid to hear the answer, so I just shrugged and smiled. "I just tag along with him, to be honest. He does all the real investigating. I'm more there to make my editor happy and get some stories on the local crime beat."

Whether Jack believed my lie or not I couldn't tell. His face remained stony as he leaned across the bar to kiss me on the cheek, and then barely above a whisper, he said, "I look forward to seeing you one more time before I leave, Poppy McGuire."

I smiled and nodded as that same flowery scent filled my nose, but now I knew where I'd smelled that before. He didn't wait to know how I felt about us getting together again before he left Sunset Ridge. He simply turned on his heels and walked out the front door of

McGuire's, not even saying goodbye to my father when he came out from the stockroom and asked him where he was going.

"That was odd. He didn't even say goodbye. Is he coming back?"

I looked over at my father at the end of the bar and shook my head. "I don't know, but something's wrong with him. I think it was something I said."

"What did you say?" he asked in a way that told me he thought I'd intentionally chased yet another man off.

"Nothing bad, Dad. You act like I meant to make him leave," I said as my defensiveness inched higher with each moment.

He began unpacking the boxes he'd brought out from the stockroom, ignoring my comment entirely. "Well, I wanted to talk to him about maybe buying some of his photos for the bar. He showed me a few and I think with some nice frames they could look really good hanging on the walls in this place. Bring a little worldliness right here to Sunset Ridge."

"Jack's a photojournalist, Dad. What were you going to buy? Pictures of war torn countries with bombed out buildings? I'm not sure that would really work for the look you have going on here."

My father grimaced, huffing his disgust at my teasing. "I don't know about those things, but the pictures he showed me were of a forest in Germany, I think he told me. I really liked them because they looked so much like the woods we have around here."

"Well, I'm sure you'll get a chance to speak to him again. I don't think he's leaving today."

My father continued to stock the bar as I thought about Cherise and what she'd said. Something didn't fit there, but what? Needing to make sure she was okay, I called Alex for her number but Craig answered instead.

"Hey Craig, where's Alex?"

Whispering into the phone, he said, "The Chief just called him into his office and it doesn't sound good. I think your victim's brother is in there complaining about how long it's taking to solve your case."

"What? Why would he do that?" I wondered aloud. "What's he saying?"

"I don't know since I can't hear everything, but that woman you two brought in today to question keeps coming up. I think he thinks she did it."

None of this made any sense. Why would Jack go to the station to complain to Derek? Was it what I said about her claiming he knew she'd be out of town?

"Craig, I need the number for that woman. Her name is Cherise Reynolds. It should be in Alex's little notebook he carries around."

He said nothing for a minute before coming back to the phone. "I can't find it, Poppy. Do you think he has it on him?"

I had a sinking feeling he did, but on the chance he'd taken it out of his pocket, I knew where he'd have put it. "Check his top right drawer, Craig. It might be there."

The sound of the drawer opening came through the phone and then Craig said, "It's not here. Sorry, Poppy. I don't think he'll be that long with Derek, though. The yelling has already stopped, so he should be out soon."

I didn't have time to wait for Alex. If Jack was trying to convince the police that Cherise killed Lee and failed, I had a feeling I knew where he'd go next. I ended the call and stuffed my phone back into my bag before kissing my father on the cheek.

"Now you're going? What was that call about?"

"I think I figured out who murdered Lee Reynolds. Do me a favor, okay? If Alex asks, tell him I went out to Cherise Reynolds' house. I just want to check something and then I'll be back."

Before he could ask me to explain who the killer was, I ran out of the bar and the few blocks to my house to get my car. I needed to get out to Cherise's before Jack did or I might not be able to prove my theory.

Putting the gas to the floor, I sped away from Barn Street on my way to her house as all the pieces of this case rambled through my brain. The eye drop poisoning. The gun. The two ex-wives. All this time and we'd been looking at Lee Reynolds' murder all wrong.

It had been love at the heart of this case all along.

Chapter Eighteen

CHERISE'S HOUSE STOOD dark against the dusk sky, a white splotch in a sea of orange and yellow streaks flooding the horizon. My heart slamming into my chest, I ran from the car to her front door and hoped to God I'd gotten there in time. I knocked three times on the door but got no answer. Looking around, I saw no workmen's trucks or any cars at all.

Had she not returned here after being questioned at the station?

I knocked again and waited, and then a sound from inside the house hit my ears. A moaning sound. Was she in there?

"Cherise, it's Poppy McGuire," I yelled, suddenly worried I wasn't helping her but instead interrupting something. "I just came out to see if you're okay."

I listened for a reply but only heard the same moaning sound once again. Jiggling the door knob, I found it open and praying I wasn't about to walk in on her with someone, I pushed open the door and walked into the dark living room.

"Cherise, can you hear me? Is everything okay? I wanted to see if you were all right after the interrogation," I called out as I gingerly made my way through the darkness to the kitchen to turn on a light.

A faint voice from her bedroom answered quietly, "Poppy, help." Hands out in front of my body to prevent me from running headlong into some piece of furniture, I hurried to where the sound came from and fumbled in the darkness to turn on the nightstand lamp next to her bed. What I saw when the room was lit up made my heart leap into my throat.

There on the floor in between her bedroom and bathroom lay Cherise in a puddle of blood. Shot in the back just like Lee, she clung to life. I raced over to her and saw she had little time left, so I quickly called 911 and hoped I wasn't too late.

Then as I waited for the ambulance to come to her rescue, I sat down on the floor next to her and quietly promised her everything would be okay, even though I wasn't sure of that at all as I watched her eyes close.

"Open your eyes, Cherise!" I ordered each time her eyelids fluttered closed, terrified every time would be the last. "Open your eyes and look at me! I'm right here, Cherise. I called the ambulance and they're coming, so I need you to hold on."

She obeyed my command to open her eyes and tried to speak, but she couldn't. Taking her trembling hand in mine, I held it and quietly told her how much I loved her new house and how when she got out of the hospital she'd move on to the next room she planned to remodel. She never answered, but I hoped she knew I was there with her.

When the ambulance arrived, the EMTs hurriedly got her out of there, leaving me alone in that house that would someday be beautiful again. I called Alex to tell him what had happened and that I thought I knew who killed Lee Reynolds.

He answered on the first ring and I quietly said, "Cherise was shot this afternoon after she got home from the police station. The ambulance just took her to the hospital, but I don't know if she's going to make it."

Just saying those words as I stood not five feet away from the pool of her blood on the bathroom floor made it so real, and whatever haze I'd been in since finding her lifted and I began to cry.

"Poppy, are you okay? Where are you? Are you still out at her house?" Alex asked in rapid-fire succession.

I couldn't stop the tears to answer his questions, so he continued to talk, his voice soothing me like always. "It's okay, Poppy. The hospital will take care of her and fix her up. You probably saved her life."

The thought that my coming out to check on her may have saved her made my crying ease up. Taking a deep breath, I calmed myself as much as I could and said, "I wanted to make sure she was okay, so I drove out to the house. I know who did this, Alex."

"Yeah, I do too, but we'll talk about that later. For right now, I need you to get back here. I want you to stay on the phone with me and get out of that house, Poppy."

I looked down at the white tile floor in the bathroom to see the dark red blood. "I should clean up here, Alex. She doesn't have anyone else to help her and it's going to stain the floor."

"Poppy, listen to me. I want you to leave there and come home now. Don't worry about what's on the floor. Just get out of there and into your car."

With one last look at the blood, I started to cry again. "I should have seen it earlier, Alex. If I had, she might not be on her way to the hospital and clinging to life."

"I'm coming out there, so just get to your car and lock the doors. Do you understand me, Poppy? Get to your car right now."

Alex's words reverberated in my head, and I realized what he'd just said. Wiping my tears from under my eyes, I took a deep breath once again. "No, I can get home on my own. I'm okay. I'll be fine."

He didn't sound like he believed me, but I knew he didn't want to fight now. "I want you to talk to me the whole way back so I know you're okay."

Slowly, I made my way to the front door of Cherise's house, noticing in the light bloody marks on the doorframes and walls. "Alex, there are fingerprints all over this place. Those beautiful front rooms of hers have bloody fingerprints but they don't have any ridges like normal ones."

"They're probably from the ambulance crew as they were taking her out. Are you almost to your car?"

I heard the concern in his voice and suddenly felt like I should ease his mind. "Yeah, but I'll be okay, Alex."

My words sounded faraway, like someone else was speaking them. In comparison, his seemed loud and demanding, his voice verging on panic as each moment passed.

"Poppy, I want you to drive back directly to the police station. I'll meet you here and you can tell me everything, okay?"

"Okay."

But then I remembered my father possibly all alone with Jack and everything in my brain snapped into place. "No, I have to go see my father. I have to make sure he's okay."

I started the car and began driving back to Sunset Ridge as Alex explained how he'd check on my father and make sure he wasn't in any danger, but I still needed to see him for myself.

"Poppy, why don't you call him on your way back just to put your mind at ease?" he suggested, clearly understanding he wasn't going to convince me on this issue.

"While I'm driving? Aren't cops against driving and talking on cell phones?" I asked as I pushed the gas and sped down the highway.

"Damnit, Poppy, just do as I say and get back here," he answered, his voice exasperated.

"Okay, okay. I'll call him. At the rate I'm driving, I should be back to Sunset Ridge in way less than an hour. I'll see you when I get to the station."

Alex was silent for a moment and then in a far less worried voice, he said, "Just be careful, Poppy. I don't want to see anything happen to you."

"I'll be fine, Alex. I'll see you in a few."

I ended the call with him and immediately called my father. His phone rang and I thought it would go to voicemail, but just before it did, he answered in his usual way.

"Hi, honey."

"Hi, Dad. I just wanted to call and see if you're okay. Are you at the bar?"

He didn't answer, and after a long pause, he finally said, "Actually, I'm over at your place. There was a problem at the bar with the pipes, and I had to close for the night. The plumber said the house might have water problems until he gets there tomorrow to fix everything, so I was hoping you wouldn't mind if I spent a night or two with you."

"Of course! I'd love that," I said as relief washed over me. "You sound pretty shaken up about it. That house is old, though, so you shouldn't be surprised that the plumbing would go eventually."

"Yeah, I guess. When will you be home?"

"You sound pretty eager to see your only daughter, Dad. I should be there in about a half hour. When I get there, after I take a shower I'll make us some dinner. Sound good?"

"Sounds good, Elizabeth. I'll see you soon," he said in a somber voice, using my given name, something he usually saved for when he was serious about something.

"You okay, Dad? I know it'll be a big expense, but you're going to be fine."

He began to tell me everything was good, but the reception on my phone failed and all I heard was a crackling noise in my ear before the call dropped. I tried to call him back, but it went directly to voicemail. No worries. I'd be home in a few minutes, and then I'd make him a good dinner so he could forget his plumbing troubles for at least a little while.

I PULLED INTO my driveway to see Alex waiting for me in his car with a look of relief on his face. Quickly jumping out, he rushed toward me as the evidence of blood on my arms and hands came into focus.

"Damnit, Poppy! Why didn't you come to the station like I told you to? And why didn't you wait for me before going out to Cherise's? You might have been hurt. As it is, you're covered in blood. Not exactly a good thing to see first thing."

Looking down, I saw just how bad I looked with all that blood on me. "I'm sorry. I had a hunch and worried that if I didn't get out there she might get hurt. I guess I was too late."

Alex brushed my hair off my forehead and smiled. "I talked to the hospital there. She's going to be okay. She lost a lot of blood, but you got there in the nick of time. A few minutes more and she might have bled out. Luckily, the bullet only grazed an artery."

A sense of relief like I'd never felt came over me. I hadn't been able to prevent Cherise from getting hurt, but at least I'd been there to make sure she didn't die. I didn't know why, but I began to cry. Maybe it was because of all I'd been through that day, or maybe they were tears of happiness. Whatever the reason, I stood there in my driveway sobbing like a baby.

"It's okay. Everything's going to be okay," Alex said as he pulled me into his arms. "You did good, Poppy. I just wish you would have waited for me."

I let my head lean against his chest and loved how safe I felt with him holding me. Like I could tell him anything and it would be okay.

In between sobs, I said, "I guess I wasn't thinking. I'm sorry."

He tilted my head back and smiled down at me. "Remember how partners have each other's backs? That's not just something I say just to hear myself talk. You could have gotten hurt or worse out there. I don't know what I would have done if that had happened."

The concern in his deep brown eyes touched me. I hadn't meant to worry him or anyone else, but it felt good to know it had worried him.

"I just figured you had your hands full with the case, especially since Craig told me Jack came by the station to complain about how you were handling the case."

The mention of Jack Reynolds made me shudder with embarrassment, and I hung my head. Once again, I'd picked the wrong man.

"I'm never too busy to follow my partner's gut. You know that." He tilted my head up to face him again. "But what's this about? You can't even look me in the eye."

I closed my eyes so I wouldn't have to face him when I admitted the truth. "I thought he really liked me. I just wanted to be someone different than the person everyone in this town thinks I am."

For a long moment, Alex remained silent as I waited to hear him tell me I was worrying about nothing or everyone made mistakes. He was good for those kinds of supportive statements when I needed them.

But he didn't say anything like that. Instead, when he finally spoke, I realized he was saying exactly what I'd wanted to hear from someone for so long.

"You're perfect just as you are, Poppy McGuire. From the first day, I knew you were someone unlike anyone else I'd ever met. You were too good for him, so don't beat yourself up for giving him a chance. It's just who you are."

I opened my eyes to see Alex smiling at me as he cradled my face like I was the most important thing in the world to him at that moment. As I stared up at him, I realized no one had ever looked at me like that before in my life.

"He was just what you thought he was. I should have

listened to you from the beginning. You never liked him. All this time your gut knew what he was when mine didn't."

A slow smile lit up Alex's face, and he softly kissed me on the forehead. "That's because I was jealous."

"You were?"

A sheepish expression came over his face. Looking away, he nodded. "Yeah, I was. I didn't have any right to be jealous, though. You're a grown woman who can choose to go with any man she likes. I guess I just got used to you always being around and I felt jealous that he was taking up so much of your time."

I thought about how we'd been together since Jack came into the picture. He had been jealous. I hadn't believed it, but in some way, I'd known all along. Just like I'd been jealous when Bethany came into his life and threatened to take up all his time.

"Jealous, huh? Well, I guess it's time for me to come clean too then."

He narrowed his eyes to slits and knitted his brows. "Come clean about what?"

As much as I wanted to look away so I didn't have to see how he felt when I told the truth about him and Bethany, I didn't and forced myself to face him. "I was jealous when you and Bethany started to date. Crazy jealous, like ridiculous teenage girl jealous."

With a big smile, he said, "Oh, I thought you were going to tell me something I didn't know."

"What? You knew? How? It's not like I was running around town telling anyone. Did my father say something to you? When I get inside, I'm going to give him a piece of my—"

Alex stopped my mouth with a kiss that made my

legs go weak. His lips tenderly caressed mine like they were meant only for me. Every cell in my body rejoiced in the feel of his hands gently holding my face and his body pressed against mine. After all those months working by his side and secretly wishing he cared for me like I cared for him, there we stood kissing for the first time. I didn't know how long we stood in the dark kissing in my driveway, but I would have been happier than I'd ever been before in my life if we never had to move from that spot and I never had to feel the loss of his lips on mine.

When he pulled away, I didn't want to open my eyes and show him how much that one kiss had meant to me, but I couldn't stop myself from wanting to see if it had meant the same to him. So I silently promised myself no matter what he looked like I could handle it and looked up into those beautiful chocolate brown eyes of his to see them telegraphing exactly what I was feeling.

And suddenly all those fears I'd had about the two of us ever being more than just work partners flooded my mind. I couldn't deny how crazy I was about him, but I couldn't lose him from my life if a romance went bad either. Alex meant too much to me to let that happen.

So even though I wanted nothing more at that moment than to feel his lips on mine kissing me again, I pulled away and pretended he hadn't just made me the happiest person in all of Sunset Ridge.

"I better get inside. My father is expecting me to cook dinner for him, and I don't want to let him down."

The disappointment in Alex's eyes was unmistakable, and for a moment I wanted to crawl into a hole and hide so I wouldn't have to see him looking at me like that. I was crazy about him, and he had finally shown he cared about me too. I should have been inviting him in to have dinner instead of pushing him away, but I couldn't.

The fear of losing him entirely from my life was stronger than the fear of never having him kiss me like that again.

"Oh, okay. Tell him I said hi. I'd planned on heading over to the bar tonight for a drink, so I'll probably just see him later," he said in a casual tone I knew was forced.

"His pipes broke, so you'll have to get your scotch at another bar tonight. I don't think McGuire's will be open for a couple days, from what he said the plumber told him."

"Oh, well. I'll just have to go someplace else in the meantime."

An awkwardness settled in between us that I knew was all my fault. In his eyes, I saw all I had to do was push that fear of losing him aside and take a chance and he'd be right there taking it with me.

I couldn't, though. He meant too much to me to have none of him at all in my life, so I'd take the work partnership and try to be happy with that.

"See you tomorrow at The Grounds?" I asked like I always did at the end of the day.

He forced a smile and nodded. "Tomorrow at The Grounds. I'll be the cop in the chair facing the door at the table in the back. Right now, I'm going to go get our killer and put this case to bed finally."

For a second, I wanted to protest him going without me, but it was for the better. I'd had a pretty full day and didn't need any more excitement. I moved to turn toward my house, and Alex's hands slid from my face, leaving my skin feeling cold without his touch. This was for the best, though. If we were only partners, I didn't have to worry about messing up and losing him.

Chapter Nineteen

I OPENED MY kitchen door and stepped into the darkness of my house as I yelled, "Dad! You didn't fall asleep on me already, did you?"

Tossing my purse on the table, I felt along the wall for the switch for the ceiling light. I turned it on and instantly understood why my father had sounded so strange on the phone just a few minutes earlier.

"Lock the door and walk into the living room," Jack said in a low voice, punctuating his command with the awful click of the hammer being pulled back on his gun.

I did as he ordered and he followed me, the gun pressed into my back between my shoulder blades. Every tiny movement reminded me that at any moment he might shoot me like he had his brother and sister-in-law.

Two steps into the living room, and I saw a sight that made my heart ache. The dim light from the end table lamp showed my father lay unconscious on the floor near the very couch Jack and I had sat on together just a few nights earlier. The absence of blood made me hope he hadn't shot him but merely knocked him out.

"Please tell me you didn't kill him. He never did anything to you, Jack. Please tell me he's okay."

Spinning me around, Jack thrust the gun toward my

face and shook his head. "I'm not a monster. Joe's okay. I wouldn't hurt someone who didn't deserve it."

His words hit me like a brick to my head. "And I deserve to be hurt? Is that what you mean, Jack?"

"I kept hoping you would settle on Cherise for the murder. You and that damn cop!"

I slowly lowered myself to the couch and looked down at my father on the floor. He would be okay, and it was probably better that he didn't see his only child being held at gunpoint by the man he thought should be her next boyfriend.

Jack's eyes flashed a wildness I wasn't sure I could talk my way out of. Logic certainly wasn't going to save me, so maybe its opposite would.

"You at least owe me some answers if you're going to kill me."

He thought about it for a moment and nodded. "Okay, I'll answer your questions. It's not like it's going to matter in the end. I'm not going to let you drag this out for hours in the hopes that someone will come by and save you, though. That's not going to happen."

And then the horror of what would really happen to my father flashed through my mind. "Oh my God! You're going to kill him after you kill me, aren't you?"

My outburst made him recoil in disgust. "Christ, you're an emotional one. He won't know a thing. He'll just never wake up."

He said that like he was graciously giving my father a gift. My head began to spin as my emotions threatened to overwhelm me. I would never get to tell my father I loved him again. Never get married and be a mother to that little girl I'd always dreamed of. Never tell Alex how I truly felt about him.

Alex! If only I hadn't basically shoved him away after he kissed me, none of this would be happening.

Well, if all I had was myself, I needed to start thinking and fast. Best to at least make an appeal for my life. No, it had never worked for even a single person on the planet in all of history, but there was a first time for everything and I had to at least try.

"Jack, you don't have to do this. If you leave right now, you could probably be out of the country by the time the sun rises. I know Alex doesn't plan to do anything until tomorrow. You can get away."

My attempt only garnered a sinister grin and a head shake. "If this was only about me, I would have been gone a long time ago. I would have disappeared into thin air like I can do so well. But there's someone I can't leave behind again."

I sat there as his expression softened at the mention of this someone else. Only a woman could make a man look like Jack did at that moment, so I asked, "Which one are you in love with?"

"Which one? Isn't it obvious?"

Confused, I shook my head. "No, but then again, I thought you liked me, so I might be the wrong person to try to figure this out. But I wouldn't put it past you to shoot a woman you cared about."

Jack sat down in front of me on the ottoman and leaned his elbows on his knees, still pointing the gun at my head but almost relaxed, as if he wanted to talk to me like a friend would. I didn't care what he wanted to talk about as long as he talked. The longer he let me live, the better chance I had of getting my father and me out of that house alive.

"It's not that I didn't like you, Poppy. You're sweet

and funny, and the sex wasn't bad."

His tepid compliment brought out my snarky side. "Thanks. You were okay too."

Waving the gun in front of my face, he said, "You know I had a feeling your heart wasn't entirely in it. That's why I said it wasn't bad. It wasn't meant as a reason for you to insult me."

"Fine. You were better than okay, if we're being honest," I admitted, hating that I wasn't lying. He had been pretty good. Bad men usually were good in bed.

He smiled broadly, brightening his face. "See? We had a good time, even if we both were thinking of other people. What's the saying—if you can't sleep with the one you love, love the one you sleep with? I didn't love you, but a good time is sort of the same thing."

I was pretty sure that saying didn't exist other than in his crazy mind, but I didn't think arguing over something like that was in my best interest. Better to get him to talk about his crime in the hope that if I kept him talking long enough maybe Alex would come by.

Not that he ever really dropped by and my brushing him off a few minutes earlier likely meant the last thing he'd want to do that night would be stopping by to see me.

"So who is she?" I asked, hoping for one of the few times in my life that anyone, even one of the town busybodies, would feel the need to come knocking on my door.

His hands moved expressively while he talked, making the gun wave as he spoke about this woman he loved. "Have you ever met someone and instantly knew you belonged with them? That's how it was for me. The first time I saw her I knew. Every time I looked into her eyes, I felt like I was home, like I finally had a place I belonged in the world."

With each word, my curiosity grew. Who was this person he so desperately loved and why wasn't he with her instead of sleeping with me for the past few days?

I opened my mouth to once again ask who she was, but a knock on my front door stopped me cold. I turned toward the sound as every muscle in my body ached to run in that direction. Jack leapt from the ottoman and grabbed my arm, pulling me to the door as he stood off to the side.

"Answer it and tell whoever it is to go away or I'll make you watch me kill your father. Do you understand?" His threat was made more intense when he painfully squeezed my bicep, making me whimper in pain.

I nodded and slowly opened the door just a crack to see the one person I'd asked God to send to me that night. Alex stood on my porch in jeans and a grey long sleeve t-shirt with a look on his face that told me he wanted to talk and he didn't plan to leave unless we did.

"Alex, I'm surprised to see you. I'm busy, but I'll see you tomorrow at the Madison Diner like we planned, right?"

"I was hoping we could sit down and talk tonight, Poppy. I think we need to."

He hadn't picked up on my hint that something was wrong, probably because what he wanted to talk about—that kiss—was preoccupying his thoughts. If I wasn't being held at gunpoint with the threat of my death and my father's and how to prevent both of them taking up every square inch of my brain, I likely would have been thinking about our kiss too.

Jack whispered low in my ear, "Tell him you're here with me and then shut the door."

"I can't right now. I'm here with Jack," I told Alex as I worked to make my eyes project the truth I couldn't say.

"Jack? You're with Jack after what happened just a few minutes ago?" he asked in a voice full of hurt. He hadn't picked up on the true meaning beneath my expression, unfortunately.

Behind me, Jack forced the gun into my back and squeezed harder on my upper arm. I wanted to cry, but I couldn't without risking three lives now, so I stifled my tears and simply nodded. "I promise we can talk at the Madison tomorrow morning."

Alex stared at me for a long moment before mouthing the words, "Step away from the door when I push on it."

He had understood something was wrong!

"Okay, Poppy. I'll see you in the morning."

I felt the gun move away from my back, and then all at once I saw Alex launch at the door. I quickly moved out of the way as much as I could as the door slammed back into Jack's face. He reacted by tightening his hold on my arm and yanking me back with him so that in just a matter of seconds, the three of us stood there in my foyer, Jack holding me to him as he pointed the gun at my head and Alex pointing his gun at Jack.

"Let her go and you might not get hurt," Alex warned him.

Laughing, Jack shook his head. "Now neither one of you is getting out of this. Your gun will be used to kill her and then you. Murder-suicide. The crime solving buddies dying together on their last case."

I suddenly feared Jack more than ever after hearing his plan and struggled against his hold to get away. Alex seemed far less flustered than I was, though.

"That's not how it's going to happen," he calmly warned. "If you don't let her go, the only person dying here tonight will be you."

"We seem to be at an impasse, except I have the bargaining chip and you have nothing," Jack threatened as he dragged me in front of him and repositioned the gun next to my head. "The way I see it, I'm the one who's going to be calling the shots here."

I waited for Alex to return with his own clever threat, but he simply looked from Jack to me and then back at him again. I guess there was no point in claiming he could do something to help me when it was more than obvious he couldn't, but I had to believe a little more manly bluster in my defense would have been nice.

"Was that how it was with you and Lee, Jack? You never got what you wanted as long as he was around so you left to see the world, a world where he wasn't always there?" Alex finally asked, surprising me since I had no idea what he meant.

Jack knew, though. I felt him tense up next to me when Alex mentioned Lee by name and even more when he talked about him not getting what he wanted.

"Don't talk about him to me! You don't know what it was like. He came first in life and then in everything after. Whatever he wanted, he got. I swear he was charmed. Even he began to think he could do no wrong, but that wasn't true. He had feet of clay just like everyone else."

Alex nodded like he understood what he was talking about. "When did you realize you loved her, Jack?"

I turned to look up at him and saw that dreamy look he'd had earlier when he talked about the woman he loved. A tiny smile tugged the corners of his mouth up, and I finally heard her name.

"The first time I met her. My brother introduced me to Jessica and I knew from the moment I looked into her eyes that I loved her. She was everything I'd ever dreamed of, and she was marrying my brother. Once again, he got whatever he wanted."

"He loved her. I've found no evidence he wasn't the best husband he could be for her," Alex said calmly as he took a step further into the living room and quickly looked around to see my father still lying unconscious on the floor.

"He was too old for her, too calm. He didn't know how to have fun. Jessica's a woman who needs excitement in her life," Jack said to counter the kind things Alex had said about Lee.

Alex stared at me as he spoke to him, and I knew what he was trying to do. If he could lull Jack into distraction, I could take a chance and try to get away. If that was going to happen, though, Alex had to get him far more relaxed because he still had his gun pointed at my head.

"Why not just tell her how you felt? She may have secretly loved you."

"I did. Right before they married, I told her how I felt—how she was all I ever thought about. How I would have done anything to have her in my life. I told her everything in my heart, and she told me she wished things could be different because she cared for me too. We'd never even kissed, and we loved each other. But Lee had the kind of money she needed to feel safe and secure, so she couldn't walk away from him. She'd always dreamed of living the life of her dreams, and I couldn't deny her that. So I walked away and devoted my time to my career so one day I'd have enough money and prestige to give her the life she wanted. I never stopped loving her, though. Never."

His words struck me dumbfounded. I had no inkling Jack Reynolds had any feelings like he talked about for anyone. He'd been the glib world traveler, usually bragging about something he'd done or someplace he'd traveled to. I'd never seen any hint of the man who stood next to me professing his love for the only woman he couldn't have.

Alex looked surprised by what he said too. Studying him like he was someone he hadn't seen before, he took a minute or so to let his words sink in and then asked, "So you planned his murder for years?"

"Every day I spent away from her I waited for the moment when I could return to her and say I could finally give her what she wanted. But I didn't plan on killing my brother. If only he would have just seen he didn't belong with her."

For the first time, I saw my chance to appeal to this new side of Jack. Quietly, I said, "If you didn't intend for him to die and were just defending yourself, then you really can't be blamed for his death. You and Jessica can still be together if you let me go right now. It's not too late, Jack."

He smiled like something I'd said amused him and chuckled. "You're definitely the naïve one, Poppy. No, I didn't plan to kill him, but I wasn't defending myself either. Your partner can tell you that."

I knew by where he'd shot Lee that he hadn't been

defending himself when his brother died, but it was worth a try. His feelings for Jessica might still help us, though, so I had to try to manipulate him with them.

"Don't you want to finally have a chance to be with the woman you love?"

He got a wistful look in his eyes and said, "More than you can ever know. When I finally knew I had enough to give Jessica the life she deserved, I told her. I never expected her to tell me she loved me back and wanted the two of us to run away together. I don't think I ever heard sweeter words than that day when she told me she loved me."

Jack stopped for a moment but still he didn't loosen his hold on me as he talked about finally being with Jessica. "We began meeting and talked it over each time she came to see me. After a while, I decided I would approach my brother and tell him the truth. That I loved Jessica and wanted him to give her up. But then I was sent on assignment for six months. The whole time I was gone, I missed her so much, but after two months she told me she found a way to speed things up so we could be together."

Alex said, "She began poisoning Lee with eye drops, but all that did to him was make his stomach upset."

Jack sighed. "Jessica never wanted to kill him. She isn't the smartest woman in the world, but that's not why I love her. Don't drag her into this."

Alex nodded and pretended to agree to Jack's first term. "Fine. Jessica will stay out of this. Just let Poppy go and we can talk about what happened."

I looked up at Jack hoping he might go for Alex's offer, but it was as if Jack didn't even hear him. He began talking about when he returned from being on assignment and they continued their relationship once more.

"When I got back, she told me the eye drop thing hadn't worked. I thought I could live with having only part of her in my life. She began coming to see me in DC every Thursday afternoon because she knew he worked late that one day a week. But somehow he found out because two weeks ago she told me we couldn't see each other anymore until I told him the truth and got him to let her go. So I called my brother and we agreed to meet at the Hotel Piermont where I always stayed when I came to town."

I couldn't help but feel his choice of lodging when he came to Sunset Ridge was fitting.

"So you decided to kill him in the woods right past the hotel and finally have Jessica all to yourself," Alex said in a voice full of judgment.

"No, it wasn't like that!" Jack protested, defensive for the first time since he'd begun talking about his affair with his brother's wife. "It wasn't. But as I was driving here something in me changed. I knew he wouldn't let her go. I'm not even sure he loved her anymore, but he wouldn't let me have her. I knew it. So I stopped at Cherise's. I knew from talking to her that she'd be out of town at her sister's, but my former sister-in-law still loved me, even if my brother had treated her like shit, so of course she said I could stay over when I asked."

"So that's how you got Cherise's gun," I wondered aloud.

"And you took her gun and shot your brother in the back," Alex said, succinctly summarizing his crime.

Jack nodded and held me tighter to him. "Well, I guess all I need to know before we finish all this is how you figured it out since your lovely sidekick here had no clue what I'd done. Well, before this afternoon, I guess."

"The chalk," Alex said calmly.

"No way. How?"

"You left a fingerprint on the piece of chalk and we matched it to the fingerprints you left on your glass at McGuire's."

"A fingerprint on chalk. How?" Jack asked, his voice filled with an odd curiosity.

"Chalk isn't just chalk. It's covered in a very thin layer of plastic to hold the chalk together. You took all that care to not leave fingerprints on the gun or anywhere on your brother, but the extra effort you took to try to throw us off did you in," Alex explained.

Jack slung his arm around my shoulders and whispered in my ear, "I see why you like him, Poppy. He's sharp and quite the man. He's got that whole knight in shining armor thing going for him too. I hope you can forgive me for using you through all this, though. I've never been like your partner here."

I looked at Alex as Jack spoke and saw in his expression that now was my chance to get away, so I lifted my leg and kicked back into Jack's shin. He screamed out in pain and Alex lunged for the gun as it dropped from his hand when he grabbed his injured leg. I jumped out of the way as Alex pushed him to the floor and aimed his gun at Jack head.

"Jack Reynolds, you're under arrest for the murder of your brother, Lee Reynolds."

Trying to get my wits about me, I relaxed for a moment as Alex recited Jack his rights and called the station for backup. Suddenly, I remembered my father still unconscious on the floor across the room. While Alex handcuffed our killer, I ran over to the couch and saw my father hadn't seen anything that had happened, thankfully.

"Dad, can you hear me?" I said in his ear to wake him. "Are you okay?"

His eyelids slowly opened and he winced in pain, his hand immediately moving to the back of his head where a golf ball sized goose egg had formed. Dazed, he looked around and asked, "What happened?"

I looked back at Alex as he dragged Jack out to the police car that had just pulled up in front of my house and smiled. Turning to face my father, I kissed him on the forehead. "We just solved our case. That's all. Oh, and you got hit on the head by our killer, one Jack Reynolds."

"I'm sorry, Poppy. He forced me to call you and bring him here. I thought I could overpower him, but he hit me and I guess he knocked me out."

Just like my father to think he could defeat the bad guy.

"It's okay, Dad. We got him, so it's all over now. How about I get you an ice pack and we sit on the couch until you feel better?"

"Okay. Sounds good."

I helped him up to the couch and trotted off to the kitchen to get him that ice pack to stop the swelling. On my way back, I looked out the front door and saw Alex putting Jack into the back of the squad car.

As Craig drove off to the police station, Alex smiled up from the street. "I wasn't kidding when I said I wanted to talk to you. When all this is over, I'll be back and we'll have that talk."

I wasn't sure what I'd say when we had that talk, but I'd be there waiting for him like a partner should be.

Chapter Twenty

MY FATHER KISSED me on the cheek and gave me one of those broad, Irish smiles that brought out the faded blue of his eyes. "Thanks for letting me stay until I got my wits back, but it's about time I get back home and open the bar before my regulars think I've skipped town."

I smiled at his devotion to souls most people in Sunset Ridge considered plain old drunks. They were his regulars, a group of men who were so much more than just guys who drank too often at McGuire's. These men were people who cared about one another, even as much of the world had decided there wasn't much to care about anymore. That my father worried about them was a testament to who he was far more than the business he ran.

"Did you ever finally convince Andrew to get that prostate exam or is he still being stubborn?"

Lifting his chin in pride, my father answered, "Oh, we got him to that doctor. It took a little prodding, but we all told him we weren't going to lose him to some disease because he was embarrassed to go through what every one of us had already gone through."

"I'm glad you guys take care of one another, Dad.

They're good guys, your regulars."

He nodded and turned to open my kitchen door before he stopped and looked back at me. "I think that's why I like your partner so much. You know that?"

Unsure what he meant, I shook my head. "No, Dad. What do you mean?"

"You and Alex, you take care of one another. He came over here tonight because you were on his mind. If he hadn't, I don't know that you and I would be standing here talking like this. And I know you take care of him too."

"We're just partners, Dad. Nothing else," I said, attempting to convince myself as much as him.

"Well, you two are great partners. Don't forget that, Poppy."

I kissed him goodbye again and gently ran my fingertips over the slowly shrinking goose egg on the back of his head. "I won't, Dad. You sure you don't want me to give you a ride back to your place?"

He waved off my suggestion. "No. I'm fine. I'll see you tomorrow?"

"Of course."

"Good. Rest up tonight. You deserve it, Elizabeth."

I watched my father walk down the stairs from my kitchen door and down my driveway until he was swallowed up by the darkness and thanked God he'd survived Jack Reynolds' attack.

As I closed the door to head back into the living room to curl up on my favorite chair for the night, a stab of regret jabbed me for being the reason my father ended up in danger in the first place. On her death bed, my mother had made me promise I'd look out for him just as she'd made him make the same promise about me. I'd never forgotten that, yet my desire for romance with Jack Reynolds had made me go back on that promise, even if it was unintentionally.

Looking up, I silently apologized for my foolishness and hoped my mother understood. In my haste to get to know a man, I'd let him get close to the most important man in my life. For that, I prayed she saw it hadn't been because of thoughtlessness.

My phone vibrated across the coffee table in front of me, and leaning down to read the message, I saw it was from Alex. As usual, he said very little, but the four simple words he'd sent me said it all.

We need to talk.

My fingers trembled as they hovered over the tiny keyboard on my phone. We did need to talk, but I didn't know what I'd say or what he'd say. Was he going to tell me he wanted us to be more than just work partners? I still couldn't bring myself to think of that without a spike of fear exploding inside me every time, not from us getting together but from what might happen if it all went bad.

While my thoughts marched through my mind, I typed back a message and hoped when the time came that I'd make the right decision.

I'm here. Come over when you're finished.

His response came immediately.

I'm outside your door.

Then I heard a knock that made my heart leap in my chest. I wasn't sure I was ready to have this conversation, but it couldn't be put off. Whatever we had to say, now was the time.

I opened my front door to see Alex standing there in the same clothes he'd worn a few hours earlier when he came to talk to me and ended up saving my life. Again. His expression was the same calm one I usually saw, but I had a sense underneath that façade he was a swirl of emotions like I was.

Or maybe that was just wishful thinking.

"Hey, did everything work out at the station?" I asked lamely, grasping for something to say that didn't have to do with us and that kiss.

"Yeah, it went fine. We have Jessica there too, and she's confessed to dosing Lee with the eye drops and getting the money every month from Jack. She probably won't be charged with attempted murder, though, since the eye drops were never going to do much more than make him sick to his stomach."

"True."

I stood there looking out at him as the truth of what Jack and Jessica had done for love hit me. Both had been willing to kill a man who by all accounts had never done anything to his wife but adore her. Jessica's selfishness in wanting to have her cake and eat it too had set into motion a series of events that ended with poor Lee Reynolds' death, and for what? Now Jack and Jessica would never spend another day together again.

All of that had happened because of love. I suddenly hated the idea.

"Can I come in or do you want to continue having this discussion on your front porch?" Alex asked, rousing me from my thoughts about love and the destruction it wrought.

I stepped back and opened the door for him to come in. "Sure. Let's talk in the living room."

We walked to the couch and sat down next to one another. My brain noted that was the first time we'd ever done that. Usually Alex sat across from me on another piece of furniture when we sat together anywhere.

As my mind fixated on tiny details to avoid the bigger issues he was there to discuss, he turned to face me, making the cushion I sat on sink toward him. I caught myself just before I slid into his legs, hating how physics and my furniture had chosen to work against me in my effort to remain aloof.

"I thought we should talk about what happened earlier," Alex said in a low voice bristling with emotion.

I struggled to sit normally as I nodded. "Yeah, I guess we should."

Suddenly I understood how my father's friend Andrew felt about his prostate exam. I didn't want to talk about that kiss any more than he had wanted to hear the snap of that glove on his doctor's hand or what would follow.

Alex swallowed hard and said, "You know I care about you, Poppy. I don't have to tell you that."

A strange tone sat under his words. I couldn't be sure, but he sounded like the next words out of his mouth would be to explain to me how he'd made a mistake by kissing me. In a flash, I changed from not being sure I wanted more with him to being offended he might not want that from me.

"Sure. Sure. I know that," I mumbled, waiting for the next thing he'd say.

"It's just that I'd hate to make a mistake that we

couldn't come back from. I don't want to repeat the mistake I made with Bethany."

The two mentions of the word mistake and Bethany's name hit my brain like three successive sledgehammer blows. Stunned, I tried to not let my face show how hurt I felt hearing being with me compared to a mistake and even worse, compared to his relationship with Bethany.

I stammered out, "Oh, yeah. Yeah, well, I can certainly see that, I guess. Sure."

I absolutely could not see how our getting together would be a mistake, at least not in the way he was saying it. And saying anything we might be could ever be like the superficial nothing relationship he'd had with Bethany? I wanted to scream at the top of my lungs, "How could you think so little of me?"

Of course, I didn't. He wouldn't understand it if I did anyway. He had no idea of how many times I'd stewed in my jealousy over them being together, hating that someone I cared about had chosen her of all people to date.

So I channeled all my courage into one sentence I couldn't believe I was saying. "You know, Alex, that kiss doesn't have to mean anything. We can just forget it. It's not like we can't do that."

His brown eyes instantly filled with a look of hurt. "Forget it? Is that what you want to do?"

And there it was all on my shoulders. Whatever might come from that one incredible, knee-buckling kiss could cease to exist with just a simple statement from me. All I had to say was I could forget it and act like it never happened.

The problem was I couldn't. From the minute Alex

walked out of my house with Jack in handcuffs and our case was over, I'd had two thoughts occupying my brain. The first was would my father be okay, and the second was a replay of how Alex's lips felt on mine as he kissed me out in my driveway.

No kiss had ever held as much promise and as much threat to my future. He had no idea how impossible it would be for me to ever forget that kiss.

Knowing he waited for an answer, I focused my gaze on my hands as they sat in my lap and mumbled, "I'm not sure I could, to be honest."

The sound of a quiet sigh made me look up at him, and I saw those lips that had kissed mine and made my legs feel like jelly spread into a smile that lit up his face. I guess he couldn't forget that kiss either.

"So we don't forget it," he said in a way that sounded like a formal declaration.

"I need to know whatever happens or doesn't happen won't affect us working together, Alex. Getting to work with you on cases means a lot to me, more than you can probably understand and more than I can probably explain. I don't want to lose that."

His expression grew serious. Knitting his brows, he frowned and asked, "Why would you lose that?"

Before I could form the right answer, my brain and heart conspired together and sent a stream of worries out of my mouth. "Because what if we do take this further and then you realize that I'm not different than Bethany—that you aren't ready for anything with me either? I don't think I'm anything like her and whatever we might be would be anything like that, but what if the end result is the same? And then after you don't want to feel awkward at work so you decide that working with me can't happen anymore. I would hate for that to happen."

At the touch of his hand, I stopped my rambling and looked down at where his fingers met mine. That was the kind of effect he had on me. One touch and everything in my mind simply dissolved into nothingness compared to how his skin on mine made me feel.

"Is that what you're worried about? I wouldn't do that to you, Poppy. You're my best friend, the person I'm closest to in this world. I'd miss you as much as you'd miss me if we didn't work together. Probably more since you have other people in your life to fill the void. I have no one."

I closed my eyes and hung my head, overwhelmed by the feelings he brought out in me. His words touched my heart. The feel of his hand on mine made me crave more of him. It was like sensory overload, and I didn't know if I wanted to run away or beg for more.

But I didn't see anything of that in him as he sat there next to me practically making me crazy over him.

"Alex, why did you kiss me?"

He didn't answer but instead looked away, and I was sure he was merely taking the time to craft a kind response that wouldn't hurt my feelings because I didn't create the whirlwind of emotions in him like he did in me. I watched as he set his jaw and slowly turned back to face me with a look that made my heart skip a beat. Whatever I made him feel, I had a feeling it was written all over his face in the expression of anguish he wore.

"I stayed away from the world for a long time, Poppy. I hated myself for letting Helena die. I blamed myself. I decided I'd never take the chance that would happen ever again. So I closed myself off in that house away from everyone and for years I was alone."

He stopped for a moment and I finished his thought with what he'd told me so many times before. "And then I showed up one night to trespass on your property."

Alex smiled and nodded. "Then you showed up one night and everything changed. You brought me back to life, even though you never intended to do that. I'm a cop again because of you. I have a life again because of you. Why would I not want to kiss you?"

"So it was like a thank you kiss?" I asked, all at once sad and relieved, my brain not knowing what to think about all he'd said.

He leaned in toward me and pressed his forehead to mine as he whispered, "No, it wasn't a thank you kiss. It was an I was worried you were hurt kiss. It was I didn't want to think about a world without you in it kiss."

I leaned back and looked into his eyes. "That's some kiss," I joked.

"It was, don't you think?"

"It was."

It had been a kiss that took my breath away, made my knees buckle, and made my brain whirl with possibilities and fears. Now that we'd talked about it, though, it was merely a kiss that I never wanted to forget because it had been with Alex.

"So what happens now?" I asked, knowing he no more had the answers than I did.

Arching one eyebrow, he grinned. "We do what we always do. We solve crimes. After that, I don't know. I guess we'll have to figure that out along the way."

I studied the man in front of me with his dark brown eyes that told me things when his words said little and that boyish smile he wore when he was truly happy. I didn't know what I exactly felt for him, but my belief I'd be able to remain as just his work partner faded away as I sat there, and I didn't care.

His answer hadn't been the most romantic and probably would have upset a woman looking for a happily ever after, but I wasn't that type of woman. I liked a mystery, and if Alex Montero was anything, he was definitely a mystery. I planned to enjoy myself as I unraveled the clues that would lead me to finding out who he truly was.

And if there was more kissing and other pleasures along the way, all the better.

Poppy and Alex return in The Darkest Hour:
A Poppy McGuire Mystery
(Poppy McGuire Mysteries #4)

About The Author

Anina Collins has always loved a good mystery. From Agatha Christie's Hercule Poirot to Sir Arthur Conan Doyle's famous detective Sherlock Holmes to Dan Brown's intrepid Professor Robert Langdon, she's spent some of her favorite reading times with mystery novels. When she's not writing her favorite mystery couple, she can be found watching entirely too much Supernatural and dreaming about the beach.

Visit Anina's Facebook page at facebook.com/Anina-Collins-429334270597293 for news about her books, along with giveaways and other fun stuff!

And sign up for her newsletter today for exclusive news first! Visit her website at aninacollins.com for more details.

Books by Anina Collins:
The Eleventh Hour (Poppy McGuire Mysteries #1)
After Hours (Poppy McGuire Mysteries #2)
Top of the Hour (Poppy McGuire Mysteries #3)

And look for the next book in the series, **The Darkest Hour (Poppy McGuire Mysteries #4)**, coming JULY 2016!

www.ingramcontent.com/pod-product-compliance
Lightning Source LLC
Chambersburg PA
CBHW030326200626
46816CB00006BA/1947